THE ASCENSION

Lauren Hudson

Publisher Page
an imprint of Headline Books, Inc.
Terra Alta, WV

The Ascension

by Lauren Hudson

copyright ©2017 Lauren Hudson

To order additional copies of this book or for book publishing information, or to contact the author:

Publisher Page
P.O. Box 52, Terra Alta, WV 26764

Tel: 304-789-3001
Email: mybook@headlinebooks.com
www.HeadlineBooks.com

Publisher Page is an imprint of Headline Books

Cover design by Kevin T. Kelly / www.kevintkelly.com

ISBN 13: 9781882658756

Library of Congress Control Number: 2016950288

For my brother, Robbie,
because how can I write a book
about siblings without having
an awesome one of my own?

I

The stately grandfather clock chimed from the bottom floor of the small mansion, ringing not one, not two, but twelve times. The multiple dings signaled the beginning of a brand new day. However, this would not be a typical day for Desdemona Anchor. Today marked the start of a very new year of life for the now fifteen-year-old beauty. Desdemona smiled to herself and lightly sang "Happy Birthday" under her breath. Pulling the fluffy, purple comforter up to her chin, she yawned and closed her eyes, wanting to get a good night's rest before her "surprise" birthday celebration the following afternoon.

Desdemona's mom always believed fifteen marked the start of a new life for her only daughter. *Why fifteen?* Desdemona did not know. She always wondered why fifteen mattered rather than the classic sixteen, but she never argued with her soccer mom mother. After all, whenever an argument occurred in the Anchor household, her mom brought out the classic "I'm your mom. Do what I say" verse. Desdemona would simply stop talking, not wanting to bicker with the only person she could completely trust in her life.

Speaking of Stacy Anchor… A voice drifted through the dry wall, reaching Desdemona's ears as muffled waves of sound. Stacy talked excitedly to her best friend about the surprise party she planned for her "sweet baby Mona" tomorrow and how "excited Mona was going to be."

As Desdemona began to laugh at her mom's giddiness about her birthday, her world began to twist and swirl and turn.

Body shivering, eyes fluttering, something hauled her out of the bedroom and into a memory not her own.

Beeping noises pierced silence. Darkness enveloped her, except for a large overhead light shining onto a screaming woman, writhing in a hospital bed. She scrambled and ran, rushing around the dark, blurry room frantically searching for something. Pulling open dark drawers, she ran her hands all around the tables and desks until she felt a sharp pain in her index finger.

Desdemona picked up the syringe by the sharp needle. She wiped the blood drawn from her finger on the desk, wincing slightly. Sprinting towards the bedside, she placed the syringe on a table next to a man wearing a white lab coat holding three babies in his arms. The doctor passed the children to her. After he injected the struggling woman, she fell still. For the smallest moment, everything became silent. Everything stopped. No one moved. Not an inch.

Finally, the doctor let out a large sigh and the door cracked open from across the room.

"Has she been silenced?" A woman, gray haired, although not more than sixty, poked her head in and asked.

"Yes, Mom," Desdemona heard herself saying. "You may enter." But wait. This wasn't her mother. She had never seen this woman in her life. Wrinkly skin, frail hands, and yet bright, intelligent eyes. Although Desdemona did not know this woman, she intuitively felt an eerie connection with her.

"Which child would you like?" The doctor asked the woman referred to as 'Mom.'"

The woman walked over to where Desdemona struggled with the three sleeping babies and inspected each of them closely. She reached out and caressed each of their cheeks, smiling when she reached the larger baby girl in Desdemona's left arm.

Her teeth shone in the dimly lit room as she spoke, "This one."

Desdemona gladly handed the child to the woman and watched while she debated over a name.

"Jinx. Yes, she looks like a Jinx," the woman concluded. The name Jinx struck Desdemona as being quite odd, but she decided against speaking up.

The doctor gazed at the two remaining children, finally resting his eyes on the lone boy of the trio. "I will take the boy home and name him Felix."

She passed the baby boy to the stocky built man, leaving the smallest girl in her arms.

The baby's blue eyes gleamed in the darkness as she tugged at Desdemona's brown hair. But Desdemona wasn't a brunette. She had been a blonde her entire life.

"That one's got an attitude. Much like her mother," the gray haired woman motioned at the girl in Desdemona's arms. "What ever will you name her?"

A lingering hesitation engulfed the room in silence.

"Desdemona. I will name her Desdemona."

Light streamed into the room, filling the darkness. Desdemona gripped the sheets, terrified and confused as she screamed into the night. She breathed heavily as her mother rushed into her room, pulling her in a tight hug. "Shh shh, it's okay. Everything's fine," her mother whispered in her ear. The shaking of Desdemona's body slowed to a stop, as did her panting. Tears rolled slowly, despite the horror she felt in the pit of her stomach.

Desdemona finally pulled away from the hug and stared at her purple sheets.

"Mona, what's wrong, baby? What happened?" Her mom talked in a voice calmer than it should have been. With a quick glance, Desdemona saw 12:02 p.m. on the clock by her bed. *Only two minutes passed? How can that even be possible?* She thought, running a hand through her bangs. An expression of realization crossed her mom's face, a look which left in an instant.

"Well, go on. It's just me here," her mom urged. Taking a deep breath, Desdemona began to recap the scene to Stacy, stopping every few sentences to collect her thoughts. A look of fear grew and filled her mother's face as she told of her vision in full detail. Towards the end, Stacy Anchor only half listened. She knew the memory. Not only did she know it, she had lived it.

"We have to go," Stacy frantically ordered. "Don't ask questions. I'll explain everything when we get there." Little did they know, just across town, another family found itself in the midst of a similar, harrowing phenomenon.

Blankets pulled over his head, Felix Anchor slept deeply. Outside the door stood his father, cake in hand, waiting for the clock to strike midnight. Marcus Anchor burst into his son's room, loudly singing "Happy Birthday" in his deep baritone voice.

"Happy birthday to you! Happy birthday to you!" he sang, shaking his son gently. He laughed as he continued singing and sat the cake down on the wooden nightstand.

Felix blinked open his eyes, still facing towards the wall and not his father. He smacked his hands over his ears.

"Couldn't this have waited until tomorrow morning, Dad?" Felix complained, hating his dad's punctuality for every single step in life.

"Of course not," Marcus cheered at the end of the song. "It's your fifteenth birthday! Such a big milestone for you!"

Felix wondered why his dad preferred fifteen instead of the normal sixteen, but Marcus raised him so as not to argue with family tradition.

Planning on telling Marcus to leave him alone now—they could repeat this tomorrow morning—Felix flipped over to face his father. At the sight of his father's smiling face, Felix's mind went fuzzy and swirled outside itself.

Deep blue engulfed everything in a dome-like room. Objects and images cluttered his line of sight. Felix, knowing he didn't belong, desperately looked for a way out of the dome. Somewhere in the back of his mind, without knowing the object of his search, he knew he wouldn't be free until he found something. Keeping a steady head, Felix stumbled along an uneven path, falling and scraping his knees more than once. In some spots, he felt his legs ache as he climbed steep mountains, but every time the road would even out and become smooth for a while.

Without warning, the road ended and the space turned bright yellow. On the last brick of the road, he gazed upon a bizarre cake, icing and all, floating.

"If this is another happy birthday trick from my father, I'm going to kill him as soon as I get out," Felix whispered to himself.

But then, images began to form and crowd around the cake. His father now held the frosted delicacy. Not long after, a blurry version of Felix himself faded into the cake. The Felix clone, all smiles, laughed with his father as another shape drifted into the vision. The other shape, fainter, never appeared to stabilize.

The room darkened to a light shade of grey as Felix's stepmother drifted into the picture, holding a lighter. Her small hands lit the candles steadily, a dramatic change from her state just before she passed away a few years ago. They all smiled and sang happy birthday. Felix joined in and sang, despite the song being dedicated to him. Just as he was about to blow out fifteen candles, the walls of the dome began to close in on him and Felix number two disappeared, along with Dad number two and ghost Mom.

The dome grew darker and darker and began to shake; the walls appeared to close in on him. Felix frantically scanned the dome for an escape route, to no avail. The walls were roughly ten meters from Felix now. Five meters. Four. Three. Two. One!

Screaming at the top of his lungs, Felix found himself wrapped in his father's arms, but it hardly felt like a hug. More like a restraint. His heart raced at the speed of light and his thoughts clouded.

"Felix! Felix!" Marcus shouted. "Son!"

It took a few minutes for Felix to find his voice. "There was a dome and it changed colors, with a road, and you, and Mom, and me and it was closing in." He spewed quickly.

"Whoa, whoa, whoa, stay calm. Slow down. I can't understand you," his father soothed quietly.

After a few more seconds of recollection, Felix recited his experience and watched as his father's expression filled with surprise. Then it changed to fear.

Urgency filled his father's voice. "We have to go. Please don't ask questions. I will explain everything when we get there." They had no idea just a few streets away, one final girl would also be receiving her fifteenth birthday "present."

Enjoying the late hours of the night, Jinx Anchor had practically become nocturnal. At night Jinx could think, assess problems, and work them out. The darkness of the night quieted her mind's worries, allowing Jinx to think rationally without interruptions from others.

The clock on her computer screen read 11:59, which meant Jinx still had approximately three hours and one minute to stay awake until it was her time to hit the sack. The computer screen illuminated the dark living room, making it feel slightly less lonely, but Jinx knew she was never really alone. Her grandma was just a shout away at all times. An old, spiritual kook, Hilga Anchor had a young mind for a woman of seventy-two. She kept the room cluttered with dream catchers and other spiritual objects to ward off mythological creatures Jinx didn't quite understand.

A sudden, clanking noise interrupted the peaceful silence and Jinx jumped up, rushing to her grandmother's aid. She ran into the kitchen and found her grandmother on her hands and knees, searching for a large hard plastic cup which clanked on the linoleum floor just a few moments ago. The clock on the stove signaled the mark of midnight as Jinx reached down into the darkness to help her grandmother find the cup.

"Happy birthday, J," her grandmother smiled, reaching for the hiding cup. As Hilga's hand reached the cup, Jinx's fingertips bumped into her wrist and the world went swimming out of focus.

Lightning flashed across the sky at dusk and rain fell by the ton. Hair soaked, weapons bared, Jinx watched as a bystander while an alternate version of herself stood back to back with two other kids. One, a beautiful yellow haired girl and the second, a skinny boy with shaggy blond hair. Each of them terrified, gasping for breath, as if they faced a near-death experience. Each gripped the other's hand, creating a triangle with their arms.

A shape appeared from the shadows and although Jinx could not make out the face, instincts took over. She feared this dangerous woman, but why? Suddenly, the triangle connecting the trio began to glow and shimmer. The shape screamed and raged at the trio, desperately attempting to break the chain, but the teens didn't budge. An unseen power created a bond between their hands. Jinx locked eyes with each member of the trio. Despite the three connecting with one another, to Jinx their faces remained unclear and blurry, fading in and out.

The blonde haired girl shouted something at the shape but the sound of cracking thunder drowned her out.

The boy yelled as well, but Jinx couldn't understand him. He spoke gibberish.

Finally, Jinx herself screeched something at the shape, without even knowing what or why. Jinx no longer controlled her own actions.

As lightning crackled overhead, striking the ground just a few feet from Jinx, she heard herself shout to the others at the top of her lungs. "Trust me!"

Jinx wasn't sure when the tears started or when the screaming began, but a state of uncontrollable hysteria overtook her. Her grandmother pinned Jinx's arms down to her side and pushed her knees on top of Jinx's legs. Jinx' limited movement led her to stop struggling.

"Now, Jinx, tell me what just happened," her grandma asked in a nervous voice.

After a few gasping breaths and multiple swipes at falling tears, Jinx slowly retold the image she just experienced.

Hilga spoke in a calm voice, but her mind raced and she struggled to comprehend. Finally, it dawned on her.

"We have to go. Please don't ask questions. I will explain everything when we get there."

Thus, the third and final pair began their journey to the Frozen Desert.

2

The summer night's moon shone brightly across the ground, mocking Desdemona's tense and stressful mood. Her mom, just a few feet in front of Desdemona, walked briskly to a destination still unknown. A heavy silence filled the open sky as they continued their trip.

"Why didn't we just take the car, Mom?" Desdemona finally asked, breaking into the noiseless night.

"Cars can be tracked and you can't be tracked," Stacy answered. She didn't even glance at her terrified daughter as she put one foot in front of the other. Desdemona's mind raced as she stared down at her feet, which appeared to be moving by themselves. Looking up at her mom, she wondered why her vision suddenly made her mother so anxious. Stacy was never one to particularly worry.

Neither of them daring to say more, they continued on.

A few silent minutes later, Stacy came to an abrupt stop. Desdemona, lost in her own thoughts, ran right into her mother.

"Sorry," Desdemona mumbled, almost inaudibly.

Stacy ignored her apology and began shuffling nervously through her purse. Scratching at the fabric, Stacy tore open a side pocket sewn shut in the purse fifteen years ago. She emerged with an old-fashioned key, holding it in her dainty hand.

They walked around to the back of an abandoned restaurant. Chilled night air swirled around the pair, encircling them as they rounded the corner. Desdemona heard a rustling noise from behind the back dumpster. They were not alone in this darkness.

The back door had been boarded up with hastily cut slabs of chopped oak wood, with rusty, brown nails in between.

Just in between two darker pieces was a clearing, where the wood had not been placed. Stacy gripped her key in a clenched fist and approached the door. A faded sign hung crooked over it. Desdemona squinted to decipher it within the darkness.

Frozen Desert... What a strange name, she thought reflectively. Aren't deserts supposed to be hot? Just as her mom placed the key in the door, another pair of baffled humans stumbled behind the restaurant.

A boy with disheveled blond hair that reflected the dimly lit area looked thoroughly terrified as he clung onto a much older man in front of him. The man, obviously trying to keep his calm, let out a sigh of relief as he laid his eyes on Stacy.

"Wow, long time no see," Stacy called. Marcus brushed off the boy who had latched himself onto his arm and ran over to greet her. They shared a quick embrace and Desdemona noticed while they were hugging, Stacy whispered something into Marcus' ear.

Marcus pulled away, concerned. "Yes, we most definitely have an issue."

There was more to the dialogue with Marcus, but Desdemona didn't get a chance to hear it. She was sucked back into the hospital scene.

Nothing changed within the scene, except this time Desdemona saw it from a different perspective. This time, her mind cluttered, rushing in a million different directions, desperately tried to go from one procedure to the next. Desdemona's muscular hands worked frantically on the struggling woman, attempting to calm her.

Desdemona heard rustling in the background. Someone else was in the room. In the back of her mind, she remembered hearing the shuffling in the last version, but she had been the one rustling the objects. As Desdemona saw the needle in her hands, the puzzle pieces began to fit together one by one. The needle within her fingers plunged into the woman and she went still. Three children squirmed in Desdemona's white-coated arms as she handed one off to the woman who made the rustling noises earlier.

The woman had long brown hair, striking green eyes...

Wow, that looks just like my mom when she was younger, she thought. Then, the last light bulb turned on inside her mind.

That man was Marcus. The woman? The woman was her mom.

This time, Desdemona didn't scream or sob, but instead, stood in shock across the street from the back of the restaurant. She wasn't sure how she ended up there, or why, but as it appears, no one followed her.

Confused and unsure, Desdemona made her way across the ghost town street and back to the group.

As she reached the opposite sidewalk, two hooded figures ducked beyond the Frozen Desert corner. Shivers flew up and down her body, from her pinky toe to the crown of her head and back again.

When she reached the back, the door that had been previously boarded up had been shoved in. She managed to glimpse the two hooded figures ducking into the door. She crawled in after them and listened as the door croaked when she pulled it closed.

The musty and heavy air smelled faintly of dead animals and burnt food from many years ago. Desdemona had an image in her mind of what to expect when she turned around to face the restaurant. But instead of having beat up, wooden chairs, red sparkly leather covered the stools. The whole restaurant had an old fifties feel that made you want to pull out a poodle skirt and do the Hand Jive. From the back room, she heard her mother talking worriedly. She rushed towards the lit up private area to hear sighs of relief at her return.

Her mom jumped up and embraced her. "Oh, Mona, where did you wander off? One moment I was talking to Marcus and the next you're just gone. When we went looking for you, you were nowhere to be found. We were afraid you'd already been taken…" Her voice trailed off and cracked with emotion.

A girl with stringy, dark black hair stood up and looked at Stacy. Desdemona recognized this girl from school. Thinking back to last semester's AP Government course, she recalled her name - Jinx. Desdemona drew a blank as to her last name. To be honest, she always thought Jinx was a little strange.

"We will answer your questions when you answer ours." Jinx's assertive personality shocked Desdemona and it obviously shocked Stacy as well.

An older woman Desdemona assumed was Jinx's grandmother addressed the party of six in a surprisingly strong voice. "We will tell you everything going on, but first we need to know your stories."

The man, Marcus, chimed in. "We know the three of you have been through traumatic experiences tonight, but please bear with us as you recap your visions for the rest of us."

Momentary silence followed, as none of the teenagers wanted to be the first to spill.

The boy, silent up to this point, cleared his throat.

"Um… I guess I will start. Hi, everyone, I'm Felix, for those who don't know. Goodness, I feel like I'm at one of those meetings where you work on your anger management issues," he laughed a little before continuing. He went on to explain his story of how he transferred to a strange place and saw his dead mother. Honestly, hearing Felix's story made Desdemona feel a lot better about her sanity.

"And when did the vision start? Tell us the exact moment you remember," Jinx's grandmother, who introduced herself as Hilga, asked Felix.

Felix scrunched his pale face up in concentration. "I guess it happened when I saw my father. I rolled over in bed to tell him to shoo and then I saw him. The moment I saw him, I kind of left my mind and entered someone else's."

The three adults in the room shared a look of confusion. The three kids in the room shifted their eyes, trying to focus on anything but their guardians.

"Um… I'll go next," Jinx announced, crossing her left leg over her right leg.

She proceeded to tell a story about seeing three teenagers back to back in a triangle, desperately trying to fend off a horrifying shape.

"And when did this start for you?" Stacy asked.

Her response was instantaneous. "I touched Grandmother's hand when we reached for a cup she dropped on the kitchen floor. The moment I touched her, it started."

Desdemona knew it was her turn for story time next and, not wanting to bear the awkward silence, she began to speak.

"Well umm… My dream thing started at the moment I heard my mom's voice through the wall talking about my surprise birthday party." Desdemona ignored the gasp coming from Stacy when she realized her daughter knew about the surprise for some time now. She told everything, not leaving out a single detail. And when she finished the first vision she proceeded to disclose the most recent one, including the part where she found herself alone on the sidewalk across the street.

"Okay…" Stacy said after some time. "Who wants to tell them?"

"Tell us what?" Jinx asked, pursing her lips.

"Are we going to die?" Felix worried aloud.

No one answered Felix's question. No one reassured the three kids of their safety; no one even made an attempt to calm their nerves. And it hung there, suspended in the stuffy air of the abandoned restaurant.

"We need to get them out of here before she realizes they've come of age," Stacy said quickly, completely ignoring Felix's question. "Take them to The House… immediately."

The three children looked at each other in confusion as all three adults rose from their chairs and hustled out of the Frozen Desert.

"Hey," Jinx yelled. "What's The House? I'm not leaving this seat until I get some answers."

Hilga whipped her head back into the open doorway, the lights framing her face. "You will follow us right now, young lady. That is, unless you want to be found by *her*."

Desdemona, Jinx, and Felix all looked at each other. Each expression mimicked the other. Fear, desperation, confusion. Without another word, the three rose to their feet and followed their families out of the Frozen Desert.

3

All six of them sat in Stacy's minivan. Apparently, speed was more important than secrecy because Stacy was all too quick to offer up her minivan to take them to their destination. Silence filled the heavy air, making it nearly unbearable for the uprooted kids. Despite their discomfort, no one said a word. The children did not ask questions and their families did not volunteer answers.

Darkness swirled in the trees beside them as they drove. With each opening in the foliage, Desdemona's stomach churned. *What lurked in the trees and made her mom drive so fast? What happened in her mind earlier? What had she seen? What in the world is happening to her?*

Finally, Jinx broke Desdemona's inner questionnaire. "So… what are we doing about sleeping arrangements? It's nearly 3:00 a.m. and I would like to stop somewhere and maybe get some Arby's or Subway before we sleep." Nobody answered her. Hilga ignored her question and apparently so did everyone else. Desdemona looked over just quick enough to see Jinx open her mouth, as if to repeat her question, but then closed it again before speaking. Desdemona guessed everyone had been asking their own inner questions.

Head pounding, heart throbbing, Desdemona decided she should probably try to get some sleep. Taking one more look out at the dark night, she glanced at the stars in the sky and noticed the gleam of a street sign that read "Baton Rulle 4 miles."

Baton Rulle... What a weird name for a city. Desdemona thought before closing her eyes and drifting into the night.

After what felt like only a few minutes of peace, Desdemona awoke to another flurry of activity. The car violently skidded to a stop on the side of a cobblestone street. Marcus jumped out of the car and sprinted into a large house. Stacy and Hilga leapt out of the car and opened the door for the three teenagers in the back. All three hesitated, confused, sleepy, and disoriented.

Stacy shook her daughter's arm. "Mona, you need to get up. Get out of the car." Desdemona, deciding not to argue with her mom right now, tumbled out of the car and nearly landed face first on to the cobblestone. Rubbing her chin with the palm of her hand, she groaned. Strong, but surprisingly soft hands lifted her up. When she turned around, she saw a kind smile on Felix's face.

"It's alright. I'm pretty clumsy too," he shrugged.

Desdemona noticed how his shoulders were broad, yet curved and rounded. What a strange combination.

Hilga, followed by a very angry and confused Jinx, soon joined the group in front of the large house. For the first time, Desdemona turned to really look at the building. About five stone steps led up to a building made entirely of the same cobblestone which lined the street. Though the building appeared to be no more than five stories high, it towered over the other structures on the street. Each story had four windows, two on each side.

Stacy, motioning for the group to follow, made her way up the steps to the door. A dark brass handle adorned the large, light colored wooden door, in sharp contrast with the cobblestone building. Above the door, in bold letters, it read 1021 Pisa Drive, Boston, Massachusetts. Stacy put her hand on the knob, muttered something inaudibly under her breath, and turned it to open the door.

The second her feet touched the stone floors inside the building, a strong aroma hit Desdemona. A mixture of the smell of sunscreen and the beach - hands down the best smell of Desdemona's young life. With each deep breath, she remembered the favorite place her mom used to take her at Destin Beach in Florida.

Felix also breathed in the irresistible smell of The House, but to him, it was a much different scent. To Felix, The House sported an aroma of freshly washed clothing and grilled steak, his favorite smells from his very own house.

But Jinx experienced something of her own accord. Jinx enjoyed a fragrance of The House which resembled the blackberry jam Hilga made every season when the blackberries were just right.

Taking in the intoxicating smell, Desdemona raised her eyes to look up, realizing for the first time the building was much larger than she predicted.

Five stories? No way this thing is five stories… Desdemona thought. Slowly counting some of the floors, Desdemona counted twenty-three until she lost track. The high ceiling and open foyer allowed her to see all the way to the top. She had only seen four windows on each floor outside, but there appeared to be at least thirty rooms on each floor.

"Okay, am I being punked right now?" Jinx asked, obviously annoyed. "Because if I am, I would like to applaud the person who contributed to the special effects of this building."

Sarcastically clapping, Jinx followed closely behind Desdemona, who nervously began to twist her hair in her right hand. As she counted the floors, Desdemona began to notice kids, no younger than her, poking their heads out of the doors. While the lobby area they stood in remained silent, Desdemona soon realized everyone above was watching their group.

Felix hadn't said a word this entire time. Instead, he seemed to be looking at the ground, nervously counting his steps. He rubbed his temples, as if he had a bad headache.

I'm right there with you, Felix. Desdemona thought, as her own head began to pound.

Stacy and Hilga began to approach a desk where Marcus stood, talking briskly to a tall man behind it. After listening to Marcus, the man stepped out from behind the desk and placidly, yet deliberately, made his way to the trio. He held his head high in the air and looked down at the three from under his spectacles. His graying hair showed he was much older. The look in his stormy, gray eyes held years of wisdom and intelligence.

21

"Ah, the Anchors. How good it is to finally meet you," The man exclaimed excitedly with a youthful tone not exactly matching his appearance. "I was expecting to see you guys soon enough. How are you? How do you feel?"

"It smells so good in here." Desdemona noted appreciatively.

Mr. Belton nodded. "Ah, yes. I would imagine it does, but The House has a different perfume to every Asterian who enters its doors. In fact, The House takes upon a mixture of everyone's favorite aromas.

Jinx stared at Mr. Belton, appalled and confused. "I don't know about these two, but I'm confused and I think we all deserve some answers."

"I agree," Felix spoke up, wiping his shaggy blond hair out of his face. "We were dragged from our homes on our birthdays and I would like to know why."

"Have you told them anything yet?" The man with the gray hair asked.

Marcus shook his head. "No, we were waiting for you to explain everything to them. You can do it better than we can."

"Ah, yes, I suppose so. Come along then. We can go into my office and I will give you the answers to all of your questions, or nearly all of them as I can figure," the man noted.

Desdemona felt a slight touch on her arm and turned around to see her mom. "Mona... now is the time I should be leaving."

Stopping in her tracks, Desdemona turned to totally face Stacy. "Wait, no. You can't just leave me like this. I'm confused and scared. You're the only one I can trust anymore..."

Desdemona's mom had a pained expression on her face. "You won't trust me after you hear the whole story. We needed to get you to the safety of The House. I love you but baby, I must leave now. Those are the rules."

Wanting to argue, but not wishing to make her mom angry, Desdemona threw her arms around Stacy. "I'll miss you. I love you."

"I love you too, Mona. Call me, sweetheart," Stacy whispered in reply.

When Desdemona pulled away, she noticed Felix saying a wet, tear-filled goodbye to his father. Jinx gave a brisk, yet heartfelt hug to Hilga and all three pulled away from their children.

"Don't forget to call." Stacy yelled back to Desdemona. Waving her hands high in the air, Desdemona said one last goodbye to her mother. All three disappeared out the large wooden door. Desdemona, Jinx, and Felix turned to face the man.

The man watched their goodbyes with great interest and with a sweeping hand gesture, motioned the trio to follow him into a door behind the desk where they had first found him. Like Stacy had done, he held his hand on the door knob, whispered something under his breath and the door swung open.

So weird... Desdemona thought.

It really is weird, isn't it? A voice said in Desdemona's head, startling her. But she immediately recognized the voice as the soft, determined tone of Felix. She looked over at him in desperation only to see his face mimicking hers. He shrugged.

I guess we will find out soon... Felix's voice trailed off in her mind again. Desdemona nodded, following Jinx and the man inside the office.

The room they entered had ceilings as high as the rest of the building with large, glass windows rising up to the rafters. A large mahogany desk, much like the one outside the office, sat in the far right corner of the room. A small, quaint sitting area occupied the middle of the room, with three red plush chairs across from one blue chair.

The man sat down in the blue chair and motioned for the trio to sit down across from him. Desdemona sat on the left, with Felix next to her and Jinx to the right.

"I guess proper introductions are much needed on my part. I am Jason Belton, headmaster, bookkeeper, and executive of The House. You, however, can address me as Mr. Belton"

"The House?" Jinx asked with a snarky, irritated smirk.

"Ah, yes. The House is a training center for those much like you," Mr. Belton told them.

Desdemona stayed silent, patiently waiting for him to continue. When no one said anything, he finally spoke again. "The three of you are what we call Asterians. Asterians are much like specialized wizards, you could say. I mean this in the sense that Asterians, unlike wizards, only have one power they work on perfecting over the course of many years. Our history spans many centuries, originating in Eastern Europe, later rapidly spreading to the United States. Unfortunately, fewer and fewer Asterians have been identified each year. Often, Asterian powers pass from parents to children, sometimes skipping generations, and sometimes Asterians do not even recognize their powers. But with such gifted parents, you most likely will be as well."

Jinx cut him off. "But no one in my family has any special powers."

"Not in mine either," Desdemona noted. Felix shook his head in agreement.

Mr. Belton let out a small, haughty laugh. "All three of you are wrong. Your family is very gifted. Perhaps the most gifted we have ever seen."

After seeing the look of confusion on the kid's faces, Mr. Belton hurried his explanation. "You are triplets. The people who have taken care of you love you, but they are not your true parents. Your family here begins with Hilga, who is grandmother to all three of you. Marcus and Stacy are your aunt and uncle. Your real mother was … not exactly 'mother' material."

"Well…" Felix spoke up. "What happened to our real mother?"

Mr. Belton shook his head, hesitating. Finally, he answered. "Stacy, Marcus, and Jane, your mother, were three of the most talented siblings ever to train here at The House. Often, siblings' powers go hand in hand with one another. Siblings can work together as a team. Stacy could slow down the use of someone else's powers. Marcus could read and interpret other Asterians' gifts. Your real mother, Jane, became the most powerful of her siblings. With a single touch, she could strip others of their powers entirely and use them as her own. With a great gift like hers, of course Jane needed to be very careful about how she used it."

"And was she careful?" Desdemona asked, leaning on the edge of her chair, listening intently.

"Jane Anchor? Jane Anchor was never careful. Jane began to abuse her power and wreak havoc on The House. She would strip other powerful teens of their gifts, including Stacy and Marcus, Her own siblings. Eventually, it got to a point where we had no choice. We expelled Jane from our training center for good."

"So what happened to her?" Jinx questioned.

Mr. Belton took a deep breath. "No one heard from her for several years. One day, about fifteen years ago, we heard Jane gave birth to triplets, a boy and two girls. Knowing you could be more powerful than even her, Stacy, Hilga, and Marcus took the three of you and hid you from her, protecting your powers. No one has seen your mother since that day."

4

"Well, where is she now?" Felix asked, nervously twisting his fingers and looking around, as if he expected Jane to pop out from the walls at any moment.

"I can't quite answer that for you, young man. But I can tell you we believe her to be alive, somewhere," Mr. Belton answered, getting up to pace in front of his chair.

Jinx tilted her head to the side in skepticism. "How can you possibly know?"

"We know she's alive because she hasn't yet been reported otherwise. The Asterian Society, a league of the most powerful, wise Asterians ever to have lived, reports all deaths. Jane Anchor has yet to be found as such."

Suddenly, a light rapping was heard on the door.

"Who is it?" Mr. Belton yelled.

"It's Margret," a sweet voice answered from the other side. "I was told to come take the Anchors to their rooms."

Mr. Belton told Margret to come in and a petite, striking red haired girl entered the office. Felix's eyes went wide at the sight of the girl and she smiled softly at him.

"Ah yes. I think it would be best for them to go get settled," Mr. Belton agreed.

"Wait," Jinx stopped and stood up. "I'm still confused. What does this have to do with any of us?"

Mr. Belton turned to look once more at Jinx. "Why, of course, you are here to begin your Ascension."

"What in the heck does that mean?" replied Jinx. Despite the fire in her eyes, her question did not faze Mr. Belton. "All Asterians who come of age must join us at The House, away from their parents, to train for a period of time. You have much to learn. The four of us will continue this conversation tomorrow in the training wing. Right now, Margret will show the three of you to your rooms in the living wing. It's late and I know each of you has had a lot to process tonight."

You don't say, Felix's voice drifted into Desdemona's mind. Desdemona giggled softly, mentally agreeing with him and trying to ignore the uncomfortable feeling she got at the thought of some stranger inside of her head.

"Run along now. You have a long day ahead of you tomorrow. You will find all your things from your rooms at home have been moved into your rooms here."

Margret waited expectantly as the three siblings followed her out the door of the office. Once the door shut behind them, Desdemona turned to look at her.

"So, what's your um… gift?"

Margret smiled a beautiful, soft smile and said in the sweetest tone, "Felix, I need you to run down the street to the grocery and buy twelve pounds of cat food, will you? Do that for me?"

Without a word, Felix turned and began to walk out the door. Margret's smile fell and Felix stopped in his tracks. She smiled again. "Come back now, Felix."

He made his way back to the group and when he stood beside Desdemona once more, Margret let her smile down. He stopped walking.

"What just happened to me?" Felix asked.

"My power is one of persuasion. I can make any boy do what I ask of him with a simple smile and a command," Margret explained sweetly.

Desdemona nearly jumped with excitement. "That's so awesome. I hope my power is as cool at that."

Margret giggled one of the purest laughs Desdemona ever heard and began to walk. The trio followed closely behind, looking extremely clumsy behind Margret's graceful step. As they walked, Desdemona looked up at the high-arching ceilings and once again saw the faces of many others peering down.

Creepy... Desdemona thought to herself.

Why are they all looking at us like that? Felix asked in Desdemona's mind. Desdemona shrugged and shook her head, just as confused as Felix.

Margret finally stopped near another wooden door and placed her hand on the frame of it. She whispered something under her breath and the door opened to what appeared to be an elevator.

Stepping in, Margret motioned to a wall entirely covered in buttons. "The floors in The House range from floor 1, the lobby, all the way to floor 365." Her hand glided on the left side of the buttons, which lit up in groups of different colors. "The green buttons, floors 2-150, is the living wing. These are where you will find all of your rooms and living areas. The red buttons, which are floors 151-250, is where you will find all of your training rooms and arenas. The blue buttons, floors 251-300, include all eating areas and entertainment centers. Finally, the yellow buttons, floors 301-365, are the classrooms where you learn all about the Asterians."

Felix, overwhelmed by the size of The House, wondered if he would ever manage to find his way around. He imagined months of taking wrong turns in the corridors and ending up on the other side of the giant school.

Margret pressed a green button, floor 111, and the elevator shot up. Desdemona assumed this was the floor of their room and desperately hoped she would remember it later when she needed it.

The elevator, which seemed to be moving at least 80 miles per hour, stopped at floor 111 with a loud ding. Margret flowed out of the elevator with Jinx, Felix, and Desdemona and entered a dimly lit hallway. The hallway was long - longer than Desdemona's eyes could see.

"We have divided the rooms here at The House by family. As the Anchor family, you will be sharing a suite."

Jinx opened her mouth to protest about having to share a room with people she hardly knew, but Margret cut her off with a wave of her hand.

"Before you freak out on me, you each get your own personal room within the suite. Since Asterian powers center around family heritage and past gifts, your rooms connect in a suite to strengthen your relationship as siblings," Margret smiled politely at Jinx, who was obviously still unhappy with the living situation.

Jinx curled her hands into fists. "Strengthen our relationship as siblings? I don't even know these people. I don't know a single thing about them and now you want us living together and calling ourselves brother and sister? Maybe this works for these two softies, but not for me." Jinx turned to face Desdemona and Felix. "I don't know you and I don't have any desire to change that. And I would say sorry, but I'm not."

Jinx defiantly whipped around, flipping her short hair behind her, and stomped to the elevator.

"You don't know how to use that elevator, Jinx," Margret reminded her. "Please come back so we can work this out."

Jinx, more frustrated than ever now, groaned in annoyance and stomped down the stone steps to the left of the elevator.

Desdemona and Felix both looked at Margret, as if expecting her to know what to do. Margret sighed and told the pair that every crowd had one, a hothead, and the only way to deal with them was to let them cool off.

"But shouldn't we go find her? She doesn't know her way around this..." Felix hesitated, "...place yet and I'm worried she'll run into trouble."

"Yeah, I guess that would be best," Margret agreed. "There's a boy on the 110th floor who can identify any person's exact location within a hundred mile radius. Let's go to him."

Desdemona and Felix both followed Margret down a single flight of steps. Desdemona noticed cobwebs in the corners of the ceiling.

Gross. Someone should really clean this place, Desdemona thought to herself. Everything was peaceful until Margret stepped down the last step and her ballet flats made a clink on the stone. The entire stairwell swirled out of focus and Desdemona's mind went black.

When surroundings started to come to her, Desdemona found herself in the same stairwell, except here, cobwebs no longer sat idle in the corners. Her feet hit the stone stairs silently as she ran. When she reached the last step, a loud clinking, echoing noise filled the stairwell. Her mind ran wild, pulsing with an anger and fear stronger than anything she ever experienced.

"They're crazy if they think I'm really going to believe I have powers. What do they think I am? Five?" Desdemona asked herself with a deep, dark laugh. She realized it happened again - she spoke with a voice and laughed with a laugh not her own. Desdemona kept running down the steps until she reached an open doorway. Here, she exited the stairwell into a dimly lit room. Two figures stood there, a boy and a girl. Though she could not see their faces, body language showed their displeasure with her.

"Jane, it's okay," The boy said, reaching out to her. His hand brushed her arm and she flinched away, swatting at his touch.

The girl stepped into the light and her face looked a lot like a younger version of someone Desdemona had seen before…

"J, we know you're scared, but we promise, everything you're hearing is true. You really do have these powers. You're one of the strongest Asterians here," the girl said.

Desdemona's mind rambled on and on, searching for the right words. "I don't… I don't want this. I never asked for this. I just want to go back to high school and have a normal teenage life." Desdemona shrieked, throwing her hands up in the air. Tears began to stream down her face and she started to turn around and flee, but a hand closing around her wrist stopped her.

"We're your siblings, J. We know this is a lot for you to process. It is for all of us, but we have to stick together. We're a team, remember?" The girl said, pulling Desdemona into a tight hug. She felt the boy's arms wrap around both of the girls and Desdemona's vision faded.

Strong hands touched at Desdemona's face, feeling her forehead. She opened her eyes just in time to see Felix's face close to hers, inspecting her carefully. When she looked at him, his face immediately flushed with relief.

"Oh, thank goodness, you're alive. I swear, I thought you were dead," Felix said, putting his hand over his heart.

Desdemona laughed weakly and sat up slowly. She noticed Margret leaning against the wall near the cobwebs.

"And she wasn't even concerned," Felix gasped, exasperated. "She didn't even flinch when you fell."

Margret giggled at him, placing her hand delicately over her pink lips to muffle the sound. "I knew it had something to do with your powers. I don't know what your powers are, but I knew that was it. As soon as I made sure you didn't hit your head on the stone, I stopped worrying, unlike this goofball over here."

Felix's eyes widened as Margret mentioned him and then he smiled goofily, further proving her comment.

"C'mon, Felix. We need to go find Jinx right now," Desdemona ordered, rising to her feet. Thinking about the dark room seen in her vision, Desdemona knew Jinx's exact location. Margret started to follow them as they continued down another flight, but Desdemona put her hand up, stopping her. "This is something Felix and I need to do. Alone."

Margret didn't put up a fight, but Felix sure did. "Wait, no," he shouted. "She's the only one who knows her way around this building."

Desdemona waved lightly to Margret and pulled Felix down the steps. As she walked, she began to explain things to him. "I know where I'm going," Desdemona stated.

"How? Are you okay? You had a pretty big incident back there," Felix asked, this time questioning her sanity.

Desdemona took a big breath. "I had a vision. About the past. That's my power. I can see the past."

Felix's eyes opened with surprise and his jaw dropped only slightly before he promptly closed it and waited for her to continue.

"What I saw this time, I think, was our mom. Not our fake moms, but our real mom. A girl ran down this same stairwell, scared of this place and angry out of her mind. When she got down the steps, she noticed a boy and a girl, Marcus and Stacy. They comforted her, reassured her everything was going to be alright. They called her Jane..."

Just as she finished informing Felix of her vision, they reached the same dimly lit room. Except this time, she saw just one shape in the shadows. The slight curves in the shadow proved it to be a girl and the short, out-of-control hair told it to be Jinx. She breathed heavily from the darkness and took a single step into the light. The faded darkness made Jinx's features look more pointed than normal and Desdemona saw the haze in her eyes.

Felix took one step into the empty, stone room. "Jinx..." he started hesitantly. She took another step back, making him hold his hands up in surrender. "Hey, talk to us."

Jinx huffed in protest, crossing her arms. "I don't want to talk. Leave me alone."

Felix looked back at Desdemona in desperation.

Do we leave? Felix asked in her mind. Desdemona shook her head fiercely. They would not run away.

"You know," Desdemona started. "Neither of us are exactly wrapping our heads around this either. Nothing gives you the right to run away and leave the two of us here to face all this."

Jinx cocked her head to the side, daring Desdemona to say more. She got her wish. Desdemona pointed a finger at her. "And you know, Felix and I aren't thrilled about it either, but you don't see us getting so worked up."

Her voice rose a pitch in frustration with Jinx and only then did Desdemona realize she had been the one getting worked up. Felix took a small step back to stand next to Desdemona and put a hand on her arm.

"Actually, I do see you getting worked up." Jinx accused, taking a few steps closer to them. She towered over Desdemona and when she stood less than three feet from her, it became obvious who would win if a fight were to begin.

Felix stepped in between them. "Look, girls, we're never going to get anywhere if you keep fighting. The only way we're ever going to work something out is if we talk." Jinx stared down at Desdemona with squinted eyes while she lifted her chin to glare back. Finally, Desdemona took a step back from her, retreating.

Felix let out a sigh of relief at the averted crisis. "Why don't we all get some sleep and we can discuss more in the morning?"

Jinx still appeared to be opposed. "I don't feel comfortable sleeping there."

Desdemona opened her mouth, ready to tell Jinx off for being so selfish, but Felix shot her a glance and she shut up.

"It's just one night for now, Jinx," Felix persuaded. "If you're still opposed to it tomorrow, we can try to work something out. It's been a really, really long day."

The girls nodded in agreement and they slowly made their way back up the steps they had just come down. The stairwell became utterly silent, except for the light pitter-patter of footsteps. When they reached floor 111, Margret stood waiting at the door for them.

"Your handprints have been programmed into the doors here. Simply place your palm on the wood and say your last name. That will get you into any room in this Training Center," Margret informed them.

Without another word, Felix placed his hand on the wood of the door and whispered "Anchor." The door swung open into a small hallway. He saw four doors, three on the right and one on the left. Three bedrooms on the right with a very large bathroom on the left, big enough for the three of them. Desdemona opened the door to the first room and saw dark blue color with white trim, a desk to the left and a twin sized bed in the middle of the room. Beaten up licenses plates littered the walls.

"This looks just like my room at my house…" Felix whispered to himself in awe. Jinx ignored his comment, opened the door to the second room, walked in and slammed it shut behind her.

I guess that's her room, Desdemona thought to herself.

Sighing at the sight of Jinx's shut door, Desdemona waved lightly to Felix and went into the third room. Purple, just like her room at home, with all of the stuff in her bedroom prior to this crazy day.

Not even bothering to change out of her clothes, Desdemona flung herself onto the queen-size bed. She pulled the covers up to her chin and closed her eyes, but her mind wouldn't rest. She worried about Jinx.

How could this girl be Desdemona's sister? No doubt, they hadn't exactly started off on the right foot. She gripped the sheets tight, desperately wanting to get along with Jinx.

You'll get along with her someday, Felix's voice drifted into her mind from the other room.

Desdemona huffed, annoyed with even Felix at this point. *Stop doing that. It makes me uncomfortable you can get inside my head.*

Don't let it, Felix said. His voice whispered in her mind. *I can't control it yet, but this is my power. I can see the present through people's thoughts.*

Desdemona thought quickly. *Have you pushed into Jinx's mind?*

No, Felix answered. *Like I said, I can't control it yet. Her mind seems more guarded than yours.*

Desdemona thought about this for a second, wondering if people's minds looked like their personalities.

Get some sleep. Felix ordered her and then left, saying nothing more. Desdemona turned on her side and looked at the string of Christmas lights which hung year-round in her room.

"It looks just like home," Desdemona heard herself whisper before finally falling into a deep sleep.

5

When Felix and Desdemona awoke the next morning, they saw one special change of clothes laid outside each of their rooms. The clothing looked like a stretchy material which would fit tightly, almost like a wetsuit. The red fabric had a small, stitched in name just below the neckline. It read *Anchor* in fancy, curved white calligraphy. A note had been placed on top of the outfits. In neat penmanship, the note read:

Put on the training outfits and report to room 161 at 10:00am for your first training session. Have a great day. ~Margret

Felix's heart fluttered at the thought of Margret thinking of him and writing him a note, but before he got completely lost in his trance thinking about her beautiful red hair, Desdemona walked out of her room in the training outfit.

"Is Jinx up?" She asked, placing her hand on her hip. Desdemona pulled her golden hair back away from her face into a loose ponytail, outlining her soft features.

"I don't know," Felix answered. "Do you want to see? It's already 9:30 and we wouldn't want her to be late."

"I'm not going in there," Desdemona answered defiantly. Felix groaned, saying he would do it and knocked lightly on her door. A loud groan erupted from the other side of the door.

"Jinx…" Felix started. "We have training in thirty minutes and you need to get ready."

Suddenly, the door swung open and a sleepy eyed, messy haired Jinx appeared in the doorway. She glanced at Desdemona in her training outfit quickly then reached down to pick up her training outfit. Without another word, she shut the door in Felix's face and left him alone with Desdemona.

"Dang," Desdemona noted. Felix nodded, despondently hoping Jinx would lighten up sooner rather than later. When he went into his room to change into his training outfit, he heard a snippet of a voice that wasn't Desdemona's.

They hate- he heard. *They don't understand. They can't-*

He heard choppy, incomplete words and phrases, so much so that he couldn't even make out what the person was trying to say. Whose voice was it? He hoped from the depths of his heart he had heard Jinx's voice, but he hadn't heard her enough to know exactly what it sounded like.

After putting on his training outfit, Felix walked out into their small hallway where Desdemona sat on the ground with her arms wrapped around her legs. Soon, Jinx reluctantly joined them and they walked as siblings towards room 161. Or, as close as siblings could be after knowing each other for about ten hours.

When they exited their small hallway into the larger hallway, they found it filled with other kids around their age. Some dressed in training outfits, like the three of them, while others wore their school clothes. Light chatter and morning excitement filled the air of the hallway while the kids sat in groups of three or four. Slowly, the students started to notice the three newcomers. The loud chatter dulled to a low whisper.

Felix heard whispers of "Is that them?" and "The Anchor children?' Inside a guy's mind, he heard *Dang, that girl looks good in her training uniform.*

Felix turned to Desdemona, pointing to the guy whose voice he just heard. "That guy thinks you're hot," he whispered.

Desdemona snorted in response and tugged on Felix's wrist, leading them down the hallway to the elevator. Jinx followed behind silently.

When they reached the wooden door holding the elevator, it opened quickly to reveal a short, stubby boy with blond hair. He was no older than them, but when they entered, he looked inquisitively at the three siblings.

"The Anchor kids, right?" The boy asked excitedly. "We read about Jane Anchor in The House history the other day."

None of them knew exactly how to react, so Jinx waved him off with her hand. Desdemona, shrugging off Jinx's curtness, turned to the boy. "Umm yeah. I'm Desdemona," she introduced, sticking out her hand. "And this is Felix and that is Jinx."

The boy shook Desdemona's outstretched hand with a vivacious grip. "Is it really true you're Her kids?"

"Jane's?" Felix asked him to clarify.

The boy gasped. "So you are?"

Felix nodded and the boy looked from his left to his right, inspecting Felix as if he were an unfamiliar animal. Finally, the boy turned his eyes back to Felix's face.

"Is it true she can take away powers?" He asked with wide eyes.

Felix shrugged. "I don't know. I've never met her. I mean, I would assume it's true because that's what Mr. Belton told me."

The boy looked like he wanted to say more, but before he could, the elevator dinged and the door slid open. Jinx exited quickly. Desdemona and Felix had no choice but to follow. With a slight wave, Desdemona bid the boy goodbye.

The trio moved quickly, ignoring the students who whispered and pointed as they walked past. Soon enough, they reached room 161. The room's stone door, with its slight cracks going in all different directions, looked old, ancient really. Felix worried that pressing his hand to the door wouldn't work this time because of the stone, but he decided to give it a shot.

Pressing his hand to the cold, broken, stone, Felix whispered under his breath as the door made an awful squeaking noise. It began to inch open, each second screeching on the floor. Finally, the door opened about halfway and it came to a stop. They slid into the room and each breathed a sigh of awe when they entered.

"Whoa," Jinx noted, seeming somewhat excited for the first time since coming to The House. In all honesty, Felix would be surprised if this room didn't baffle everyone. Looking upwards into a room which had to be indoors, he saw a milky sky which stretched seemingly forever upwards. Long yellow-green grass swayed in the light breeze, reaching the middle of their ankles. Small, brightly colored flowers spotted the meadow.

In the middle of the grass stood a tall, lanky boy, no older than seventeen. Black hair flipped freely across the forehead of his chiseled, handsome face. His white cutoff tank top showed off his arm muscles. Felix heard Desdemona muffle a gasp.

I've never seen anyone look that amazing, Felix heard Desdemona think to herself. Felix elbowed Desdemona in the side, hinting to her he heard her flirty inner commentary. She elbowed him right back and began to walk towards the mysterious boy, who tilted his head to look at her.

"Ah yes," he began. "The Anchor family. I was told to expect you here today." His voice was raspy, but flowing, fluctuating up and down at just the right times. Felix saw Desdemona give her best award winning smile.

"And you are?" Felix asked him.

"I am Kade Defrates, your trainer," he answered, brushing his hair out of his deep green eyes.

Jinx narrowed her eyes at him. "Our trainer? You're too young to train us."

Suddenly, the meadow went dark and hissing noises filled the room. Slimy, scaly creatures moved below them, brushing against their feet. Desdemona shrieked beside Felix, but wind, rapidly increasing in speed, muffled her scream. Felix could feel it whip around him in a circle, making him unsteady on his feet. He began to stumble to his knees, where the snakes climbed up his legs.

He heard Jinx yell from near him. "Okay, fine. Stop it."

As if on command, light filled the meadow and everything returned to normal. Felix rose to his feet and noticed Desdemona practically shaking across the meadow. Jinx stood in place with her arms crossed over her chest, looking angrily at Kade.

"That wasn't funny. You used your powers to scare us," Jinx told him, glaring with stormy eyes.

"It might not have been funny for you," Kade agreed, tossing a pen into the air. "But it sure was funny for me and it got my point across. Yes, I'm only 17, but I can make people see illusions and completely strip them of their senses."

"How original," Jinx mocked, huffing. By this time, Desdemona made her way back to the group and stood next to Felix, who waited patiently for further instruction.

"My first job as the Anchor family trainer will be to help you discover your gifts," Kade told them, looking each of them up and down from head to toe. "Have any of you an idea what your powers could be? An inkling or a guess?"

Desdemona was the first to speak up. "I think I can see visions of the past."

Kade perked up at that idea and asked her to explain. She promptly told him of her three visions, the first two of the hospital and the third of Jane. Kade narrowed his eyes at her, nodding as she recounted each in great detail.

"And when did each of these happen?" he asked. Desdemona tilted her head, confused. Kade explained further. "I mean, what triggered these visions?"

"Well…" Desdemona thought hard. "The first was the sound of my mom's- I mean, Stacy's- voice. The second, there was a loud banging noise and the third happened when Margret's foot hit the step with a bang."

Kade nodded, not saying more about Desdemona's gift, but scribbled something on a clipboard he held. Next he turned to Felix.

"What about you?" he asked.

"I can read minds, sort of a power to see the present," Felix began. He then told Kade the story of what happened when he saw Marcus in his room the night of his birthday. He recalled how he saw his dead step mom and the hills and valleys in the vision. "I can also hear people's thoughts on and off, but I can't control when I hear them."

"And what triggered your vision that night?" Kade asked, again brushing his hair to the side. Desdemona beamed beside Felix.

"The vision? Well, it happened when I first saw Marcus in my room, holding the cake."

Kade scribbled something again and turned to Jinx. "And what about you, sassy?"

Jinx huffed at his comment and curtly told him the story of her single vision. She noted to him she didn't know what the vision was or why it came to her. When Kade asked her when it happened, she told him it happened when her hand touched Hilga's wrist.

"Well, this is surely a very interesting bunch of gifts you guys have here," Kade told them. "They're some of the most connected powers I've ever seen within siblings."

"So what does that mean?" Desdemona asked eagerly.

"It means you may be some of the most powerful Asterians ever to enter The House, but I'm sure you've already heard that before."

"Multiple times. Thanks for the input though," Jinx said with a sarcastic smirk.

Kade ignored Jinx's immature comment and continued. "I think the three of you can see the past, present, and the future, and when you put those three things together, it could be amazing."

"But why did you ask us what triggered the visions?" Felix asked.

"I wanted to try to figure out the cause of your gifts," Kade told them. "And I'll have to look into this further, but from what I can see, the visions are caused by hearing, sight, and touch."

Kade looked at each of them skeptically. "I would like to work with each of you individually before throwing you all together and working with you as a team."

Felix wasn't sure about this approach as a method to teach them team building skills as a family, but he decided not to argue with the man who could probably render him blind and deaf within a matter of seconds.

"Felix," Kade shouted. Felix snapped back to attention and stood up a little straighter. "We will start with you."

Desdemona looked very disappointed with Kade's choice of order, but didn't argue. Jinx, on the other hand, looked ready to get out of the room as quickly as possible.

"Girls, I would like to work with Felix. So, if you could please step out of the room, that would be delightful," Kade ordered in a sweet, yet authoritative voice. "Don't wait outside. It could be a while. I will call you when I need another one of you."

Desdemona almost protested, but Jinx grabbed onto her arm and yanked her around, shutting her up. Without another word, the sisters swiftly exited the meadow. Felix turned to face Kade, who watched him apprehensively.

"Do you know why I began with you, Felix?" Kade asked, circling him like a vicious predator.

Though terribly afraid, Felix tried to seem like he had his thoughts together. "Because you were sick of Mona and Jinx?"

Kade let out a weak laugh, letting Felix know his joke was not appreciated. "No. I chose you because your gift confused me the most. You told me you could read minds, which I believe, but what happened with your father sounded like quite a lot more than just reading someone's mind. I almost think…" Kade trailed off.

Felix waited for him to continue, but he never did. The silence hung in the air over their heads like a storm cloud. Finally, Kade spoke. "You know what? For now, let's just focus on the mind reading thing. What am I thinking?"

Panic surged through Felix's body. He couldn't just read somebody's mind on command. "I don't… I don't know," Felix answered truthfully.

Suddenly, the room went black, with an awful high-pitched screaming noise. Terrified, Felix threw his hands over his ears. The lights flashed back on and Felix's heart rate slowed as he realized Kade hadn't moved.

"That is the problem, Mr. Anchor. The fact that you cannot control your power is the sole reason you are at this training center." Kade shouted. "Now, we have several different mind readers here, but each of them can only hear certain thoughts."

"What do you mean?" Felix gulped.

"I mean Annie Spinner can hear people's needs. Jordan Gardner's gift only works with thoughts relating to animals and nature. What can you hear?"

Felix paused, thinking over all the thoughts he has heard before. "Umm… I'm not sure exactly."

Just before the room went pitch black again, Felix heard a thought. *I wish I understood the extent of his powers.* The voice sounded much like Kade's. In fact, Felix believed he heard Kade's thoughts. Too lost in his own mind, Felix hardly realized light once again entered the room.

"I think I know," Felix shouted. Kade looked upset, but proud that Felix appeared unfazed by his powers. "I can hear one's current thoughts."

"And what did you just hear from me?" Kade asked, smirking.

Felix quickly relayed his thoughts and Kade nodded, impressed. "I hoped you would hear that one."

Felix and Kade worked with exercises for hours and hours on end that day, to the point where Felix's brain ached and his body felt drained. Each time Kade asked him once again to concentrate, to think like the person he was trying to read, he felt weaker. Eventually, he panted like a dog. He sat down on the grass and put his head in his hands.

"You've done well," Kade noted, smiling slightly. *That's weird,* Felix thought to himself. For the first time he saw a genuine smile on Kade's face. As Felix studied Kade's face, the room started to quickly spin. Felix wasn't sure if he was about to experience Kade's powers or his own.

6

One word best described Felix's surroundings: dark. The ominous ceiling above him seemed to extend forever, as did a gray cement pathway. The pathway curved in every direction. Felix saw valleys, mountains, and plains, but no matter the terrain, the path never straightened. Out of confusion, Felix began to walk the pathway. Staring at his feet, he noticed the concrete got darker as the path went into a valley. On flat land, the concrete became lighter, more neutral.

After walking for what seemed like a very long time, Felix came upon a faint apparition. Felix gazed upon an enchanting, wispy looking girl with a rounded face and the warmest light brown eyes. The pathway under and all around her turned pure white, making her look like an angel. The girl smiled warmly and Felix lifted his hand to wave, but she didn't wave back. It occurred to Felix she could not see him like he could her.

Passing around the girl slowly, Felix studied her from all angles. Her long, neatly trimmed chestnut hair contrasted with her fair, nearly see through skin. Felix felt a strong, unrequited connection. Desperate loss, as if a loved one went missing, gripped him.

Confused and slightly scared, Felix turned to leave the girl, but his first step nearly took him right into a deep, dark abyss. The path under his feet suddenly went jet black, the color of a starless night sky.

Get out of my mind. Felix heard someone yell as his surroundings blurred and twisted. Get out! The same voice yelled. The area disappeared and the meadow swirled back into focus.

Felix first noticed Kade. Kade was angry, so angry. His skin turned a light shade of red, eyes bulging.

This time, he didn't hear Kade's voice in his head. It was real and very, very loud. "Get out! Leave. NOW."

Kade pointed furiously to the door leaving the meadow. At first, Felix stood still, thinking he must be kidding. After all, Felix hadn't intended to get inside Kade's head. But when Kade yelled again and threatened to kill him if he didn't get out that second, Felix wisely opted to leave.

Scurrying out the door, Felix quietly shut it behind him and left Kade to his own company.

Unsteady and unsure, Felix didn't know what to do besides go find his siblings. Felix took the elevator to floor 111 and breathed a sigh of relief when he found the normally crowded hallway to be empty. He really wasn't in the mood to explain to a total stranger why he was panting like a dog. His footsteps made loud thuds as he ran to his room. Placing his hand on the wooden door, it swung open.

Margret stood in the small hallway leading to their rooms, smiling sweetly. Felix placed his hand over his heart, not expecting anyone to be in his room besides Jinx or Mona.

"What are you doing here? How did you get in here?" Felix asked her, resisting the urge to send her away right that instant.

Margret smiled and giggled, placing her hand on Felix's shoulder. He shrugged it off. "I'm your advisor for these first few weeks. That gives me full access to your room."

Something feels off... Felix thought to himself, squinting at Margret. "Okay… Well I would really appreciate it if you left right now. I need to talk to Jinx and Mona."

"Oh," Margret exclaimed. "They are up grabbing dinner on the food floors."

"Dinner?" Felix asked, confused as to how long he was in the meadow.

Margret nodded. "It's almost 8 o'clock."

Wow. It only seemed like a few hours to Felix, but in reality, he'd been in there almost ten hours.

"C'mon, let me show you where Jinx and Desdemona are," Margret said enthusiastically.

"Actually," Felix started. "I think I can find them on my own. Thanks though."

Something was going on with Margret and Felix didn't want to stay to find out more. He'd never been very good dealing with girls' problems. Margret cocked her head to the side, offended by Felix's denial. She once again placed her hand on his shoulder.

"Oh, please, let me help." She spoke in her excited, sweet, enthusiastic voice, much like the one she used when they first met. "I just want to do my job and help you get adjusted to the school."

Felix knew he could not say no to this beautiful, selfless girl. He sighed, giving in, as she clapped her hands in glee.

Yea! Let's go!" She shouted, smiling and running towards the door. Felix followed.

For a couple of minutes, they walked in silence. Felix broke it. "Hey," he began. "Are you okay?" The pair got on the elevator and Margret clicked a button before answering. She sighed heavily.

"Yeah… There's just this boy…" Margret trailed off. Felix internally cursed himself for asking in the first place.

When he didn't reply, Margret continued. "I think I really like him, but he's relatively new and I don't think he likes me."

"Oh," Felix awkwardly replied, not sure how to comfort her. He put his hand stiffly on her back and patted her lightly. "What's his name?"

Margret jumped away from Felix's touch so quickly he worried he'd offended her family heritage. Her eyes softened slightly and she let out a big sigh. "I don't think I'm comfortable telling that yet."

Yep, I should have just stayed out of it, Felix thought. He always knew better than to get into the business of pretty- no, beautiful- girls. Finally, the elevator dinged and the door swung open. They exited into a large circular room filled with more than a hundred tables. Restaurants of all kinds filled the walls and students sat, chattering excitedly as they ate.

"I'm sorry I snapped at you," Margret apologized. "I just want to get to know this guy better before I make any moves." Felix nodded understandingly and looked around anxiously for his siblings. His heart still raced from his encounter with Kade.

"Your sisters are over there," Margret noted, pointing to a table near the center of the circle and sure enough, there they sat. Desdemona looked exalted as a herd of students surrounded her, laughing at something she said. Jinx sat to her left, looking angry with the crowd.

"Hey, Margret. Do you want to eat with us?" Felix asked. But when he turned around, Margret was nowhere to be found.

Weird, he thought to himself. He glanced around quickly, wondering where she went, but eventually gave up and hurried over to Mona and Jinx. He concentrated hard as he approached them, hoping to pick up a few thoughts from the Asterians surrounding Mona.

This girl is so funny. A boy thought excitedly. One girl kept thinking about how much she wanted Mona's beautiful hair. Another wondered why Jinx didn't seem anything like her sister. One boy noticed him coming over and thought *I really hope that's not her boyfriend. She could do better.*

Felix cringed a little at that one, but kept walking. Eventually he leaned down to whisper in Mona's ear. "I need to talk to you. Something went so wrong in my session with Kade."

Desdemona nodded and relayed the message to Jinx beside her. All the people surrounding her looked utterly disappointed when Desdemona stood up to leave with Felix. A few boys even gave him an angry glare. Though reluctant, Jinx got up to follow them as well.

Felix hurried quickly with the girls trailing behind him. Since the training center seemed to be so busy, he figured the only place with privacy would be their rooms. When they got there, he whipped around and told them everything.

"And then I was sucked into an alternate universe and he started screaming at me, telling me to get out of his mind," Felix finished. The pair remained silent the entire time, without so much as a smart remark from Jinx.

"Wait, do you think you were actually in his mind?" Desdemona asked.

Jinx scoffed. "Don't be silly. He *reads* minds, not lives in them."

Desdemona paused for a second, thinking. Her brain seemed to be running at a hundred miles per hour. "But, if you think about it, Felix's power allows him to see the present. Wouldn't being inside someone's mind be the present?"

Felix glanced at Jinx and worked quietly, trying to push himself into her mind to test himself. Knowing she wouldn't be happy with him in her mind, he settled for a simple mind reading. *Dang, who knew this girl had a brain?*

"Hey!" Felix defended, calling Jinx out. "Mona's actually very smart."

Desdemona looked temporarily offended at the snippet she heard, but chose to ignore the comment. She pushed her question again. "Wouldn't it?"

Felix nodded, agreeing with her. "I mean, yeah. Technically, it would. It's just so overwhelming for me to use that part of my gift. It's draining."

"Draining? What do you mean?" Jinx asked, stepping momentarily out of her usual sarcastic self.

"I mean nearly every time after I enter someone's mind, I feel like I need to sleep for days. Not physically, but mentally."

The pair nodded in understanding. Jinx reached up to tug at her short hair and then crossed her arms. "I see what you mean. It happens to me after I have a really intense vision."

Felix glanced at Desdemona. *Why is she suddenly being so understanding?* Desdemona thought to herself. In all honesty, Felix wondered the same thing, but since this new side of Jinx was quite pleasant, he decided it best not to argue.

Suddenly, the trio heard a rustling noise outside the door and someone slipped a folded piece of paper against the hardwood floor. Desdemona turned around and picked up the note. Unfolding it silently, Jinx and Felix waited for her to read it, slightly anxious.

"It's from Kade," Desdemona blushed. "It says tomorrow's training session is with me at 8am and Jinx's session is at 5pm."

AH! Felix jumped as he heard Desdemona scream excitedly in her mind. *A whole nine hours with Kade.*

"Wait…" Felix wondered aloud. "Do you have a crush on Kade?"

Desdemona's eyes went wide and she slapped him on the arm. "Stop snooping on my personal thoughts."

"You never answered the question," Jinx noted.

Desdemona blushed all shades of red as she nodded her head excitedly, her blonde hair shaking with her. "He's just so cute and mysterious."

Felix smiled softly at Desdemona's excitement about spending time with this boy. She seemed very happy about it, which made Felix's heart swell. He had begun to care for these girls and not in a friendship type of way. Felix now had siblings - a relationship that, one day, could be much stronger than friendship.

7

Desdemona bounded with excitement towards the training room, skipping down the halls. She noticed a familiar swish of red hair and looked over to see Margret rushing to catch up with her.

"Mona," Margret called in a voice pure enough to be a song. Desdemona slowed her pace to let Margret match her stride. "Off to training I see? With Kade, right?"

Desdemona nodded excitedly, smiling and blushing furiously at the mention of his name.

Margret noticed her blush and giggled in agreement. "Oh, trust me, I understand. Kade is by far the best looking Asterian in this whole House. Probably in the whole Asterian race really."

Desdemona laughed along with her and the two girls went on and on about his dreamy hair and mysterious eyes before they reached the outside of the training room.

"Well, I hope you have fun with Mr. Handsome," Margret called, breaking the stride in her skip just long enough to laugh and smirk at Desdemona. Desdemona smiled back and turned to enter the training meadow, which was bright with the noon day sunlight. Flowers popped up from the tall grass and tickled Desdemona's ankles as she noticed the beautiful boy perched on the stone bench in the center of the daisies.

"Kade," Desdemona shouted in delight, skipping over to sit next to him.

But the moment she sat down, the meadow went black and she heard the sounds of hissing snakes. Teeth nipped at

Desdemona's ankles as she screamed and jumped up. The second her butt left the bench, the sound faded and Kade brought her back to the meadow.

"What was that for?" Desdemona shrieked, angrily.

"I'm just preparing you, Mona," Kade informed her. "You're such a bright and delightful girl- maybe even too much so. The Asterian world isn't always rainbows and sunshine, especially with a mother like yours."

At the mention of her mother, Desdemona bit her lip as a tense silence fell over the meadow, allowing the only sound to be the swish of the wind and the chirp of the birds.

Finally, Kade broke the silence. "Alright, let's get to work. You have visions of the past and sounds trigger them. Perfect." Kade snarked, sarcastically.

At this, Desdemona put her hands on her hips and looked Kade square in the eye. "What is up with you right now? I was actually looking forward to this training, but you're being all passive aggressive."

Kade sighed heavily and ran his hand through his hair. At the sound of his sigh, Desdemona felt the familiar pang in her stomach and the meadow swirled out of view.

Desdemona found herself outside, next to a snow-covered swing set. Desdemona, whose hair was now chestnut brown, lifted her hands to the sky; by doing so, the snow fell harder, covering the ground with white fluff. A boy with cropped dark hair laughed with glee. The boy plopped himself down in the snow, moving his arms and legs in syncopation to create an outline of his form.

"Look, Haze. I made a snow angel," the boy yelled. At this, Desdemona chuckled, feeling love swell inside her chest before the snowy backyard began to fade from her view.

Desdemona came back to find herself sitting in the tall grass of the meadow, wide eyed and confused.

"What did you just see?" Kade asked, sitting down next to her. The past, angry demeanor faded to leave only a concerned teacher, a comforting listener and a caring friend.

At 5pm, just in time for her training session, Jinx groaned as she opened the door to the meadow. Only this time, instead of being bright, like a summer morning, Kade cast the meadow in near darkness, lit only by a simple dim red and orange sunset. Red and brown leaves crunched under her feet from nearby bushes. Jinx internally cursed at the sight of him sitting on a small stone bench which wasn't there yesterday. But when he lifted his eyes as she approached him, butterflies turned in her stomach.

No. Stop. Ever since she met Kade that first day, she knew he was cute. More than cute even. He was hot, but she never had an attraction like this to a boy. It made her nervous, to be honest. With her lack of experience in the field of the male species, she thought it best to simply suppress her attraction to her mentor.

"I was worried you wouldn't show," Kade called when she got closer.

"I shouldn't have," Jinx told him, putting her hand on her hip defiantly. "What's up with this room? It used to be brighter."

Kade looked around, as if just noticing the change in scenery. "Ah yes. This meadow only shows up when a new Asterian needs their initial training. Since we only have three of you, the meadow will be dying off as you train. Once you complete your first step training, the room will go black and it will not reappear until new Asterians are on their way."

Jinx felt an ugly pang of sadness as she realized the beautiful room would soon be gone. She pushed back the feeling, trying to ignore the emotion of weakness. That's how Jinx always thought of sadness- as a weakness. When a certain level of attraction to something occurs, it allows a person to become vulnerable to rejection. That rejection hinders the brain and weakens the body. It was best to avoid getting attached.

"So here's what we know," Kade started, changing the subject. "You can see the future and that sense of sight is triggered by a touch."

"Yeah. I know," Jinx said curtly, crossing her arms.

"I want you to start by clearing your mind of all things distracting you from your power," Kade ordered. Jinx gave a heavy sigh and attempted to push all other things from her thoughts. When it was otherwise empty, she gave Kade a short nod.

"Is it cleared?" Kade asked.

"I already told you yes." Jinx raised her voice slightly, very annoyed.

The room went dark from Kade's powers and Jinx heard the rustling of movement from Kade. She stood rooted to the spot, knowing the lights would return soon enough.

Just as planned, the red glow returned and Kade stood right in front of her, towering over her small frame. She tried to ignore the racing of her heart at his closeness.

"Look at me, Jinx," Kade ordered. Jinx raised her eyes to meet his. "There are things out there. Things that wouldn't hesitate to kill you in an instant. If you don't stop being so stubborn about losing your old life, they will kill you and you won't even get a taste of your new one. Being gifted is a privilege some would die for and you act like you don't even care."

"That's because I don't," Jinx yelled.

"But you do care," Kade told her. "I know you care. You care about your life. You care about your siblings. You care about this world. Listen to me now. I have a bad feeling in my gut. A bad feeling someone who we thought had gone forever isn't gone and if you don't get your head out of your ego, it could be the end of things as we know them."

To this, Jinx didn't have anything to say. Kade finally found a way to shut her up.

"Good. Now let's get to work," Kade ordered. Jinx cleared her mind as previously ordered.

From then on, the pair moved into an extremely productive training session. They learned how to control Jinx's visions by triggering them with touch. Finally, when beads of sweat dripped from Jinx's hairline, Kade called it a night. Near complete darkness seemed to swallow the meadow. The leaves, almost all fallen from the trees, scattered the ground. Jinx nearly completed her first step training.

"You did well today," Kade noted. "All three of you progressed very nicely."

"Desdemona, too?" Jinx couldn't help but ask. Half of her almost hoped Desdemona failed her training with Kade.

That's mean, Jinx caught herself thinking. The voice from Jinx's subconscious called this one right. Saying that about her... her sister was very rude.

"Desdemona did well," Kade informed her. "She was very eager to learn. Sometimes too eager, which made it hard for her to clear her mind."

Jinx nodded awkwardly. "Yeah, she's a little over-excited at times."

"Funny that you seem to be the exact opposite. The three of you each have such different personalities. I feel this will make you very powerful."

"I don't understand though. Why does everyone say we're so much more powerful than other Asterians?" Jinx asked.

Kade sat down on the stone bench once again, motioning for Jinx to sit down next to him. The stone froze her skin when she sat, but she did not flinch.

"I'm sure Mr. Belton has told you of your mother's powers. She can take away anyone's powers with a single touch. He told you about Jane taking away the powers of her own siblings, Stacy and Marcus.

"But," Jinx wondered. "Why did she do it?"

"Back when your mother was still at school, it didn't take her long to realize she possessed stronger, more dangerous abilities. Mr. Belton urged her to look to the light, rather than the darkness, but she only cared about becoming more powerful. He watched her grow up from an innocent, young girl to a power-hungry, evil woman. After taking powers from many students, Mr. Belton finally sent her away. As she left, she promised they had not seen the last of her."

"Then what happened?" Jinx asked, on the edge of her seat.

"True to her promise, Jane went around taking the powers of all the Asterians she could get her hands on, literally. She said that one day every Asterian would be under her control. The thing that scared Mr. Belton was she could do it. She really could. With the threat of their powers being stripped hanging over Asterian heads, she could get them to do nearly anything. She promised after she gained complete power, she would give her most loyal subjects their powers back."

"But... what stopped her?" Jinx asked, with genuine curiosity and concern written all over her face. Kade smiled slightly at the idea that she was beginning to really care.

"It can't be traced down to one single thing that stopped her, but it all started with a boy. Despite being so power hungry, there was one very handsome man who turned her head. His name was Alexander. They went to school together for quite a few years. Once he started following her and helping her on the way to greatness, she fell for him," Kade told Jinx.

"Wait? Is this Alexander guy our dad...?"

"What a smart girl you are, Jinx," Kade praised. "Soon after, Jane became pregnant with you and your siblings. It infuriated her that she let herself be seduced by Alexander and distracted from her quest for power. We can only be thankful Alexander succeeded."

"The power of you and your siblings became so strong inside of Jane, it made her weak. On the day of your birth, she hardly mustered the will to struggle when she saw Marcus was her doctor. After some sedation, you were born and given to Hilga. Sometime after they took you and your siblings away, Jane woke up. Losing her babies and perhaps her powers changed Jane. She disappeared from the hospital and has never been seen since."

Jinx remained quiet for a moment before taking in a shaky breath. "Do you think she is still alive?"

"I would think so. Jane was strong and after fifteen years, I'm sure she regained some or all of her strength. I'm only worried that..." Kade trailed off.

"What? What are you worried about?"

Kade shook his head. "Now is not the time to express concerns like that to you. You have much more schooling and training to do."

Jinx opened her mouth to argue, but Kade took her hand quickly, shutting her up. She flinched at his touch and nearly pulled her hand away, but the look in his eyes stopped her.

"Be careful, Jinx," Kade told her in a whispered voice. She shrunk away from the serious look on his face and focused on the now dark sky. As if reading her mind, he stood up and informed her it was time to leave, breaking the moment. Kade walked towards the door and held it open for her as she followed. As she exited, the room began to slowly disappear behind her.

Kade stopped her at the door and she turned to face him. Kade's devilishly handsome smile played on his face. "Just try not to get yourself killed, kid."

8

The next day all three Anchor siblings found themselves in a different uniform than before. Today they wore their sleek and stretchy attire, allowing a wide range of movement. All three of them fidgeted outside a closed door marked "training room #177" in italics on the wood. Although Felix tried to open it like they had been taught, it didn't budge and they just figured they should wait until someone came and opened it for them. Jinx slid her back down the wall and sat to the right side of the door, hands twiddling in her lap. Desdemona did the same on the opposite side before Felix sat down next to her. She sighed deeply.

"You okay?" Felix asked, concerned. Desdemona just nodded, further proving she wasn't okay.

"C'mon Mona. I haven't known you for that long, but you are my sister I guess. So tell me what's really bothering you." After she didn't say anything, he focused quickly on Desdemona's mind. It was blue, which he figured depicted sadness. Looking around quickly, he heard the voice of Stacy and a faint image of her smiling face swirling around.

I miss her was all Felix heard in Desdemona's thoughts before a deep, loud voice roughly pulled him out of his concentration.

"Good," Kade shouted as he swaggered up to the three sitting on the floor. "I'm glad you found the right room."

Felix noticed Jinx glare at Kade, but this look differed from her usual snarls at him. More like a half-glare, paired with a slight smile. What in the world was going on there?

Whatever was happening, Kade didn't seem to notice and walked right up to the door, opening it with a single whisper. The three siblings all rose to their feet and followed their mentor inside the large room.

Weapons lined every single stone on the walls of the brightly lit room. Someone mounted everything from knives to bows and arrows to flamethrowers, ready at any moment to be used. A couple of other students threw large knives at sparring dummies. Felix flinched when a burly girl threw the shard of metal right through the dummies' heart.

I do not want to mess with her, Felix heard Desdemona think to herself. He shook his head in agreement and turned his attention to two brothers who fought roughly with gleaming swords, sending loud strike noises throughout the room. Right next to them, a girl stood alone firing arrows at bags of flour. Every five arrows or so, the bag would burst open, spilling white everywhere, and she would move on to the next one.

"The number of arrows it takes her to burst that bag equals the number of arrows it would take to kill an attacker," Kade mentioned as he noticed Felix watching the girl. "By the fifth arrow, she might be killed. She needs to be more accurate."

Personally, Felix thought he was being slightly harsh, but better harsh than dead.

"Are we going to watch other people train while we just stand here? Or will we get to throw some knives too?" Jinx asked, actually seeming fairly interested in this task.

Kade rolled his eyes and motioned for the trio to follow. Once they reached the opposite corner of the room, away from any other Asterians training, he stopped and turned to face them. The shiny black of Kade's mentor uniform glinted off the metal of the weapons on the wall. Felix glanced over at Desdemona, who looked ready to drool all over Kade.

"Alright, we are here today to find your weapon of choice. Now, do any of you have fighting experience?" Kade asked. None of them answered, for none of them had ever needed to use a weapon. Stacy, Marcus, and Hilga made sure they all had been safe and sound. Felix never once even felt threatened until just days before when his life turned upside down.

"That's what I thought. We will just have to start from scratch," Kade declared. "Just like each Asterian has a certain power, each Asterian typically has a specific connection with a type of weapon. With that weapon and that weapon only will you be at your most powerful. Any other weapon will feel like dead weight in your hands."

"That's so inconvenient. I want to be able to fight with every weapon around me." Jinx spat, motioning to the walls of weapons around them.

"Not everything is about your convenience, Jinx," Kade reminded her. Though she still looked quite annoyed, Jinx simply folded her arms across her chest and huffed.

Kade gave her a warning look as to say 'don't cross me' and continued speaking. "Alright, I'm going to start each of you out with a single weapon." He motioned to three very beaten up dummies to the right. "You have five chances to knock these practice dummies to the ground with your weapon. If you don't, you know it's not the weapon for you."

Kade turned around to face the wall of killing machines, scanning it quickly. First, he called over Desdemona, who looked thrilled to be chosen first. He first paired Mona with a bow and arrow, which she shot brilliantly. To everyone's surprise, she knocked over the dummy with only her second arrow.

"You're a natural, Mona," Kade shouted, high-fiving her as she strutted back with three arrows left in her quiver. She smiled proudly as he informed Desdemona she could keep the bow and arrow, for it was now hers.

Jinx looked uncomfortable when Kade handed her a sword. Picking it up, she swung it with speed but missed the target. The same happened with the other four. Kade decided to move on to another weapon, handing Jinx a rack of gleaming knives. When she held them this time, she looked confident and put together. Lining up right in front of the dummy, Jinx threw the knives with such precision, the dummy ended up sliced in half.

"I think you're going to need a new dummy," Jinx called as she leaned over the two cleanly cut pieces of fabric. Kade let out a loud shout of laughter, which seemed out of character for him. He walked over to Jinx and patted her on the shoulder, smiling.

Jinx beamed back at him, leaving Felix to wonder once again what was going on there.

Desdemona had her bow and Jinx had her knives. This left only Felix without a weapon.

"Felix," Kade called abruptly, motioning curtly for Felix to join him. Feeling a little anxious, Felix glanced nervously at his sisters. Desdemona gave him a little wave and pushed him lightly towards Kade.

"So… Umm… Which weapon is the one for me, you think?" Felix asked with a nervous laugh. At first, Kade didn't answer. Then, he reached up and grabbed an axe from the wall.

"You're a big guy. Try this." Kade dropped it into Felix's hands and he almost fell over with the weight of the blade.

"Kade, I really don't think that…" Felix began.

Kade threw his arm up, shooing Felix towards the dummies. "Give it a throw."

Mustering up all his strength, Felix lifted the axe up and positioned it to throw. With a grunt, he launched it across the room. As he watched it fly, he realized he threw it harder than he thought he could. But the axe wedged itself into the wall about fifteen feet above its target with a loud bang.

Feeling slightly awkward and very out of his element, Felix turned to Kade with an expectant look.

"What are you waiting for?" Kade asked. "You've got four more throws."

Felix turned on his heel and nervously shuffled to dislodge the axe from the wall. With the ax too high to reach, Felix grabbed the ladder positioned to the left of the dummy and climbed it to retrieve the weapon.

When he returned, axe in hand, he threw it again. And again and again and again. All four times it missed the target by a long shot. After the fourth throw the ax almost went backwards and Felix managed to hit the ceiling with the fifth. Finally, Kade agreed the axe could not be Felix's weapon of choice.

Surveying the wall of weapons, Kade landed on a sword with a shiny metal blade and a sturdy, black handle. Pulling it down from the hook, Kade tossed it to Felix. Reacting quickly, Felix lunged to catch the blade and prevent it from hitting the concrete floor with a clatter. To everyone's, (including his) surprise, the hilt landed directly in the palm of his smooth hand. Despite being extremely heavy, the sword felt very lightweight, unlike the axe. Feeling fairly nimble with the sword, he approached the dummies on the far end of the room. With a single swipe, the far left dummy's head came tumbling to the ground. Then the second. Then the third.

Felix turned around confidently, swirling the sword in his hand. Pride welled up in his chest when he noticed the surprised faces of his siblings. Kade nodded his head slowly in approval.

"Felix," Mona yelled excitedly, clapping her hands. "That was amazing!"

"Yeah, amazing he actually acted like a man and not a squeamish little boy," Jinx said quietly, just loud enough for Felix to hear. Unfazed by her backhanded comment, Felix swaggered over to the group, beaming.

"Alright," Kade grinned. "Now the real fun begins."

After their session in the training room, Felix, Desdemona, and Jinx were greeted by Margret, who was standing, perfectly poised, outside. She held a pink duffle bag in her hand with the initials *MGB* inscribed in blue polka dots. Felix felt his heart beat in his chest as she bounded towards his new family.

"Hi, guys!" She greeted them excitedly. "How did your session go? Well, I hope it went well. I assume you all got your weapons. You know, I remember how scared I was the day I first got my weapon of choice. But once my trainer put it in my hand, I just knew this staff was the one for me. Oh, I do hope you guys had the same experience."

Jinx felt a laugh rise up in her throat as she watched this girl bubble in excitement over some weapon they would never need to use anyway. Honestly, when would they ever be in any real danger here?

"Anyway," Margret continued. "I have your school uniforms and your class schedules. You've got three classes today, one before lunch and two after."

Out of her pink duffle bag, Margret pulled three uniforms, all of which were khaki pants with a white button up shirt. On the left shoulder of each, *Anchor* had been inscribed in red thread. After the uniforms came the schedules. She handed each of them their class papers and began to explain.

"Your class before lunch is Intro to Asterian Life. This is a required class for all new Asterians, kind of like a formal welcome to our world, where you will learn about the Asterian Society, its laws, and some of the formal customs of Asterians. Then you go up to the rec area to get lunch. When you come back, you have Asterian History, which is actually a very interesting course and then Prophesying Visions 101. All the families here in The House have a specialized course based on their gift category. Since your powers allow you to see visions and dreams, you will be placed here with other Asterians like you to help you interpret them."

"Holy Asterian! That's a lot of classes," Felix exclaimed.

Jinx turned in disbelief towards her brother. "I cannot believe you just said 'holy Asterian.'"

Felix grinned. "It's going to catch on soon and all the Asterians will be saying it. You'll see."

Jinx sighed, hoping this conversation was finished, but then Margret opened her mouth again and continued to ramble in her soft, yet excited tone.

"We also offer the basic courses of writing and math, which you will have to take eventually. Not to mention the great electives The House has. They're so fun! We have human operation classes- which in my opinion are completely terrifying- and psychology and telekinesis training and my personal favorite, animal training."

Desdemona stared at Margret with wide eyes as the girl rambled on about courses and classes and training. Looking down to focus on her schedule in her hand, she realized they needed to get to Intro to Asterian Life in ten minutes.

"Hey, Margret." Desdemona interrupted. "Sorry to cut you off, but we have to get to class in ten minutes…"

Margret nodded excitedly. "Oh, yeah, sorry. Your class is up in room 333, so I hope you enjoy."

As Felix walked past Margret to get to the elevator, he couldn't ignore the tingles he felt through his spine as his arm brushed hers. Butterflies arose in his stomach as she smiled at him one last time before they entered the elevator.

Up in another dimly lit hallway, Felix found himself walking into room 333. Per usual, he whispered their household name before the door allowed him in.

Now, he expected the classrooms at The House to look much like his classrooms in public school, but he should have known better.

The ceilings rose high above the Anchor's heads, their walls filled to the brim with documents and portraits galore. Wooden chairs sat at wooden desks, each with an "Asterian Life 101" textbook lying flat on the oak. As the Anchors took their seats, a wide-eyed, stumpy man pulled a world map over the whiteboard. His white handkerchief hung haphazardously out of his wrinkled suit as his top hat sat crookedly on top of his wild, grey hair. As more students began to fill in, he excitedly straightened up his desk, which was surprisingly neat for someone so unkempt.

Once all ten Asterians took their seats, the teacher opened his mouth, beginning his introduction with a toothless smile. "Hello class. My name is Mr. Linkley, your teacher for this all important course. Ah, I love having new Asterians here. It's my favorite class, you know? Intro to Asterian Life. I just love being the first to induct new Asterians into their life of good deeds."

Wow, he's quite the nut job, Felix heard Jinx think. Felix thought for a moment, agreeing with her that this man was way off, but not necessarily believing it was a bad thing. After all, only a few days before they learned they were members of a secret race. They were all a little off, weren't they?

"Now, first, I would like to go around and have everyone share their powers and their names, okay?" Mr. Linkley announced. Some of the teenagers groaned, feeling like kindergarteners again, while others appeared frightened, like their first day of high school.

Mr. Linkley pointed to a red haired girl with freckles in the first desk. She, along with her identical brother, stood up and introduced themselves. "Hi, my name is Jackie French and I can make plants grow," the girl announced.

"I'm George French and I can control movement of the plants Jackie grows," the brother announced. Mr. Linkley clapped his hands excitedly, ranting on about how excited flora powers made him, while everyone else clapped with him, awkwardly.

The other two families introduced themselves in much the same way. The first, the Heaths, were three brothers with powers of brute strength. The second, the Poppers, were two girls with electricity coming from their bodies. And with each one, Mr. Linkley promptly clapped his wrinkly hands.

But a clap did not come when the Anchors said their introductions. Instead, Mr. Linkley's mouth gaped, wide-eyed.

"Wow! It is you?" Mr. Linkley gasped. Felix put his hand on the back of his neck, uncomfortably, and exchanged a glance with his equally distressed sisters. At their awkward expressions, Mr. Linkely seemed to realize their discomfort and began to apologize profusely.

"Oh, dear me. I'm so sorry, for I have been very gauche. Please forgive me. I have always wondered what made Jane Anchor disappear. What are your powers, young-uns?" Mr. Linkley asked excitedly.

Felix soon realized, after a few seconds of tense silence, his sisters would not speak up. So, Felix spoke for them. "Uh... Desdemona here can see the past; I can see the present and Jinx can see...uh... the future."

Mr. Linkely's eyes grew wide with excitement once again, but he appeared to make an attempt to compose himself. Nodding quickly, Mr. Linkley clapped and returned to the front of the room. "Now, I am sure many of you wonder what you are supposed to do as Asterians. I'm sure you're wondering what the purpose of all this fuss is. Well, the best way for me to explain it would be to talk about some examples. Do you remember, a couple of years ago, hearing on the news about a woman who talked a man out of jumping from the Golden Gate Bridge in San Francisco? About how she saved his life?"

Everyone in the class nodded their heads, intrigued already.

"An Asterian with a power of persuasion came to his rescue. Remember hearing about a train whose brakes failed and all the passengers were going to be killed upon impact with another passenger train? An Asterian on board had a knack for mechanics. And what about last year when that devastating hurricane moved along a path to New York? That hurricane veered out to sea with the help of our own Mr. Belton. He's got a thing with manipulating water."

One of the Heath brothers raised his hand hesitantly. "I don't think I'm really picking up on what you're trying to say? So… we just basically prevent catastrophes?"

"Yes and no, Mr. Heath," Mr. Linkely answered. "Asterians have been on Earth since the dawn of time, almost like guardian angels. When someone's about to have a catastrophe, Asterians can prevent many of them. That's why many of you will feel the urge to help others, even if they are people with whom you do not take a particular liking."

Jinx zoned out for a moment, wondering why- if Asterians were supposed to save lives- Jane took so many. However, she held her tongue, knowing a large classroom setting like this was not the right time to ask such a serious question. Mr. Linkley moved on to enthuse about all the classes offered here and all the training each family would go through during their five years spent at The House. Finally, as the class came to a close, he mentioned something Felix hadn't heard before.

"And finally, I'd like to give an intro on the Asterian Society. This is a league of the most prestigious and talented Asterians known to date. They make the laws and regulations for the Asterian world as well as keeping an eye on Asterians to make sure they use their powers for good and not for evil."

At this, Felix's mind flashed towards his mother. He wondered if Jane herself had been condemned by the Asterian Society. He wondered if she tried to fight the Society or, instead, fled into hiding to escape her true fate. Whatever the answers were, Felix didn't know. But he hoped he would have them soon.

9

"We're what?" Jinx raised her eyebrows in disbelief. A few other Asterians turned their heads to glance at Jinx. Kade had called the Anchor siblings into the recreation area early in the morning, nearly two months after their first day at The House.

"You're telling me this is a regular event here?" Desdemona asked Kade.

Kade nodded. "Yes. Every year, all families in The House gather for the Hunt."

"And so this Hunt is some sort of scavenger hunt?" Felix questioned.

"Yes," Kade answered. "Mr. Belton blows the start horn at the stroke of midnight on the first Friday of the new year. Every year, the object to find is a new one. For example, two years ago, it was a huge sack of gold coins. Last year, Asterians raced to find a cornucopia of antique Asterian weapons."

"So what is the prize this year?" Desdemona wondered aloud.

Kade took a single glance at each of the siblings, letting the suspense build. Finally, he answered her. "This year, the prize is the Asterian Jewel."

"What is that? Some kind of enchanted rock?" Jinx asked sarcastically.

Kade, appearing to be in a better-than-usual mood, chuckled at Jinx's comment. "Actually, you're more or less right. The Asterian Jewel has been known to enhance powers, especially when used within a family."

"So tell us the rules of this Hunt?" Felix asked, leaning back on the arm of the plush couch behind him.

"It's fairly simple," Kade responded. "There are only four rules. One, you must stay together as a family, but you can make alliances with other families. Two, the prize can be hidden anywhere within The House, including secret, sealed passageways. Three, you must not do serious physical harm to another Asterian. Doing so will have you expelled from the Hunt for the rest of your time here at the House. Four, your weapons can only be used to block power attacks from other Asterians and for no other purpose."

Jinx thought for a moment, doing some math in her head. "The stroke of midnight on the first Friday of the new year… But that's tonight."

Kade smiled at the wide-eyed Asterians before reaching in his bag and grabbing three outfits. He tossed them their Hunt uniforms- pitch black jumpsuits with stretchy, flexible material and "Anchor" imprinted in red stitching.

"Anchors, this is where my assistance for the Hunt ends. Arrive in training room 249 by 11:45. Be ready for a long night."

Jinx, Desdemona, and Felix all felt quite awkward as they rode the elevator to room 249 in their black outfits at 11:40 that night. Despite the fact that every other Asterian suited up in the same jumpsuit, the Anchor kids couldn't help but feel highly out of place. After all, they were among the newest Asterians to The House.

Jinx, who always silently worked the angles, thought about what the Hunt could mean for them. The buzz about their family name hadn't stopped, but not all of it was good. She hadn't figured out yet whether they were famous or infamous. Maybe the Hunt could be their ticket to earn some real respect. They will surely be underdogs, but Jinx knew they shouldn't be underestimated.

When the elevator finally slowed to a stop, the door opened with a ding, revealing only one room in the short hallway spread before them. Like all the other rooms, it had a wooden door. But that's where the similarity ended. Unlike other floors, some of which seemed to have innumerable rooms and doors, the trio gazed upon a single, spectacular entrance. This door spread wide across the wall, much larger than any other. Plaques spread themselves along the wood. Gleaming golden in the low lighting, with over 100 different plaques mounted to the door, each carrying their own inscriptions.

Felix took a step towards the door, placing his hand on the first of the plaques. "The Hamilton Family - 1913 Hunt Champions," he read aloud. "Whoa. These are all the winners of the Hunt. Each family who wins gets a golden plaque."

A high pitched voice chirped behind them. "Of course. Receiving a golden plaque is one of the biggest honors an Asterian can achieve." The Anchor siblings turned around to see a short blonde haired girl standing next to a taller, thicker blond boy. Without a doubt, they were siblings.

"And we're hoping to get that golden plaque tomorrow, aren't we, Kat?" the boy smiled at his sister enthusiastically.

"We're going to try our best, like everyone does," Kat answered. She extended her arm to shake the Anchors' hands. "I'm Kat Hamilton and this is my brother, Jared. As I see you've noticed, our great grandparents won the first ever Hunt," she pointed out quite shyly. "Our parents expect us to win it. You know, to bring good fortune to the family name."

"Those are some big shoes to fill," Desdemona sympathized. She felt for these kids. While the Hamiltons tried to uphold their good family name, the Anchors just wanted to clear their family name tonight. If one thing could take the edge off Jane's cursed name, it had to be the Hunt.

"Alright, well, we'll see you inside. Good luck." Jared enthused, towing his sister behind him as he opened the enormous doors and strode past. Desdemona, right at Jared's heels, followed him in, with Felix and Jinx close behind. Jinx appeared more involved in Asterian life than ever before. Desdemona guessed Jinx's competitive spirit kicked in just in time for the Hunt.

Desdemona's jaw fell nearly to the ground when she passed through the entryway of the large door. Behind the door, The House hid an enormous arena, with ceilings seeming to touch the sky and walls appearing as large as the entire House itself.

The dust on the arena floor flowed through the area as nearly two hundred excited Asterians loitered about, waiting for the beginning of the Hunt. Mr. Belton sat in the middle of nine tall, gold chairs high above the arena floor. To his left sat Kade, who nodded a greeting at the triplets. Seven other Asterians, whom Desdemona assumed were the other Trainers in The House, surrounded Mr. Belton. Just as Desdemona felt excitement begin to build in her stomach, Mr. Belton stood up, raising one hand. Immediately all the Asterians went silent, turning their attention to the superintendent.

Mr. Belton beamed at all of his young Asterians, eager to begin their Hunt. "Now, as I am sure your trainers have told you, the prize for this Hunt is the Asterian Jewel, but I must warn you. This is a very powerful artifact, not to be taken lightly. As such, I have checked with each of your trainers to ensure your trustworthiness with this prize. So please, do not let us down."

All the teenagers nodded, turning to their siblings to chatter enthusiastically. Mr. Belton reached for what appeared to be a conch shell sitting on a pedestal in front of the nine chairs, but paused.

"I must remind you anyone who seriously harms another House member will be disqualified from all further Hunts. Use your powers wisely, young Asterians."

And with that, Mr. Belton raised the shell to his lips, blowing into it. A shrill, powerful tone flew from the end of the shell and the Hunt began.

10

The sides of the Arena rose to the high ceilings, creating large openings for Asterians to exit the arena. As soon as the openings appeared, every family sprinted from the arena into the rest of The House, searching desperately for the Asterian Jewel. Only the Anchors and a few other families remained, making a game plan.

"Guys," Jinx began. "This will be a piece of cake. Our powers were made for this."

"What do you mean?" Felix asked.

Jinx laughed as if she couldn't believe he didn't see the simplicity of the task at hand. "I can see the future. All I need to do is envision the Asterian Jewel and I can find out wherever it is hidden in The House."

"But you can't always tell exact locations in your visions, Jinx," Desdemona reminded her.

"Maybe I can see the area around it. Maybe I'll be able to see which wing or which floor it is hidden on. It's worth a shot if you ask me."

"Alright, give it a go, J." Felix approved. "I can look into Mr. Belton's mind to see if he's thinking about the stone and Desdemona can look into the past to maybe see Mr. Belton hiding the stone." Jinx agreed and reached to touch the dusty floor, allowing her competitive spirit to guide her into the vision.

Jinx found herself in a dimly lit hallway, like all of the hallways at The House. Glancing around, she noticed the hallway was totally empty except for her and her siblings, who stood on either side of her.

"Where is it?" Felix asked Jinx. Jinx didn't answer him at first. Instead, she threw her hand up to silence him. Without thinking, Jinx felt her feet move on their own. As she glanced up at the numbers next to the rooms, she caught a glimpse of room 279 - the entertainment wing. Desdemona and Felix followed quickly at her heels, but slammed into her back as Jinx came to an abrupt stop.

"Why did you stop? Keep going." Desdemona ordered.

"No," Jinx responded. "It's in here." Jinx turned quickly into room 285, jiggling at the doorknob only to realize it was locked. Of course. Of course they would lock the door with the Jewel.

"Bobby pin," Jinx demanded, holding out her hand. Desdemona reached up to her long ponytail and pulled out the metal, knowing a piece of hair too short to fit in her ponytail would soon be falling limply down the back of her neck.

Jinx fiddled with the lock for about five minutes as Desdemona and Felix stood watch, making sure no other Asterians saw them. Finally, the door clicked open, making an odd creaking noise. Expecting something much more fear-inducing, Jinx felt her spirits drop when the door opened to reveal a simple rec room. With an orange couch and multiple game consoles hooked up to the flat screen, it looked like all the other rec rooms. Nothing special to see here.

Jinx came out of her vision with a sigh, thinking her vision could not be correct. Mr. Belton would not have hidden the Jewel in a place as casual as a recreational room.

At that moment both Felix and Desdemona exited their visions. Desdemona shared first, excited about her vision. "I saw Mr. Belton in one of the rec rooms. He walked around with the Jewel in his hand and looked for a place to hide it in that room. He looked at an orange couch."

Suddenly, Jinx felt more hope as to the validity of her vision after hearing Desdemona's view of the past. Felix, the next to share, added even more excitement to the anticipation-filled air. "Mr. Belton thought about a couch in one of the rec rooms. I'm not sure which room though."

Jinx finished his thought for him. "I know which one. I saw us going into room 285 and when we opened it, we saw an orange couch."

"What are we waiting for? We have to go." Desdemona shouted excitedly. Now the last family remaining in the arena, the Anchor siblings ran through the open walls and into the full chaos of the Hunt.

Just as they exited the arena, Desdemona almost ran head first into two dueling families. Two siblings stood with heads pulled close. The fingers of one sibling sparked with fire and she cupped balls of flames in her hands. The other flicked her hands at the three siblings standing across from them, causing the fire to fly across the room at other Asterians. The three jumped to the side, dodging a fire ball and gathering their counter attack. The siblings smiled sneakily at each other and suddenly began to merge, morphing and twisting into each other. Soon, their individual features became indistinguishable, with one oversized powerful Asterian left where three once stood.

Desdemona glanced at the terrified faces of the two fire controlling siblings and shared a panicked look with Felix. "We gotta get out of here."

The Anchor siblings broke into a sprint, leaving the dueling Asterians to their own fight. They ran full speed towards the elevator. Jinx clicked the button wildly, but looked up to find a sign that read "elevator turned off for Hunt."

"Of course they would turn them off. Let's go to the stairs." Jinx yelled, turning and running from the elevator. As they ran, chaos abounded. Asterians everywhere fought one another, each family trying to keep the other from making any progress. A fierce looking girl with silver hair took one look at a scrawny boy and he froze, as though encased in ice. She yelled at her sister, telling her to run for the stairs. Walking back slowly, always keeping her eyes on the boy, the girl kept him frozen. But the minute she turned her back to follow her sister, the straggly boy gasped, able to move again.

Don't want to meet her anytime soon, Felix heard Desdemona think. He laughed a little as they ran, finally making it to the staircase. Placing her hand on the wooden door and whispering her name, the door to the staircase swung open. Not wasting even a second, Jinx began to run up the stairs, siblings at her heels. As she turned the corner up to the next flight, she ran smack first into the chest of a tall boy. Glancing past his towering frame, she saw another nearly identical boy behind him. The first boy reached his hand slowly, placing his hand on Jinx's shoulder. At his touch, Jinx felt searing pain rush through her body.

Trying to navigate through the pain, Jinx reached her arm up to push his hand off her shoulder just as Desdemona ran up to knee him in the stomach. Instantly, the pain subsided and Jinx grabbed Desdemona's hand, tugging her up the stairs, away from the pair of boys. Felix followed quickly, running even faster than before. Finally, the Anchors made it to the floor containing the rec rooms and pushed the door open to reveal a dark hallway, just like the one in Jinx's vision.

"Where is it?" Felix asked, just as Jinx expected he would. Jinx stopped, holding her hand up and thinking. Finally, she saw room 285 and picked the lock quickly. Just as Jinx envisioned, they entered a regular rec room with an orange couch and a flat screen.

"Ok... What now?" Desdemona asked. "This is where all our visions stopped."

"Are we even sure it's in here?" Felix questioned.

Jinx turned, snapping at him. "Do you have a better idea?" When he didn't answer her, she ordered, "then get looking."

The siblings searched hurriedly, knowing their time alone in the room would be limited. Any minute now, another family would think to check this room.

After about ten minutes, Desdemona threw her hands up, frustrated. "Guys, I don't think the Jewel is in here."

"Wait a minute..." Felix thought aloud. "Kade said the prizes can be in secret passageways. And what's the one thing we all saw in our visions?"

Desdemona and Jinx answered at the same time, enthused. "The couch."

"Help me move it." Jinx said. All the Anchor siblings grabbed a side of the bright orange couch and lugged it across the room, leaving wood underneath it exposed. Sure enough, one of the wooden boards had been raised slightly. Pulling at the wood, Felix wrenched the floorboard up.

"I don't see any Asterian Jewel in there," Desdemona noted, leaning over the hole in the ground.

"Did you really think they were going to make it that easy?" Jinx asked. "We have to go in." Without waiting for their reply, Jinx knelt down and scooted through the pitch black hole, praying the drop wasn't far. Much to her relief, her feet hit the inside of the passageway almost immediately. The broken floorboards only went up to her chest.

"Well… what do we do about this?" Felix wondered.

"We're going to have to crawl, I guess," Desdemona suggested. Immediately, Jinx ducked down on her hands and knees and began to crawl. Desdemona came down next with Felix close behind.

I hear something… Felix heard a deep, raspy voice inside of his head. *The Asterians have found the passageway.*

"Guys, we're on the right track, which is great, but there's something up ahead," Felix whispered to his sisters.

Jinx came to an abrupt stop at the front, causing Desdemona to run into her in the dark. The hard, concrete floor under Desdemona's hands and knees scratched at her skin as she felt Felix also run into her. As though making up for her lack of sight, Desdemona's other senses appeared heightened. She could feel every crevice under her fingertips and could hear every movement from the floors above them.

"What do you mean?" Jinx whispered back.

"I mean I heard someone's thoughts. It was a deep voice, almost eerie sounding…" Felix's voice trailed off.

Jinx looked back in the direction of her brother and sister. Although she couldn't see them, she knew they were looking at her as well. "Hey, this is the Hunt. They're not going to put anything in there we can't defeat. We can do this," Jinx reassured.

At that moment, the Anchors heard a smashing noise ahead and Desdemona felt herself being pulled into a vision.

Desdemona stood in a large cavern with lanterns reaching to high ceilings. Pillars rose behind a pedestal, on top of which sat a bowl. Inside the bowl, the Asterian Jewel glowed brightly. Desdemona ran her hand through her short, cropped hair. Looking down at her clothes, she noticed the fabric of a trainer's uniform clung tightly to her skin. She heard whispering from a small opening in the wall. The voices drifted into the tall cavern and Desdemona recognized the voice unmistakably as Jinx's. From the moment Desdemona heard the voices, she felt her skin begin to pull and stretch in all different directions. Just as she felt she would split in half, she did just that. A second version of herself, a short, brawny man Desdemona recognized as having stood near Mr. Belton just before the start of the Hunt, now stood by her side. Desdemona continued to split and divide until over a hundred versions of herself - or himself - appeared. Desdemona turned and stood behind one of the columns, accidentally making a clattering noise as she ran into the pedestal holding the prize for the Hunt.

Desdemona felt herself being pulled out of the vision and took a moment to recover before recounting the story to her siblings.

"So are we supposed to defeat over 100 of one of the trainers at The House?" Felix asked incredulously.

Desdemona shook her head, but then realized neither of her siblings could see her motion. "I don't know," she answered.

"Well, we're not going to find out how to do this by just sitting here. Let's keep crawling," Jinx said. Without waiting for a response, Jinx continued to move, getting closer and closer to the multiplied trainer. Soon, the Anchors reached the end of the cramped tunnel and came out into the tall cavern – the one Desdemona just envisioned.

As expected, over one hundred of one man stood, multiplied, all over the cavern. The Asterian Jewel glowed in the bowl on the pedestal. Jinx took a step to the side to let Felix and Desdemona out of the tunnel. Although all three siblings expected the men to attack them all at once, they did not. Instead, they spoke all at once, like a chorus.

"Find the one of us that is real and we will bestow upon you the Asterian Jewel." They harmonized in the same eerie, raspy tone Felix heard in his head.

"Holy crap, that was the scariest thing I have ever heard in my entire life," Jinx whispered under her breath. Felix nodded in agreement, neither of them wanting to be the first to move. Instead, Desdemona confidently strode over to one of the columns, remembering the real man walked behind one. Glancing behind all the other columns, Desdemona found only one other duplicate.

"You two," Desdemona shouted at the two men hiding behind the columns. "Get out here."

The two men, identical in appearance from everything to the tinniest birth mark to the cowlick in their hair, stepped forward, standing in front of the Jewel as if guarding it. Desdemona studied them closely, trying desperately to differentiate them.

"Guys, a little help, please," Desdemona stage-whispered to Felix and Jinx. Quickly, they stepped up to her side.

"How do you know it's one of these two?" Jinx questioned, skeptically.

Desdemona answered her without a glance, still studying the two men. "In my vision, I was the real man and I stepped behind a pillar just as we crawled into this chamber. So, I know the real man is behind one of these pillars. I just don't know which one exactly."

"Hey," Felix whispered, "do you think the clones have thoughts? If they don't, then I can find the real one by searching through his mind."

Desdemona and Jinx nodded eagerly and Felix let his powers wander, searching the chamber for any trace of a mind. Sure enough, he only heard three sets of thoughts; One from Jinx, another from Desdemona, and the last from the same deep voice he heard earlier.

As Desdemona promised, the thoughts came from one of the two men standing in front of them.

Why are they so silent? How is this kid doing this? Felix heard the man think. After hearing this single thought, Felix pointed to the man standing on the left.

"It's this one," Felix answered. The hundred clones merged back into the original man with a single flash.

All three Anchor siblings staggered back as they glanced at the man, now alone, in front of them.

"Congratulations, Anchors," the man greeted. "The Jewel is yours."

With these words, he stepped aside to clear a path towards the pedestal. Jinx ran towards the Asterian Jewel, which glowed a bright white, and cupped it in both of her hands. The stone was smooth on the top, like the prefect skipping rock. However, large spikes like mini mountains covered the bottom of the Jewel.

"We did it," Jinx yelled enthusiastically, passing the Jewel to her brother and sister, who squeezed her tightly in a hug.

Just as the Anchors continued to celebrate, a large alarm sounded from above, making a shrill, buzzing noise.

"Attention, young Asterians," Mr. Belton's voice came through the speakers. "The Hunt has been won. Please make your way back to the Arena for a celebration."

"Ugh. We have to make our way back through that tunnel again?" Jinx groaned, moving towards the tunnel opening.

As she continued to complain, an unknown tall woman stepped out of the shadows of the chamber. Finally recognizing her as another trainer at The House, Felix smiled bashfully.

"It is quite impressive that triplets in their first few months here at The House won the Hunt. I think a celebration is in order," the woman congratulated. She extended her hands to the Anchors as well as the other trainer. Felix, Desdemona, and the trainer grabbed onto her arm, touching her skin.

"What are we doing?" Jinx asked.

"My power is one of transportation over short distances. I can take you back to the arena, unless you prefer to go back through the tunnel."

"Nope, I think I'm good," Jinx answered, sprinting over to join her siblings with the woman.

Desdemona closed her eyes, slightly nervous for her first transportation. But when she opened them again, she found herself back in the arena. Without moving, they arrived in a completely different place.

"Wow! You're really good at that," Felix praised.

The tall woman laughed. "I've had years of practice."

The woman marched up to the landing where Mr. Belton, along with all the other trainers, stood. Slowly, all the other Asterians filed into the arena, kicking up the dusty floor. Felix heard snippets of despondent thoughts, each wondering who won and why they themselves were not the winners.

Once the arena filled with young Asterians, Mr. Belton stood up, his voice booming. "Attention! We have a brand new winner of the Hunt, a family that has never won before." For a moment, Mr. Belton let the suspense hang in the air, allowing everyone to wonder which family possessed the Jewel at this very moment. "Our winners for this year are Jinx, Felix, and Desdemona Anchor. Allow me to break out the Asterian Ale to celebrate this fantastic victory."

The large walls of the arena lifted once again to reveal long lunch tables, each adorned with hundreds of copper goblets. Smoke arose from the top of the cups and each Asterian rushed to grab a drink.

Desdemona, Felix, and Jinx felt themselves being pushed from behind and stumbled to grab a goblet. Peering over the edge of the copper, Desdemona noticed the smoke came from a clear liquid, almost like water. However, she felt this wasn't just water.

"Is this really Asterian Ale?" Felix asked.

"I would imagine so," Desdemona answered.

Jinx sniffed the liquid, glancing around as all the other teens gulped down their cups. "Someone else try it first."

Felix shrugged and brought the cup to his lips, letting the clear liquid run down his throat. A hint of strawberry and mint rushed down his throat, tantalizing his taste buds.

"This is great, guys. Try it," Felix said. Both of his sisters tried the Ale, sighing in agreement as they too enjoyed the berry flavor. Continuing to drink their Asterian Ale, the Anchor triplets celebrated their victory.

Felix felt people who had never spoken a word to him slap him on the back in congratulations. Desdemona found herself surrounded, per usual, but this time everyone wanted to know how they did it, how they found the Asterian Jewel.

The other Asterians didn't embrace Jinx as they did Felix and Desdemona, but Jinx didn't mind. She closed her hands tightly around the stone, smiling softly. They did it. They really won.

II

The weeks following the Hunt were chaotic. The Anchor siblings enjoyed their new found celebrity status, with everyone asking what they planned to do with the Jewel. However, after about three weeks, the excitement died down and life continued normally – or at least as normal as life could be at The House.

Mona, Felix and Jinx spent mornings in the training room with their weapons, throwing knives, shooting arrows, and cutting heads off dummies. They then attended a few classes, often finding facts about Asterian powers to be intriguing and their prophecy class, divine. The trio had free time to eat lunch and in the late afternoons they mingled with other Asterians.

Nights became the most rigorous. Kade spent hours and hours with them developing their powers as a team. Each sibling attempted to focus on one objective, to see the same thing with clarity, past, present and future. Sometimes it worked. Sometimes it didn't. Kade insisted repetition would be the future key to putting their powers together if a real life situation ever called for it.

Tonight they focused on using their powers in chronological order. Their visions became the most clear and descriptive when occurring in order, with Desdemona first seeing the past, Felix seeing the present, then Jinx seeing the future.

"Desdemona, go. Conjure up a vision about the lunch menu three weeks ago," Kade ordered. At the sound of the word "lunch", Desdemona phased out, being pulled out of her own mind.

The white, florescent lunch menu in The House's cafeteria slowly became clear. She noticed the sound of excited voices speaking, even being able to make out some conversations. She'd never been able to do that before. Her red hair bounced against her shoulders, proving to her she was in a body not her own. Just as she read the lunch menu, she managed to overhear a conversation occurring closely behind her.

"No. Please don't do it. Stop!" a girl whispered frantically. She recognized the sweet voice immediately. It was Margret. Turning around conspicuously, Desdemona looked to see to whom Margret had been talking. When she looked at Margret from the corner of her eye, Desdemona noticed no one stood within ten feet of her. Was Margret talking to herself? I need to get out, Desdemona thought. Something isn't right here.

Pulling herself out of the vision, Desdemona came back to the present gasping for air.

"Why did it take you so long?" Kade asked impatiently, hands on his hips.

Trying to control her breathing, Desdemona placed a manicured hand over her quickly beating heart. "We need to find Margret. I think she's in trouble. I have a bad feeling."

Although Desdemona insisted they go find her now, Kade demanded an explanation. Reluctantly, she gave it to him, starting with the fact that she could now hear conversations without intending to hear them. She then moved on to the freaky one she wished she hadn't heard.

Kade's eyes got wide. "You're right. We need to find her immediately."

The four of them sprinted out of the room and into the halls, intending to go up to Margret's room. Just as they reached the elevator, they turned a corner and bumped right into Mr. Belton.

"Mr. Belton, what are you doing up so late?" Kade asked politely.

"It's about one of our students," Mr. Belton answered. A bead of sweat formed between his bunched up brows, proving to everyone his obvious concern about something.

"Is it about Margret?" Desdemona butted in.

Mr. Belton nodded. "You haven't seen her right?" All four of them shook their heads. "The four of you need to come to my office this instant please."

Down in Mr. Belton's office, the air was thick and heavy with anticipation.

"When did you last see Margret?" Mr. Belton questioned them.

"A long, long time ago," Felix answered, obviously worried for the pretty girl.

"Maybe it's for the best," Jinx added. "She was always obnoxiously chatty anyway."

Desdemona smacked Jinx on the arm. "Jinx, this is a serious matter."

"I'm just saying," Jinx added. "She seems a little weird…"

Before Jinx finished her thought, a loud crack shook Mr. Belton's office and a thick cloud of gray smoke slithered around the room like a serpent. When the smoke thickened and it became nearly impossible to see, a bright, blue light illuminated the wooden room.

An evil cackle erupted as the illumination took form and Desdemona gripped Felix's hand. The form took the shape of a woman, a woman who looked a lot like an older version of Jinx. An audible gasp came from Jinx when she realized…

This woman was their mother.

"Ah," the smooth voice of their mother said. "How good it is to see my children again, all grown up."

Desdemona swallowed back a lump in her throat as Jane referred to them as her children. Squeezing Felix's hand, Desdemona could only imagine the thoughts Felix heard. They must be so frantic and jumbled and afraid.

"What are you doing here, Jane?" Kade asked, voice steady. The hardened expression on his face showed no fear, as if the woman who rendered so many Asterians powerless didn't faze him at all.

"Just here to pass on a message to my kids," Jane responded in a casual voice. Then, all at once, her lackadaisical demeanor shifted into a terrifying seriousness. "Listen here, you three. You know Margret? Sweet, beautiful Margret? Been a while since you've seen her hasn't it? Why is that?"

No one answered.

"Answer me," Jane shrieked, throwing her hands up in fury.

To everyone's surprise, Jinx answered in a calm, collected tone. "We don't know why that is, Jane."

Satisfied, Jane continued. "I took her. I kidnapped Margret and she's being held hostage here at the top of Truchas Peak, the tallest mountain in Santa Fe, New Mexico. She has seven days to live before I strip her of her powers and let the mountain lions of the Truchas Peak have at her. Make your choice wisely, children. You can come here and bring her safely back home or you can leave your dear friend here to die. Imagine the guilt you would have to live with if you let her be killed when you could have saved her. You're good little Asterians, trying to save the world, aren't you?"

Jane moved to the side and a high-pitched, girly scream filled the room. It was very obvious the scream was Margret's. On the heels of her scream, the blue light went out, the smoke cleared, and the room grew dark.

For a moment, no one spoke. All five of them tried to comprehend what they just witnessed and how it happened. The three siblings shared glances mixed with confusion, terror, and surprise.

"It's a trap," Kade finally noted, breaking the silence. "She wants to get you up to the top of the mountain to take your powers, or worse."

"So what if she does? We can't just leave Margret up there." Felix countered.

"Oh shut up. You just feel that way because you think you have a chance with her, but she's way out of your league anyway," Jinx informed him.

Felix's expression faltered slightly, but then he shook it off and continued. He turned to Desdemona and Jinx, talking directly to them. "What would Hilga and Stacy say if they realized you left one of your friends to die at the hands of Jane? I know Marcus would be furious. This is our chance to make a difference. This is our chance to change the course of history, the story everyone has told about Jane being this invincible Asterian. We can change that."

"You're not going. This is way too dangerous," Kade ordered. "Even if all three of you went, your powers wouldn't be enough to defeat her."

"I don't believe that one bit. We need to go. We can do this," Felix told him, standing his ground.

For a moment, Felix and Kade both stared at each other. Kade's stormy eyes flared up in rage at the opposition of his student.

"Hey." Desdemona butted in. "Why don't we let Mr. Belton decide? He is the headmaster."

All eyes flipped to Mr. Belton as the fire in Kade's face extinguished. Mr. Belton tapped nervously on the wood of his desk, his brow furrowed in thought. "Kade, what is the status of their training? The truth."

"Their training has come along very nicely," replied Kade.

"And how powerful have they become? The truth." Mr. Belton inquired further.

Kade reluctantly admitted, "Mr. Belton, together, with a bit of further development, their powers will be extraordinary."

With that, Mr. Belton announced, "We will let the Anchor siblings decide. But, the vote must be unanimous."

Kade shook his head in anger, frustrated with the headmaster's decision. Jinx, Felix, and Desdemona looked at each other again.

I say yes and I know Felix does too, but I'm worried about what Jinx will say. Felix heard Desdemona's voice inside his head. He tended to agree with her. They had to convince Jinx.

Felix, stepping up and taking charge, stated, "I say we go." Desdemona quickly agreed with him.

Jinx, as expected, hesitated. She ran her hand through her hair in frustration. "It isn't my job to go save a girl who went and got herself kidnapped."

"True Asterians feel a tug, a yearning, to help those in need. But if you're not ready, if you're not up to it….," Mr. Belton trailed off. Well, that proved what side he was on. Mr. Belton knew how to push buttons.

"Imagine what Hilga would want you to do," Felix reminded her. He could only imagine the face of the sweet, old grandmother if she found out her granddaughter let an innocent girl wither away in the mountains.

This made Jinx think hard. She would never ever want to do anything to disappoint Hilga - the one person in her life whose opinion she genuinely cared about. She knew Felix was right. "Alright," Jinx started with a sigh. "I'll go."

Desdemona and Felix shared a proud smile, mentally high-fiving each other. Kade, knowing he lost, sat down in one of the blue, felt armchairs and rubbed his temples, as if he had a horrendous headache.

"I want to come with you," Kade whispered, barely audible to the other four in the room.

"What?" Jinx asked, scrunching up her eyebrows.

"I said," Kade repeated. "I am coming with you. I'm not just going to let my three students go off all the way across the country without the guidance of their mentor. What kind of teacher would that make me? And plus, I could be very beneficial to you in battle."

Battle... Whoa, we're going to be fighting... For real, Felix heard Desdemona think. He pushed into her mind and reassured her.

But, that's what we've trained for, isn't it? Wouldn't want these past few months to go to waste. We can do this. We have to do this.

Desdemona smiled softly at Felix, silently thanking him.

As Mr. Belton discussed travel plans with the triplets, Kade paced the room anxiously. His hand flew through his shaggy hair and his eyes flared with a mixture of anticipation and fear. For the first time, Jinx realized she was seeing some emotion from Kade. Her cold heart softened at the sight of him upset and she got the foreign urge to comfort him, pat him on the head, rub his back, anything. Weirded out and a little disgusted by her own emotions, Jinx turned away from Kade and re-joined the conversation. Or re-joined it as much as she ever did.

Meanwhile, Mr. Belton talked of travel plans, ranting on and on. "I can get you a flight out tomorrow night at 9pm and set up a car to take you to the bottom of the mountain. We need to pack each of you backpacks, filled with food and water and lots of extra clothes. I'd imagine it's freezing up there at the top of Truchas."

"Hey," Kade interrupted, ending Mr. Belton's extensive rant. "Why don't we let the Anchors go get some rest? They've had a long physical and emotional day. You and I can work out the plans tonight while they sleep."

Mr. Belton nodded furiously, shooing Felix, Desdemona, and Jinx to their rooms and ordering them to get some "shut-eye" immediately. But his cheery, excitable mood shifted the minute the wooden door closed behind them. Mr. Belton turned to Kade with a more serious expression, one never seen by Kade in their ten years together. His normally warm brown eyes fell to a deep black and his mouth, set in a strict line, fully revealed his previously disguised worry.

"Why did you let them go?" Kade asked Mr. Belton with a huff.

Shutting his eyes, he breathed deeply. "In the end, we would not have been able to stop them and even if we could, they wouldn't have been able to live with themselves. You just have to get these kids home safely."

Kade immediately felt the pressure on his chest like a barbell. "I fully intend to, Sir," he answered, reassuring himself almost as much as he was Mr. Belton.

"It won't be easy," Mr. Belton reminded him. "This is Jane Anchor we're talking about. Everyone who has crossed her before has failed miserably. If you lose, Jane will take their gifts, their lives, or all of the above. If the Anchor kids are as powerful as you say and Jane takes their gifts, it's a safe bet Jane will come back to The House and try to end Asterian life as we know it.

12

The sun began to set just as the wheels of the plane lifted off the ground and the wings took over. An orange flame of light streamed through the window and fell onto Jinx's face. She shut the window shade with shaking hands and took deep breaths, one after the other. Jinx reached instinctively for her knife at her hip, only to remind herself Kade ordered them to secure all weapons in their checked luggage. Instead, she reached down in her backpack and pulled out a small cloth bag which contained their prize from the Hunt.

Taking the Jewel out and cupping it in her hand, Jinx admired the beautiful emerald, wondering about the true extent of its powers. She could hear Desdemona and Felix across the aisle pointing excitedly at the clouds as the plane shot through them like water. Personally, Jinx didn't enjoy the fact that the plane passed through the clouds. In fact, Jinx didn't like the idea of planes at all. Rubbing her sweaty hands on her shorts, Jinx blinked rapidly, a nervous habit of hers.

"Are you okay?" Kade asked Jinx from the seat beside her. Jinx snapped her head towards him, ready to bark and scowl. But the minute she saw his big eyes filled with genuine concern for her, she softened. Something about this boy made Jinx feel crazy things…made her want to do crazy things. Like be nice.

"Yeah," Jinx answered. "Thanks for your concern, Kade."

Kade nodded, knowing Jinx wasn't telling him the truth, but deciding not to push it. She needed to be handled with care. In complete contrast with her sister, Jinx remained quiet and reserved most of the time, while you could read Desdemona like a book. Jinx might seem rude to other people, but Kade knew something special hid behind those heavily guarded walls of hers. Something sympathetic, benevolent, and even loving. Something told Kade he would eventually get to the bottom of it.

Desdemona tapped Kade on the shoulder, pointing out the window. She went on and on about how excited she felt to be on a plane and how everything seemed so much more exhilarating now that she realized her powers. "Being an Asterian just-"

Kade hit Desdemona on the shoulder, scolding her. "You can't just go around saying," he whispered "Asterian" to her. "It's not something we just go around telling everyone."

"Well why not?" Desdemona tilted her head in question.

"I can't explain it to you now," Kade told her. "I'll explain it to you soon. But not here. Not now."

With the seriousness of his tone, Desdemona fell quiet.

As the sun set further into the horizon, other passengers on the plane slowly fell asleep. Kade glanced over at Felix and Desdemona, who fell fast asleep on each other. Turning his head to check on Jinx, he caught a glimpse of her dark eyes before they snapped shut, trying to hide from him.

"I know you're not asleep, Jinx," Kade informed her. She sighed heavily and opened her eyes. "C'mon, tell me what's going on."

Kade could practically see the walls build up inside Jinx. He could hear the bricks stacking up on one another; smell the cement being used to seal them together. "I'm fine. Really," Jinx lied.

Even though he knew he wouldn't get a real answer, Kade couldn't help but feel his hopes sink to the pit of his stomach.

"You know Jinx, it's not good to keep everything bottled up like this. I may not be able to read minds like Felix, but I've known you long enough to know something is up. I'm not going to push you to talk about it, but when you do finally want to let me in, I'll be here."

Jinx made eye contact with him for just a second, but she broke it just as quickly as she once again closed her eyes.

Roughly three hours later, Felix woke up to the sound of the captain's voice over the loud speaker. "We are now beginning our descent into Albuquerque International Airport. Please stow all carry-ons and switch all electronic devices to the off position."

Groggy and disoriented, Felix shook Desdemona awake. Desdemona opened her eyes slowly but surely and reached her arms up above her head to stretch.

"We should be landing in about twenty minutes," Kade informed them. With a face as hard as stone, Felix wondered if he slept at all on the flight despite it being nearly one in the morning. "I want us all to stay together. Talk to no one and I mean no one. We will get our luggage from baggage claim and immediately go meet the driver to take us to Truchas."

As they sluggishly filed off of the plane, Kade led them towards baggage claim. People talked excitedly around the group, murmuring to their friends and family members about their upcoming trips. Felix couldn't help but feel a pang of jealousy as he noticed three siblings, two girls and a boy, playing tag around one of the waiting areas. All three laughed and squealed with glee as they ran from the smallest girl.

That could have been us, Felix heard Desdemona think. *If our mom hadn't been a weird psycho Asterian.*

But she was and she is, Felix pushed into her mind and reminded her. *And that's why we're on this trip. We're going to end her power once and for all.*

Desdemona nodded, taking a final, sorrowful glance at the happy children. Kade, staying a good distance in front of the triplets, followed the signs in the airport that read "baggage claim." He had one job for the day and that was to get these kids safely into the car and on their way to the bottom of Truchas Peak.

Suddenly, he felt a tap on his shoulder and Kade whirled around, powers ready, only to come face to face with a sickly Jinx.

"Kade, I feel strange. Something is wrong," Jinx informed him, holding her stomach.

Eyes growing big, Kade stuttered over his words. If there was anything he wasn't okay with handling, it was sick girls. "Um... Do you think you're going to throw up?"

Jinx shook her head. "It's not like that. I have this feeling something is wrong. Like if we don't change something, we're going to be badly injured."

Kade took a deep breath. Thank goodness it was just badly injured and not throwing up. "Do you mean it feels like you need to see something in the future?"

"I don't know. I've never felt it before. But I've also never used my powers in a dangerous situation," Jinx answered. As they reached the baggage claim and stopped in front of the moving conveyor belt, Jinx noticed her black suitcase with the green luggage tag. Reaching up to grab the bag, Jinx tried to pull it off the belt but felt a vision coming on. Dropping the bag back onto the belt, Jinx turned to Kade.

"Gettt tthhhee lluggaggg," Jinx said, slurring her words a little. Sitting down quickly at the feet of Felix and Desdemona, Jinx closed her eyes and let the picture consume her.

A tall, burly man greeted Desdemona, Felix, Kade, and Jinx with a cheery grin. His dark black hair, cropped short under his chauffeur hat, revealed black eyes.

Creepy, Jinx thought to herself. Why is he driving a car? He's big enough to be a wrestler.

The man, introducing himself as Andrew, smiled politely again and reached for Desdemona's bag, placing it carefully in the trunk of the van. Shooting him a thankful smile, Desdemona flipped her hair and blushed.

Unbelievable. Why is she trying to flirt with our driver?

The man reached for their remaining bags. After he finished loading the black van, he politely opened the door and Desdemona was the first one in. Felix, then Jinx, then Kade followed her. Settling into the plush seats, Jinx reveled in the thought she would have roughly another hour to sleep before having to get up.

Just as she closed her eyes, the door slammed shut behind Kade and locked with a snap. A green mist began flowing from the floorboards. Desdemona pulled furiously at the door handle, to no avail. Jinx's vision grew cloudy as her thoughts twisted and turned inside her jumbled mind. Desdemona stopped pulling at the door, knocked out cold on the opposite side of the car. Before she blacked out, Jinx turned just in time to see Andrew's cheery smile turn to a devilish grin.

"We can't go with our driver. He's working with Jane." Jinx shouted, pulling herself out of her vision. Calming her breathing, she took Felix's outstretched hand and hauled herself up onto her feet. Jinx ran her hand through her hair and breathed deeply before she began replaying the events of her vision to Kade and her siblings.

"Wow," Kade started. "You're right. We really can't go with him."

"But how are we going to get to the bottom of the mountain? It's an hour drive, probably a whole day's walk. We don't have time to waste." Felix mentioned. Kade understood his concern about wasting precious time. They were already at the tail end of the first day, but he didn't see any other choice. Kade would not risk putting the Anchor siblings in a car with anyone. Not after this.

Retrieving the remaining bags from the conveyor, Kade thought quickly. They couldn't trust even a cab driver, nor were any of them old enough to rent a car. Kade had only one choice.

Coming back to the group, Kade ran his plan by Desdemona, Jinx, and Felix. "Felix, I need you to extend the range of your mind reading. Look for a particularly gullible person, young, too nice for their own good. Desdemona, once Felix targets someone, I want you to look into their past. Find out about any past dumb mistakes they've made. Jinx, this is your chance to finally use your powers in the real world. We're going to hijack a car."

13

All three Anchor siblings worked, nervously attending to their given tasks. Regardless of the fact that stealing a car went against everything Felix learned growing up, he was "all in." Walking would take too long and this could be their only chance to save Margret's life. Felix zoned in on a ditzy girl whose thoughts ran around in her mind like rabbits in a field of carrots. Perfect. Desdemona quickly saw her being manipulated in her past, which caused her to feel a little bad for the poor girl. Jinx spun quickly into the future, realizing if they worked fast this would get them to Truchas.

But the future had a habit of changing. There was no guarantee.

"Are we ready? We need to get moving," Kade asked, reminding them of their time constraint. As if they could forget.

"There's a red headed woman outside this door. She's carrying a large, blue purse. Can't miss her," Felix informed him. Quickly, they headed out the doors of the airport into the warm New Mexico air. As Felix said, the woman was nearly impossible to miss. Her frizzy red hair stuck out in the dry heat of Albuquerque and the freckles on her pale skin stood out like a sore thumb. She talked loquaciously on the phone, popping her bubble gum.

Kade, pushing his hair out of his eyes, left the bags with the trio along with an order to follow closely once chaos broke out. They all three stared at him with questioning eyes, but decided to let him have at it. Once Kade reached the woman, he tapped her on the shoulder and leaned onto her small, red car with one arm, creating a barrier. She turned around, afraid at first, but after seeing the suggestive look in his eyes, softened up.

Kade reached up, taking a strand of her hair in his hand. "You've got such beautiful hair, ma'am. You're really quite breathtaking."

The woman, now fully blushed, thanked him as she stuttered. Kade glanced quickly down at his target: the keys hanging out of her left pocket.

"And your eyes... Wow," Kade complimented once more. As soon as he believed her to be appropriately flustered he made his move. As quick as lightning, Kade blocked all the senses of everyone around him besides Desdemona, Jinx, and Felix.

At first, the three didn't know what to do. Everyone around them became dead silent, confused even. But then, just as Kade warned, chaos broke out. Women began running like men, while men began screaming like women. Kade quickly grabbed the keys from the woman's pocket and clicked the car unlocked.

"What are you waiting for?" Kade yelled. "Put the bags in the car. I can't hold all these people forever."

Frantically, each Anchor child put their bags in the trunk along with Kade's. Piling in, Kade walked slowly around to the driver's seat, making sure everyone remained under his influence. As soon as the keys hit the ignition and the Honda shifted into drive, Kade released all his "subjects," restoring their senses and driving furiously out of the airport terminal.

Kade drove as fast as possible, taking weird and sudden turns to make sure no one followed them out. Finally, once they reached a mostly deserted road far away from the airport, he slowed...

"That was so awesome," Jinx yelled in the passenger's seat. Her eyes lit up like never before and she appeared high on adrenaline. "Let's do it again!"

"Whoa there J." Felix called from the back. "Stealing cars isn't something we can do all that often, so I would figure it's not a good thing to get addicted to."

Kade stole a quick glance at Jinx, happy to see her excited about something in this world for once. Maybe he was finally getting to her.

"Umm…" Desdemona began. "Kade, do you know where we're going?"

"Not a single clue. But, if you look to the left, there's a mountain range. See," Kade pointed with one finger as all three turned to gaze out the window like children. "The tallest one, the one with the snow covered peak, is Truchas. Don't worry. We will get there."

Everyone seemed to accept this, which led to silence filling the car. Desdemona occasionally pointed out a funny looking plant, while Felix would compare the look of the landscape to theirs at home. At home, tall fir trees spotted the hills, but here the tallest plants were no higher than Felix himself. Oranges, yellows and browns. No greens. Anywhere.

"Oh," Desdemona yelled, breaking the silence. Everyone in the car besides Kade flinched at the sudden noise. "Kade. You said you would tell me why we couldn't tell anyone about Asterians once you got the chance. You have the chance now, right?

Kade thought for a moment. "Well, as you learned during your time at The House, Asterians are sort of like guardian angels, more or less. If the humans knew they were being protected by another species, there is no telling what those crazy people would try to do. Some of them would go out and be reckless for no reason just because they think they can do it without getting hurt."

All three Anchor siblings nodded, understanding, but then Jinx paused, finally asking a question she never had the courage to bring up at The House.

"But wait, if we're supposed to help people, that doesn't explain why our mother became such a bad woman. Why did she go around and use her powers for evil when she could have been saving people's lives?"

"Your mother's power is funny." Kade answered. "And not in the good way. About a hundred years ago, an Asterian named Jargon mastered powers of manipulation. He could hypnotize people into doing the right thing, but he decided to use his power to convince people what's actually wrong was right. He overthrew The House, absolutely wrecking Asterian life as everyone knew it. Going around, turning innocents against their families and friends, Jargon turned a benevolent power into something malicious. It was horrifying."

Kade paused for a moment, letting this sink in. Desdemona's pale face looked confused, while Felix pensively took it all in. Jinx, as usual, had a half scowl half smirk planted on her face.

"Mr. Belton speculates your mother's powers were created to prevent something like what Jargon did from ever happening again. Her ability to steal other's powers allowed her to overthrow anyone who tried to rampage Asterian Society. But of course, Jane also heard the story I just told you. After Mr. Belton revealed to Jane the true purpose of her powers, for some reason she went rogue. Absolutely insane."

"So basically the woman who could prevent Asterian destruction actually began causing it?" Jinx asked, scoffing. "Some great mom we have. Am I right guys?" Jinx turned around to her siblings, laughing. This girl always had a knack for laughing at inappropriate times.

Just as Felix almost scolded Jinx for making that joke at the worst time, he stopped. Jinx referred to them out loud as her siblings. Was she beginning to accept Desdemona and Felix?

Here, in their hijacked Honda on the way to some crazy tall mountain halfway across the country, the Anchor siblings took another small step towards becoming what none of them had ever truly been before - a family.

14

The sun began to light up the sky orange and red as they pulled up to the foot of the mountain range containing Truchas Peak. All three Anchor kids stretched as they woke up from their short nap in the car. Kade, who didn't sleep at all, found himself more wide eyed and bushy tailed than any of them.

"Get out, kids," Kade ordered. "We've got a lot of traveling to do before sundown."

"We're only a couple of years younger than you. You shouldn't be calling us kids," Jinx retorted as Desdemona and Felix sleepily emerged from the backseat, feet hitting the rocky terrain.

"And you shouldn't be talking back to your trainer. I may only be a few years older, but I've been at this longer than you guys," Kade answered, shooing Jinx out of the Honda. Jinx grimaced and reluctantly pulled herself from the seat.

Outside the back of the Honda, Felix and Desdemona began to transfer their heavier coats, food, and water from bulky suitcases to small satchels. They couldn't have those big suitcases weighing them down up in the mountains. The hard earth felt solid under Felix's feet as he hurled his now-filled satchel across his back. Although small, surprisingly, the satchels carried several days of food and water for four people. They wouldn't need the full six remaining days to climb Truchas and rescue Margret - if all went well.

Felix stood facing the tall mass towering over his head, just waiting to be climbed. He knew he would find Margret at the top of the highest peak. Beautiful, sweet, innocent little Margret. Felix's stomach turned at the idea of someone so stunning being hurt. He couldn't imagine all the things Jane had been doing to her. Hate burned throughout his veins as he thought about his… mother. No, not his mother. She couldn't be. Maybe biologically, but not emotionally. And that's how he planned on handling her.

"What are we going to do with the stolen car?" Desdemona asked.

"Nothing. We're going to leave it here. We can't drive it into the mountains. We have to walk from here, so we have no use for it," Kade told her, looking off into the lofty mountains above.

We have a lot of traveling ahead of us, he thought. We should start now.

"Well, what are we waiting for? No time like the present to climb one of the tallest mountains in the United States, right?" Jinx declared, bounding forward. Weird… Jinx seems really excited about this, Felix noticed.

Why is she so happy? Desdemona thought.

Who knows, but we better take what we can get. Jinx is rarely in a mood like this, Felix answered her in her mind. She turned to him, nodding, ending their mental conversation.

Slowly, their climb began. They trudged on up, one step at a time in a single file line. No one spoke much. It was silent. In fact, too silent. Something was off. Where were all the squirrels running? All the large birds flying? What about all the snakes slithering below their footsteps? Where was all the life?

"Hey Kade…" Felix called up from the back of the pack to him to the front. "Is it supposed to be this quiet?"

Kade stopped to listen for a second. "No, it shouldn't be. When I did some research, I read the Truchas mountain range becomes noisy with varied wildlife. Where all those noises are now is beyond me."

They continued to trudge forward in silence when a low, barely discernable growl penetrated the air. Long claws skidded softly against the rocky ground as a predator stalked the group. Sharp canines rubbed against one another through its snarled mouth. It's really too bad none of them noticed these slight disturbances. If they had, their journey would have been much simpler.

They hadn't even been walking for an hour before their first obstacle appeared - a gorge nearly impossible to cross. Kade scoped out the area, noticing the trench grew so deep that blackness filled its pit. If they fell, they would surely die. Turning to both sides, he saw no fast solution like a man-made crossing or rocks forming a natural bridge.

"Hey." Jinx called. "There's a little path down here." All three of them rushed to where Jinx stood, only to see a very narrow, rocky trail leading down the side of the abyss. Across the way, Kade saw another path spiraling around the mountain.

"We don't know how deep this is. It could take days to get up and down this trench," Felix pointed out.

"Or it could take days to go around the mountain or find another way to cross it. If we start now, maybe it will be shorter than we think," Desdemona mentioned. Kade took one last scan of the area before deciding she was right. Heading around the mountain could eat up too much time.

Kade led the way, starting down the path. It was so thin that each Asterian was forced to hug the rocky wall of the abyss just to keep their footing. Kade stopped abruptly, reaching down to grab the flashlight from his bag before continuing the walk. The others did the same.

A low growl, a vicious snarl, a sharp cut of claws on the rock. But the predator managed to stay far enough back to keep these noises just out of clear earshot. Its prey remained unaware of its presence.

As they marched down the trail, darkness slowly surrounded them like a shadow. Bright light streamed from the opening, while not quite reaching the group, making them feel even more disconnected. They began feeling their way down the side of the rock and turned on their flashlights to prevent any misplaced steps. The darkness would only grow from here.

"Guys, I need to sit down," Desdemona ordered, sitting immediately and pulling her legs up to her chest. "I've got that feeling in the pit of my stomach. If I don't stop walking, I'm going to have a vision and fall off the edge of this cliff to my death." She paused, thinking. "And if you don't mind, I'd rather not."

As they came to a slight clearing where the pathway curved to provide more room for travelers, everyone curled up near her, not daring to argue with an Asterian receiving a desire to use their powers. Who knows what could happen if Desdemona missed this vision? It could mean life or death for their mission. And in this case, it really did.

Desdemona felt her shoulders hunch back as she crouched to stalk her prey. Her eyes darted back and forth from the boy to the girl, walking side by side happily, completely unaware of her presence. Completely unaware of their impending doom. Stretching out one hand, Desdemona realized her hands were no longer hers. Neither were her teeth, nor her... fur. She had fur, paws, and canines. Her stomach growled as she snarled, quickly approaching the pair. Desdemona felt a twist in her gut, wishing she could stop herself from what she knew she intended to do, not knowing if she could change it. Had it already happened? Was it real?

Suddenly she gave a loud roar, finally alerting the couple and breaking into a sprint towards them at a speed she never believed possible. Both began running for their lives in every attempt to dodge the predator. With one powerful pounce, Desdemona brought a young boy to the ground.

15

"We're being watched," Desdemona yelled, startling herself awake from her horrifying vision. Wiping the streaming tears from her face, she attempted to control the shaking of her shoulder, but with each sob, the shudders continued. Those poor kids. They'd been murdered... Desdemona had murdered them... She felt Felix snuggle up against her, providing her as much comfort as possible in the limited space on the path. Still, she was thankful for her brother's kind nature. After a while, the shudders passed and she recounted the vision to Kade, Jinx, and Felix, all of whom appeared to become quite frightened as well.

"You mean to say... you think whatever killed those people is out there watching us now?" Jinx asked.

"Well, I was the one who killed them," Desdemona noted, feeling sick to her stomach.

"It wasn't you at all," Kade assured her. "They were dead before you embodied their killer. It's the past, remember?"

"But..." Desdemona asked, shaking again. "I could've done something. I should've done something."

Felix turned Desdemona's head to look into her eyes. "Listen to me. The past is in the past. You can't change it. Ever. Your power reveals plights that have already happened - ones you can't control. You can only learn from them. Those past events can affect our present thoughts and ultimately change the course of our future. It all starts with you, Mona. This vision came to you for a reason as a warning.

At this, Desdemona nodded her head, finally calming down for good. Slowly, she rose to her feet with her hand on Felix's arm for support. Jinx watched them, feeling like an outsider on their little sibling bonding moment. Jinx couldn't back away on the narrow path, despite feeling awkward, as if intruding on their moment even though she was part of the family. She glanced over at Kade, who shuffled stiffly as well. He too, sensed a private moment.

They continued to descend into the canyon, watching it grow darker and darker with each step they took. At times, if it weren't for their flashlights, the group would scarcely have been able to see their hands in front of their faces. Oddly enough, as their sense of sight faded, Felix noticed his hearing seemed to improve. The smallest sounds, like the noise of a bug's legs scuttling on the wall next to him, filled his ears. He heard Desdemona's hair swish on her back in front of him and Kade's flashlight batteries flicker inside their casings.

"Ok, why can I hear Felix moving his tongue inside his mouth? It's making me extremely uncomfortable," Jinx said from behind Kade.

Felix let out a deep breath, taking comfort he wasn't the only one hearing weird things.

"It's because we're in the dark. Asterians' remaining senses build when one has been taken away. Your hearing helps make up for your lack of sight. If you were to touch a wall next to you right now, you would feel crevices under your fingertips you couldn't even see in the daylight." Kade informed them. "Asterians are very powerful, remember. We can't have them blinded and half deaf, now can we?"

Felix pondered over this for a moment, placing his hand on the cracking rock next to him.

How gross. Felix heard Desdemona think. *I can feel the gum on the bottom of my shoe.* Even Felix cringed at that one, silently thanking the Lord above he did not currently have any gum on his shoes.

Surprisingly enough, the trip down the side of the canyon went quickly and before they knew it, the ground leveled off again. There was nowhere else to go down. Only up.

"Can we eat? I'm really hungry," Desdemona complained. "And thirsty."

"Yeah, we can stop. It's important to stay hydrated," Kade reminded them. But if he had just forced them to keep moving, it would have made their journey much easier. If he had forced them to keep moving, they wouldn't have fallen directly into the predator's trap.

By the light of flashlights, everyone unpacked a morsel of food and just enough water to stay hydrated. They talked quietly as they ate, discussing game plans and travel arrangements.

"Look. It's dark already," Desdemona pointed up to the top of the canyon.

Felix replied. "It's probably just around dinnertime."

Desdemona heard a horrible scraping sound, a noise too light for normal ears to hear. But with her enhanced hearing, the sound of claws scratching on the rock nearby became nearly unbearable.

"Guys, listen," she ordered. Immediately, everyone quieted and noises filled the air. Grinding canines, scratching claws, soft growls, twitching ears.

"Get out your weapons. This isn't something we are going to be able to defeat with our powers. Turn off the flashlights." Kade ordered.

"Why on Earth would we do that?" Desdemona yelled back.

"Because if we turn off the lights, our hearing will get even better and we can find it by hearing." Jinx informed her. Kade, who prepared to answer the question, found himself shocked by Jinx's quick answer. He silently reminded himself not to underestimate her.

"Kade, why can't you just blind the animal with your power?" Felix asked.

"My power only works on humans. Stop talking and get out your weapons. This isn't a Q&A session."

Each Anchor kid pulled out their weapons of choice: A bow and arrow, a stack of knives, and a broad sword. Finally, they would get to use them. For real.

The scratching of the sharp nails on the rock grew louder, informing the group of their predator's rapid approach. The slosh of shaking fur filled the dark canyon. That could only mean one thing. This predator was a cat. And it was about to pounce. But the question was, on whom?

Nobody moved a muscle, but Jinx, Desdemona, Felix, and Kade all stood with their weapons at the ready. Felix attempted to steady his arm that held the sword, but fear and nerves kept it shaking.

A loud roar broke the silence, shaking Desdemona to her core. Felix then heard claws scratch off the ground and fly into the air. The sharp yell of Jinx filled the canyon, just as Felix realized who the predator targeted - Jinx.

Desdemona steadied her senses, allowing her to pinpoint the exact location of the cat on Jinx. Jinx slashed furiously, putting up a good fight against the malicious predator. Desdemona took one deep breath and fired the arrow loaded into her bow. She heard it hit the animal in the stomach with a sickening squish. It jumped, in pain, quickly off Jinx and its claws hit the ground with a scratch. Kade took one large step forward and swung with his axe, slicing the cat dead.

Felix had a momentary celebration, excited they defeated their first real enemy. But his excitement was short lived when Jinx groaned from the floor of the canyon.

He had forgotten. Jinx had been the cat's target. She had to have been badly injured.

"Quick, get the flashlights." Kade ordered. Felix listened for the buzzing of the batteries inside of the flashlight and picked two quickly off the ground. Illuminating the dark space, he shined the lights on Jinx, who looked extremely out of it.

Blood oozed from a gash in her left arm so deep Kade could almost see the bone. Quickly grabbing the first aid kit, Kade fumbled around for the needle and thread.

Normally, Kade remained extremely calm in every situation, but now, with a girl he'd grown to believe in so much, he felt a weight over his chest he'd never felt before. Kade breathed heavy as he cleaned the wound. Jinx, who remained mostly out if it, blinked her eyes rapidly. When she looked up, her eyes met Kade's and she offered a weak smile.

"If you're fixing me up then I'm probably going to die," Jinx mumbled. Kade chuckled nervously, worried he might screw this up, but relieved she still had her warped sense of humor.

After thirty rough minutes of stitching and cleansing, the blood stopped flowing from Jinx's arm. Although her clothes were caked in dust, dirt, and blood, she appeared to be fine. Desdemona and Felix, extremely worried, breathed over Kade's shoulder for the first ten minutes before he finally told them to back off. There was absolutely no way he could have ever done this with two emotional siblings in his ear.

Since Jinx, now properly sewed and extremely sleepy, appeared to have lost a lot of blood, Kade knew trying to stay on the move tonight would be pointless. They needed to finish dinner, if possible, and get some shuteye.

"The stars are everywhere out here," Desdemona whispered to Felix, her voice traveling across the canyon to Kade. "We never get to see the stars at home."

"You know, Marcus always used to tell me about the Big Dipper and the Little Dipper," Felix told Desdemona.

"What are those?" Desdemona asked.

"They're star constellations. He used to point up at the starless sky and tell me where he grew up there weren't any big city lights to take away from the beauty of the stars," Felix informed.

Desdemona paused for a moment. "Do you wish we could see the stars at home?"

"I do," Felix answered. "I think they're beautiful. And each one is different, just like people."

It slowly dawned on Kade they were lying on their backs, looking up at the far away night sky. He, too, tilted his head to gaze at the twinkling lights.

"When Stacy used to tell me about the stars, I liked to think the stars had their own little universe up there, with their own little families and wives and children."

At this, Felix laughed. "Well, I might not have ever done anything quite that... imaginative, but I did used to beg Marcus to take me somewhere to see the stars. I never guessed the first time I'd get to see this many of them would be at the bottom of a canyon with a sister I met barely four months ago."

"Crazy," Desdemona thought. "How quickly things change. The night I got my powers, I listened to my mom talk about my fifteenth birthday party, excited for the following day with my family. But then we catapulted into this insane world with another race of people we never knew existed."

"Talk about your life being flipped around in a day, right?" Felix laughed.

"More like an hour."

As Kade listened to the siblings' conversation, he felt himself reminiscing about his own family. His sister, who is who the heck knows where. His parents are for sure on some beach in the Caribbean. He was the only one who accepted his powers and developed them. He was the only one who chose to do something useful with his gifts.

Kade also remembered, as he listened to Desdemona tell stories of her childhood, just how young these kids were. Just how young he was. At barely fifteen, they couldn't even drive, yet they carried the new burden of being Asterians, had already seen combat (a rarity for Asterians) and they just recently learned about their mother, the infamous Jane Anchor. They'd never been anywhere besides Boston until they'd followed him to Santa Fe and chose to climb a mountain.

And Kade. Some of the same things happened to him at fifteen, but he'd always known about Asterians because of his parents. He just never got his powers until he turned fifteen, as did all Asterians. And here he was, just four years later, leading three kids too young to even apply for a real job, where their fate rests mostly in his hands. They relied on him. They depended on him. They trusted him. Oh, what had he gotten himself into?

16

Day 3, Felix heard Desdemona think as she rolled over sleepily in her sleeping bag next to him. *Let's try not to get killed today.*

Felix chuckled, agreeing with his sister in every way. The sun was low in the sky, illuminating the top of the canyon with flames of orange and red as it made its daily debut. The caws of mountain birds filled his ears as the crisp, morning air made him shiver under his blanket. To think, it would only get colder as they ascended the mountain.

Slowly rising from the remaining warmth of his cocoon, Felix surveyed the area. The bottom of the canyon looked severely different than he imagined in his head during last night's darkness. The walls of the canyon were a bulky, orange rock, rising tall to the sky. But unlike the original, reddish rocks he imagined would cover the floor, the canyon floor was black. Pitch black. Normally, rocks would vary in color, ranging from a deep red to a bright orange to a dull brown, but here, the entire canyon floor was one deep shade of darkness. Nerves welled up in Felix's stomach as he realized things like this don't happen naturally. This was the work of an evil Asterian, no doubt. Someone who wanted to make the canyon even darker at night… Someone who wanted to freak out enemies.

"Mona," Felix shook Desdemona's arm, waking her as she rolled to face him.

"What?" she moaned, squinting against the light of the rising sun.

"Look at the ground."

Desdemona slowly rose from her sleeping bag, but the minute her eyes hit the black ground, a sharp shriek erupted from her tiny mouth.

"What is going on? That is SO not natural." she exclaimed, mimicking Felix's thoughts exactly.

Kade ran up from where he had been sitting, awake all night next to Jinx, wide eyed and alert. "Mona, what's wrong? Why are you upset?"

"Look at the ground. Its pitch black." Mona shrieked again, putting her hands up to her face.

"Yes, it is. Thanks for your observation, hot stuff," Jinx sarcastically commented from where she was laying on the black ground. As good as it was that she was feeling well enough to be so snarky, Felix felt a pinch of annoyance. Once again, not the time, Jinx.

Kade placed a hand on Desdemona's shoulder. "Mona, it's okay. We should have figured this out last night. The canyon is not as deep as we originally believed. Someone changed the floor of the canyon to trick us, to make us think it was deeper than it really is."

"Well who would do that?" Felix asked, confused.

"Who do you think would do that, idiot?" Jinx laughed.

"Jinx, stop," Kade scolded. Surprisingly enough, Jinx followed his orders and rolled over, removing herself from the conversation. "It was your mother to say the least. Or one of your mother's servants. We didn't notice the black of the rock yesterday in the daylight because the darkness made it seem like the canyon was endless. Last night, we didn't see it because it was already dark outside." Kade rubbed his temples furiously. "We should have anticipated this. That cougar. A trap. This canyon. A trap. She's setting us up for failure before we even reach the top of the mountain."

"Well… What does that mean?" Desdemona asked, on the brink of tears.

"It means we need to keep going. And the three of you need to keep your powers on high. We can learn so much from what happened, what's happening, and what will happen."

At this, Kade left the two siblings and walked back to check on Jinx.

"Hey, J," Kade whispered close to her ear. When Jinx turned around with a slight smile on her lips, she caught herself wishing he stayed as close as she knew he had been when he whispered in her ear.

No, No, No, you don't like him. Stop it, Felix heard Jinx think to herself. Was she thinking about Kade?

"How do you feel? Well enough to continue?" Kade asked her, not wanting to pressure her into moving if she wasn't one hundred percent sure she was capable. But, they were on a schedule. And there was kind of a life on the line here.

Jinx slowly rose up, leaning on her good elbow with only a slight wince as her hurt arm swung in the makeshift sling. "Yeah. I'm great. Let's get a move on."

For her sake, Felix hoped she was being honest. They couldn't have her injuring her arm even further. I mean, a cougar nearly mauled her, so he thought she deserved a bit of a break.

But they didn't have a break. It was down to five days now before Margret dies.

They gathered their belongings as quickly as possible, rolling the sleeping bags up and stuffing them in their knapsacks. Felix offered to carry Jinx's for her, but Kade insisted he do it. In fact, Kade's insistence was actually a little weird.

Felix raised his head to look up at the side of the canyon, which contained a small path rising diagonally up the rock wall, almost identical to the one on the side across from it. This wasn't natural. Not one bit. This entire canyon had been a trap and they'd simply been caught in it.

"Do you think there will be other tricks like this one with the canyon?" Desdemona asked Kade as they began their ascent up the narrow pathway.

He nodded incessantly. "Of course. We should just be happy we caught on to her tricks as quickly as we did. Now we can work to avoid them."

Jinx, leading the group the day before, now trailed slowly behind, her sullen attitude once again returning. Felix began to notice her expression, one of mild excitement yesterday, now contained only boredom and indifference. It seemed the old Jinx returned.

As they continued to climb in silence, Felix heard Desdemona's thoughts running within her mind.

Hmmm, Felix thought to himself. *Let's see what she's thinking about.* He pushed himself into her mind and allowed his thoughts to be overcome by hers.

76 bottles of milk on the wall, 76 bottles of milk. Take one down, pass it around. 75 bottles of milk on the wall. Desdemona sang within her head. Felix couldn't help but smile as he could practically hear Desdemona's joyful voice singing with a gleeful smile plastered onto her face.

"75 bottles of milk on the wall, 75 bottles of milk. Take one down, pass it around, 74 bottles of milk on the wall." Felix sang out loud. Desdemona, walking in front of him, turned around and gave him a teasing look.

"Get out of my mind," she yelled, but when Felix continued to sing, she began as well.

"74 bottles of milk on the wall, 74 bottles of milk. Take one down, pass it around. 73 bottles of milk on the wall." They both sang, listening to their voices carry across the canyon as they walked. Eventually, Kade joined in, leaving Jinx as the only one who wasn't singing.

"Will you quit it? It's giving me a headache." Jinx accused, annoyed. On any other day, Felix and Desdemona both would have kept singing, but with her injury, they followed her request.

The rest of the trip up the mountain was relatively uneventful as the group watched the sun rise higher and higher in the sky, eventually reaching its peak directly above their heads. Noon. That was the time they reached the top of the canyon. That was also the time when Felix began to hear the voice.

They're coming. They're at the top of the canyon. Felix heard an unfamiliar voice think. A weight dropped in the pit of his stomach, a clear signal his powers were needed at this time.

Ah, there they are. Felix heard again. *Well, the blonde is actually pretty. Such a shame she'll be dead soon.*

At this, Felix almost lost it. But he knew losing his temper wouldn't help him collect his thoughts or use his power to identify the source of the voice. Scanning the area, Felix looked for any sign of life. Ahead of them, plants grew out of the crevices in the rocks and small trees sprouted from what little soil remained on the mountain side. Other than the cougar, which lay dead at the bottom of the canyon, he saw no animals. He spotted something moved ahead of them, shimmying on the rock of the mountain floor. Felix conspicuously studied the ground in front as he continued to walk, looking for a crawling animal.

She told me to hold off and let them get farther up the mountain, the voice came again. It was deep, raspy, a man's voice no doubt. *I must not attack until they get at least twenty miles from Hazel.*

Was Hazel the one giving this man orders? Felix's gut told him that wasn't so. Felix's gut told him Hazel worked for the one who gave orders. Felix's gut told him none other than Jane Anchor gave this man commands to kill her own children.

As they got closer to the moving object on the ground, Felix started to clench up with nerves. Felix let out a deep breath as he realized the "animal" was simply a cockroach. And a large cockroach at that. The thing had legs the size of Felix's fingers and a body the size of his palm. The hard shell on its back scuttled around as the cockroach ran for cover while the group stomped around him.

If I'm not careful, I'm going to get killed before I get to kill them. Felix heard the raspy voice again. This time, it seemed louder, clearer, closer. He felt chills run from the bottom of his spine to the top as he watched the large cockroach scurrying into a nearby bush. Ugh, what a gross cockroach.

"Hey…" Felix said as he ran around Desdemona to get to Kade. He leaned in to whisper into his ear. "I think we're being followed."

Kade gave him a serious look. "What makes you say that?"

"I'm hearing voices," he said quietly so as not to alarm Desdemona and Jinx. "Or more like one voice. It's deep, like a man's voice and it was very close, but now it's getting farther away."

"What was it saying?" Kade asked, keeping his eyes set ahead as they continued to walk.

Felix gulped. "That he… he was going to kill us. But not yet. He plans on killing us when we get closer to some girl named Hazel."

Kade's face momentarily lost its mask and filled with what seemed to be fear and something else, but Felix couldn't tell what. He tried to push himself in Kade's mind to understand that other emotion, but he felt a sharp push out of Kade's thoughts.

"Stop being nosy. My mind is my mind."

"How did you know I was doing that?" Felix asked.

"In case you've forgotten, I trained you. In fact, I'm still training you. I know how your powers work and I know how to stop them," Kade answered matter-of-factly.

Felix huffed, dropping the subject. They had more important things to discuss. "So… what are we supposed to do about… you know what?"

"There's nothing really we can do right now. Keep your powers on high, follow the voice and try to learn everything you can about this follower of Jane's. We will need all the information we can get when he does decide to attack."

Felix almost started to argue, saying they needed to do something now. They needed to try to figure this out before someone else gets hurt, but Kade cut him off and waved him to the back of the group. When Felix turned around, he noticed Jinx and Desdemona in a heated conversation with their heads pushed together. They both spoke in quick, quiet whispers, but stopped immediately when they noticed Felix leave Kade.

"Want to tell us what you guys were whispering about up there?" Desdemona sassed, crossing her arms.

"Just because we're girls doesn't mean we can't handle this. We're in this just as much as the two of you and we deserve some answers," Jinx added.

Felix had every intention of telling them, but he also had half the nerve to wait and keep it to himself. He loved seeing the two sisters united. Their relationship hadn't been smooth sailing. Felix thought Desdemona's little crush on Kade faded, but meanwhile Jinx had become weirdly protective of their trainer. How refreshing it was to see them teaming up against him.

"It doesn't concern you right now," Felix said snootily, turning from them as if to end of the discussion.

Felix felt a large slap on his shoulders and turned around to notice both girls stopped walking and stood like mirrors of one another with their arms over their chests.

"Well c'mon girls. We haven't got all day." Kade called from the front, turning to face the defiant sisters.

Felix, without Kade noticing, pushed into his mind quickly. *Don't tell them what's going on. They're working together for once.*

Kade pushed him out of his mind, but then turned and nodded at Felix, confirming the deal.

"We're not going anywhere until you tell us what's going on," Desdemona informed them. She looked at Jinx, who nodded in agreement with her.

"But there is a girl up at the top of that mountain who is counting on us to save her life." Felix reminded them, beginning to walk again. He felt a small hand pulling his shoulder back and whipping him around, leaving him face to face with a one-armed, angry eyed Jinx.

"I suggest you tell us what's going on right now or Mona and I have every intention of leaving you two on this mountain to die."

Felix's lips turned up in a smile as he glanced at Kade, who could barely contain his laughter. Finally, breaking down, Felix began to laugh, as did Kade. The two of them doubled over with laughter, which only further upset the two stunned girls. These sisters didn't like to be the butt of the joke.

"Ah girls, calm down," Kade said, holding back his laughter once more. "We planned on telling you. It was just so good to see the two of you getting along for once, we couldn't risk ruining it."

Desdemona and Jinx shared a startled glance, as if not realizing they became a team. Then, a small smirk showed in the corners of Jinx's mouth as her expression of anger melted to what could only be described as affection. Not quite love, but definitely affection. And that was progress.

"Alright," Kade said, going back to his usual, serious self. "We've got someone following us. But let's keep moving and I'll explain more. We're still on a time limit here and Jane's tricks have cost us at least a day so far."

As they continued on their journey, Kade explained their predicament with the voice inside of Felix's head. Because Felix already knew what was going on (despite his bad habit of zoning out), he began to once again take in his surroundings. The quick terrain changes here surprised him. He felt separated from the rest of the world. No doubt, they walked only a few miles today, but it already felt noticeably chillier than down near the canyon. The bushes changed from large, leafy blobs to piney, thin trees.

Felix raised his eyes up to the top of the mountain that stretched ahead of them. It seemed so close, but so far away. Felix shivered at the thought of Margret's powers being forcefully sucked out of her frail body. Margret, with her flawless skin and entrancing eyes, being tortured. But his stomach wasn't just churning. There was a weight in the pit of his stomach - his instincts screaming at him to use his powers.

"Guys, we need to stop," Felix informed them, halting instantly and not budging even when Desdemona bumped into him from behind.

"Felix," Kade started. "We need to move forward-"

Felix cut him off. "No we don't. I'm going to see something. I can feel it and I need to sit down before I fall and bust my head open on a rock. I hate to be an inconvenience, but we don't need a second Anchor kid hurt."

Kade nodded in agreement before reluctantly setting down his backpack, receding on his fight. Kade wouldn't win this one.

Felix, leaning up against a large rock near them, laid his head back and, staring at the sky, allowed himself to be pulled into the mind of their stalker.

Colors burst from the walls, causing a rainbow of reds, blues, and purples to fill the space. A bright painted orange road stretched out in front of him. But unlike the minds of most other people, this road laid out fairly straight and level as far as the eye could see. Felix began to walk, like he always does, but found it a much easier going without all the hills and curves in the minds of other people. Birds flew around tall trees in his mind, singing beautiful, melodious songs. Felix couldn't help but smile as he noticed a happy couple walking in front of him, hand in hand. The girl, in a vibrant pink dress, flashed the man a beautiful smile. The man, with short black hair and deep eyes, looked at her with nothing but adoration. Felix imagined this was what true love looked like.

But as they continued to walk, with Felix close behind, he noticed the woman began to fade away. Her fuchsia dress turned to a dull, pale pink and her smile fell to a tight line. The walls of the man's mind began to darken with each step. The bright purples grew to near blacks and the cheery reds deepened to the color of blood. The once straight road now began to curve, wind and rise, indicating hardships the man faced.

The woman's laughs turned to nothing but silence as she grew bored with the man's adoration and loyalty to her. Felix watched as he grasped at the fading woman, bringing her flowers, bracelets, love, anything to make her stay.

Nothing worked and soon enough, the woman's form disappeared.

The road's orange turned to black and the happy, bright walls faded to bland grey and browns. Heartbroken, the man continued down the road alone. His hands, which once held his love, now wiped tears from his torn face. Felix felt for the broken man, but then remembered he might be inside the mind of his enemy.

That's when Felix saw a face he wished he'd never see again. The painstakingly beautiful form of his mother, Jane Anchor. The treacherous, deceiving look in her eyes held nothing but trouble as she picked up the broken man, helping him along the path. She appeared to take the place of the past woman because the hilly path grew mostly flat, although the turns in the road still told the story of his heartaches and despairs. The colors came back, although dull, and once again lightened up the room.

But it differed from the connection to the woman in his past. The look on the man's face turned from love to *a hypnotic trance. Jane led him into her trap. He would never leave her side, acting as her servant for years to come.*

"There are three kids," Felix heard Jane tell the man. "I want them dead."

He watched as the man nodded eagerly, wishing to do everything in his power to make her happy. "How will I know which three kids you're looking for?'

"You'll know. They're on their way up the mountain now. There's a blonde girl, a dark haired boy, and one who looks like splitting image of me. I promise, you'll know."

"When do you want them dead?" The man asked.

"When they have four days left in their journey, I want you to attack. But, I don't want you to show yourself until they're a reasonable distance from Hazel, say twenty miles or so. And remember, I love you," Jane lied. "But if you don't succeed here, I have no choice but to take your powers."

Felix woke up with a gasp, coming back to his surroundings. Desdemona placed a hand on his shoulder in a feeble attempt to calm him. She realized how hard their visions were. Everyone needed support after them.

"I was in the man's mind. I saw everything he's thinking about right now. And I saw Jane," Felix breathed out, shuddering at the mention of her name.

Doing everything in his power to calm his breathing, Felix relayed the visions in the man's mind to Kade, Desdemona, and Jinx. "He had a perfect life. His mind had no roads with hills or curves, which I believe means blissful happiness. But then his girlfriend or wife, I don't know which, left and he just lost it. His mind became pitch black and mountains seemed to continue for miles. Jane came to him at his lowest point. She pretended to love him, but she really just used him as a servant. Now she's convinced him to murder us."

"Did you figure out what his power is?" Kade asked, intrigued.

"No," Felix answered shakily. "But it must be something very special because Jane hasn't taken it from him yet. She's planning to though. If he doesn't kill us."

Desdemona reached for Felix's hand and helped him to his feet, steadying him as he regained his footing. "It's okay, Felix. We can handle this."

"Mona is right," Kade agreed. "We *can* handle this."

"How? We don't know anything about this guy besides that he's just another guy under Jane's spell," Felix reminded everyone.

"And that's all we need to know," Jinx jumped in. "If we can prove to him that Jane is a manipulative nightmare, maybe he'll leave her cause."

Wow, that's actually a really good idea, Felix heard Desdemona think. He snickered to himself at his sister's surprised tone. She had a reason to be surprised though. Jinx wanted to help out and carry her own weight.

"That's a good idea, Jinx. If he finds out Jane's not in love with him, it will rip him apart and he will want to do anything to get back at her," Kade added.

"I mean, it's not a fool proof plan," Jinx noted. "But it's better than what any of you losers came up with."

And there she was. The usual Jinx. Desdemona rolled her eyes, laughing at Jinx's insult as they began walking again. By this point, they all knew she didn't mean it. Her insults always had a hint of sarcasm, indicating good humor. Or at least most of them did.

They hadn't been walking long before the sun began to set low in the sky, quickly falling below the mountain top that still towered above them. The orange rocks turned fiery red in the burning light of the sun as the temperature dropped rapidly. One by one, they broke out coats from their bags, snuggling into them. In a matter of days, they would go higher on the mountain and their coats could become life-savers.

As the sun became almost invisible, Felix heard a scuttling noise below his feet.

"Eww! Gross!" Desdemona shrieked. "That weird cockroach is back again. And I think it got even bigger."

When Felix turned around, sure enough, the cockroach stirred by their toes, darting across the rock into a nearby bush.

"That thing is gross beyond words," Desdemona added to her previous statement. Inside his mind, Felix agreed with her, but he wouldn't and couldn't say it out loud. He was a man. Men do not fear or become grossed out by some big cockroach on steroids.

"We should probably turn in for the night guys," Kade ordered them, dropping his bag by a nearby indention in the rock formations. Two rocks rising high above the others, creating a 70 degree angle with the ground, formed a kind of shelter. As Kade turned on his flashlights and inspected the area, he noticed how being inside the rocks made it much warmer. For the kids' sake, he hoped they could find a shelter like this every night.

"No better place to stop than here." Desdemona agreed. "I just hope that gross cockroach doesn't decide to come join us in the warmth."

"Be careful, Mona, or you'll wake up to find the cockroach in bed with you." Jinx teased. Desdemona shrieked, shoving Jinx in her good arm and glaring at her.

After eating just a smidgen of their food for the night, all four rolled out their sleeping bags, noting the darkness of the escaped sun. The only light shone in from the full moon and the bright stars hanging from the night sky.

"Someone should probably keep watch. We don't have the canyon's protection tonight. I'll take the first shift," Kade told them. "Get some sleep. I'll be waking one of you up in about two hours to keep watch."

Felix and Desdemona drifted off to sleep without a word, but for Jinx the night was restless. Her mind ran at a thousand miles per hour as she thought about the dead cougar, their stalker, Jane, and whatever else that witch had in store for them. After an hour of trying to sleep, she conceded and wiggled out of her sleeping bag, walking over to sit across from Kade. The moonlight cast their shadows on the dark rock of the ground, illuminating their faces just enough.

"Couldn't sleep," Kade said. It wasn't a question. It was as if he just knew, as if he just understood.

"I'm thinking too much," Jinx admitted to him sheepishly, rubbing up and down her arms with her hands, her nervous habit.

"Then don't think anymore," Kade ordered. "Talk. Tell me everything you're thinking."

Jinx pondered over this for a moment. She'd never opened up to… really anyone before. Hilga had been closest to her before she moved from her world and catapulted into this one. But the idea of opening up to Kade excited her, making butterflies in her stomach flutter around with joy. Jinx lowered her guard.

"Everyone says I'm just like Jane…Felix mentioned Jane herself said it when he recounted his dream. Even you told me it during one of our training sessions. I worry … if I'm so much like her… one day, I'll become her."

Kade didn't reply. Instead, he waited for her to continue, simply listening. "I had this vision once… I never told anyone about. It happened the night after Jane appeared in Mr. Belton's office. I envisioned Jane and me, standing side by side as we fought Desdemona and Felix. We tried to kill them. I woke up so afraid I vowed never to tell anyone, like maybe if I didn't tell anyone, it didn't happen or couldn't happen."

Jinx's mind ran even faster as she felt her voice shake within her throat and noticed a traitor tear slip down her cheek. Her hands shook as they moved against her arms. "And I know in a few days I'm going to have to face her, head on. And my own eyes are going to be looking back at me. And my hair is going to be on her head. And my voice is going to be yelling, but I won't be saying a word. I've always been different and now I'm afraid I know why. I'm just like her. I don't know how to stop it. I don't know how to prevent it."

As Jinx shook and cried, Kade made his way over to sit next to her in the moonlight. He laid a comforting arm on her shoulders, feeling his skin tingle at the touch.

"Jinx," he began. "That's your name. Not Jane. You may have the same eyes and the same hair and the same voice, but that doesn't mean you're the same person. Not in the slightest. You're better than her. Deep down in that heart that Jane doesn't have is a girl who laughs with excitement, smiles with joy, smirks with sarcasm, and glares with as much love as I've ever seen in stare that could kill."

Jinx turned her head to look up at him with those big eyes - no longer looking like Jane's. These eyes filled with warm, real emotion, the kind Jane lacked.

"You really think I'm nothing like her?" Jinx clarified.

"I don't think so, J. I know so."

"But what about the vision?"

"The future can change. You say it yourself all the time. The past has already happened, the present is already happening, but the future is the one thing we can change. I mean, think about it. Did you ever see this in one of those visions?"

And with that, Kade leaned in to press his lips against Jinx's, finally fulfilling his heart's own vision.

17

When the sun began to rise above the mountain once again, the air was crisp with tension. Kade, always up first despite sleeping less than everyone else, hoped Jinx would be the last to wake up.

Of course, she wasn't.

Not long after Kade set up their rations for breakfast, Jinx opened her eyes to the light shining into the cave. To her left, Desdemona slept peacefully. To her right, Felix propped up against the wall with drool falling from his chin.

Idiot. Fell asleep on his watch. We all could have died, Jinx thought to herself. She snarled at her sleeping brother, thankful his mind-reading powers didn't work while he was out like a light.

Everyone seemed to be accounted for and just as Jinx readied herself to get up for the day, she heard rustling at the front of the cave. Human footsteps, obviously. Quiet ones. That's when she remembered.

The figure moving at the front of the cave was Kade. Kade. The Kade who was their trainer. The Kade who was older than her. The Kade she kissed last night. The Kade whom she definitely should NOT have kissed last night.

Now, don't get the wrong idea. Jinx most assuredly wanted to kiss Kade. At least, she did last night. Now she wasn't so sure. Sure, he's cute, brave, and very, very handsome, but Jinx felt extremely confused and awkward about everything which happened the night before.

Finally deciding she couldn't pretend to be asleep forever, Jinx rolled up her sleeping bag. Kade, obviously aware of her shifting around, didn't begin the conversation. And Jinx sure wasn't going to do it. There they sat, in silence, until Felix and Desdemona woke up.

Desdemona first broke the silence by finally rising from her slumber. Dragging her socked feet against the hard rock, she went over to whack Felix on the head with the back of her hand, startling him awake.

"Ouch! What was that for?" he asked, rubbing the spot on his head.

"For sleeping on your watch, that's what. We could have been hurt and it would have been your fault, Felix. None of us slept on our watch, right?" Desdemona asked, gesturing to Jinx and Kade for confirmation. They both mumbled an agreement because it was true. Neither of them slept. But what was also true was that neither of them really wanted to talk about last night.

Desdemona gave them both a weird look at their short, nearly inaudible responses, but went on to give Felix one more small hit before pulling him off the ground.

"Kade," Jinx said, acknowledging him for the first time all morning.

When he answered her, his tone was one not often heard from him. His voice radiated, awkward and embarrassed, as he gave a short "what?"

"That weird cockroach on steroids is outside the door of the cave," Jinx informed him. She pointed at the enlarged bug with a disgusted affect and an outstretched arm.

"Is that thing following us? It's really gross and I want it to go away," Desdemona shrieked, averting her eyes from the repulsive six-legged insect.

Felix cringed as the ugly insect turned to look directly at him, making deliberate eye contact. Felix never tested his powers on animals, but there was no time like the present, right? Felix gathered all of his powers, held the odd eye contact and pushed into the cockroach's mind.

Ah, pretty girl, yes. I am following you, the cockroach answered in his thoughts.

Felix staggered back as he heard the same voice from the cockroach he heard the other day when he used his powers. He needed to tell Kade about this outlandish discovery immediately, but here and now was not the time or the place.

"Kade, we should get going," Felix reminded him, making intentional eye contact with Kade. Through his expression, he begged Kade to get them moving so he could inform him of what just happened.

Kade apparently got the message because he nodded quickly and hurriedly began packing, handing each kid their breakfast.

As he gave Jinx her bread, their hands brushed, skin tingling, and the bread fell to the dusty, dirty ground. Jinx was a bumbling idiot, apologizing profusely for dropping the bread and mentally being sorry for kissing him last night.

"I'm not eating that after it's been on the ground," Jinx told Kade with a sloppy expression, ignoring the tense buzz she felt in her hand earlier.

"Fine. Then you're not eating," Kade told her with a stiff and hard face.

Jinx didn't answer him as she simply started packing up her stuff and slung it over her back, ready to start another day of traveling.

If only Jinx could ignore the pang in her chest she felt for the stone-cold boy just two people in front of her.

"No, I know what I heard. That cockroach is dangerous, Kade," Felix assured him. The two boys had their heads bent together in quiet conversation, having previously promised the girls to fill them in right after.

Kade shook his head. "That's so weird though. How would a cockroach have those thoughts?"

"Well, maybe..." Felix paused, rubbing his hands together nervously. "Maybe the cockroach isn't a cockroach."

"And what else would you suggest the six legged creature with a hard exoskeleton is?" Kade asked sarcastically, raising his eyebrows, a classic Kade move that had all the girls back at The House falling at his feet.

"It has to be human," Felix told him. "It was definitely the same voice I heard earlier, in that man's mind. I'm sure of it."

Desdemona popped her head into the conversation. "Not to be nosy, but I've been listening to this conversation for like the past ten minutes and I would like to make a suggestion."

"Mona." Felix scolded. "We told you we would fill you in after we discussed it."

"Well I don't want to be filled in. I want to hear it first-hand. You guys should know that by now." Desdemona put her hands on her hips and giggled. "And besides, it's not exactly like you guys were talking quietly."

Kade and Felix shared a confused look because they both thought they were being fairly sneaky. They paced towards Desdemona, who shook her head slowly, informing them they talked well above earshot.

Kade rolled his eyes and eventually caved, turning to Desdemona. "Your suggestion?"

For a moment, Desdemona looked confused, as if she forgot her train of thought. But then, her face lit up, remembering it instantly. "Oh yeah. Maybe the cockroach is a cockroach and a human as well."

"What do you mean?" Felix asked Desdemona, confused.

"I mean," Desdemona answered. "That maybe he's both. A shapeshifter. That's his power. He can change forms at will, just like I can see the past whenever I wish."

At this, Kade's face turned up with understanding. "You're right, Desdemona. I don't know why we didn't think of this before. I've never met a shapeshifter Asterian before, but from what I've read, most can change into only one animal or extra form. I don't know this for sure though because every Asterian power is different, but it's my best guess."

"Dang," Desdemona began, laughing. "What did this guy do to the Asterian Gods to get stuck with a cockroach as his shapeshifting form?"

This, Desdemona thought was very funny because she kept laughing, her face turning a bright red within seconds. Felix smiled slyly at his crazy sister, thankful for her lightheartedness despite the fact that a man, very close to them, would surely do everything in his power to kill them.

Felix noticed Jinx hanging back, not joining in on the laughter, but also not sneering at Desdemona with her annoyed expression. Something was up, Felix knew it, but he suppressed the urge to intrude into Jinx's mind. She deserved her privacy and Felix deserved to have all of his arms and legs. He knew if she were to find out he'd been snooping in her mind, she'd be wanting to tear him from limb to limb within the hour.

He turned seriously to Desdemona. "Hey, do you want to go talk to Jinx? She seems even more off than she normally does on her bad days."

Desdemona turned around, looking at Jinx with a sorrowful expression. Jinx glanced up to find both her siblings staring at her.

"Hey," she shouted angrily. "This isn't a zoo, guys. I'm not an animal."

Although her face said anger and tension, the slight quiver in her voice said fear and confusion. Lucky for her though, neither of her siblings noticed it as they turned around, leaving her alone. That didn't stop Kade from recognizing the slight shift in her tone. Feeling a desire to cheer her up, he suppressed it. What would he even say to Jinx after last night? His lips touched hers. And he'd initiated it with one of his pupils. What if she didn't even want to kiss him? What if she became so tense because she hated him now? What if she never ever spoke to him again? What if-

Kade stopped himself mid-worry. This wasn't him. Kade never worried about being around or even talking to a girl. And now, all because of one stubborn, quirky brunette, he found himself tripping over every thought inside his head.

And he needed to snap out of it.

"Alright guys," Kade said, repressing his unwelcome nervous side and resuming his true position: a mentor, a teacher, a leader. "Felix, I need you to keep watch around this guy's mind. I want to know the minute he's planning on attacking. If he loses the element of surprise, there's no way four of us can't beat one of him. We just need to keep moving."

All three nodded, once again falling in line to move up the mountain. It grew noticeably colder as they rose up and each of them now nestled into their coats. Despite their discomfort, the cold reassured Felix. It meant they grew closer to sweet, beautiful Margret.

Just behind him, Jinx had the exact opposite feeling. The nipping winds not only sent a chill through her skin, but also through her heart. The colder it became, the closer they got to their mother. The closer they got to the woman who looked exactly like her. The closer to Jinx's vision of joining her mother.

Despite the chilly mountain air, the sun had been high in the sky all day, warming the cold ground. The weather then seemed to change in a heartbeat. Dark clouds appeared, ominously casting a shadow on the top of the mountain. The clouds suddenly burst open. Heavy, pelting rain fell from water-filled clouds, soaking the four of them through their clothes instantly.

Desdemona let out a loud groan as it poured, lightning shooting across the sky. "These clouds just came out of nowhere."

"Yeah," Felix agreed. "I read mountain weather is weird, causing drastic changes in temperature and precipitation almost immediately."

A loud clap of thunder swept through the rain, making Desdemona jump at the noise.

"Shouldn't we stop?" Jinx asked quietly, nervously, just loud enough for Desdemona to hear.

She turned around and gave Jinx a sympathetic look, agreeing with her.

"Hey, shouldn't we stop?" Desdemona echoed Jinx, louder this time. "We've come this far and I'd really rather not die by lightning. If I'm going to die, it shouldn't be this stupid - it needs to be epic."

"We can't stop." Kade yelled back over the storm. "We've still got a long way to go and only four days left to save Margret. We can't forget why we're here. We're here to save one of our own from a certain, painful death. We have to keep going."

Four days... Felix heard the deep voice think again. He'd been listening for a while now, but this appeared to be the only thing noteworthy so far. *I was told to attack when there were four days left. Today is the day. And this storm could not have come at a better time.*

Felix listened for a few more minutes, but the man now appeared to be daydreaming about Jane. Felix turned his thoughts down, like the volume on a television and ran to tell Kade what he just heard. When they told Jinx and Desdemona today was the day, Kade noticed Jinx's face turn from neutral to concern. Her arm, still in a sling, no longer hurt, but Kade understood the difficulty of fighting with just one arm. Lucky for her, her good arm, her fighting arm, remained intact.

"Can you fight?" Kade asked her quietly, almost stuttering over the question. He looked down at his feet, rolling a rock underneath his shoe self-consciously.

"What?" Jinx asked, surprised he acknowledged her again. "Oh me? Yeah, yeah, yeah, I'm good. I can fight. I mean, it doesn't even hurt at all. I'm fine. Tip top shape. One hundred percent. I'm ready.

Both Felix and Desdemona gave Jinx a weird look, confused at her sudden rambling. Their eyes grew wide as she walked ahead of their entire group, continuing on up the mountain.

"Felix," Desdemona whispered. "I think someone broke Jinx."

They began walking once again, but this time their order switched. Jinx led, with Kade a good distance behind her. Then came Felix, while Desdemona brought up the rear. No one really said much, but silence didn't exist as the rain continued to pound the ground and thunder rocked the mountain. The disorienting clash of thunder overtook all sound, including the usual noise of footsteps around them.

It was so loud that Felix didn't notice when the footfalls of Desdemona ceased to follow him.

It was so loud that Felix didn't hear her scream, muffled by her own coat.

It was so loud that Felix didn't notice Desdemona disappeared.

18

The storm began to calm down finally and the sun appeared, reaching high in the sky.

"It's around noon. That's good. We've covered a lot of ground already despite the storm," Kade informed them all, pointing up to the top of the mountain, which was a bit closer than before. This made Felix's chest swell with hope, allowing him to entertain the idea they really would save Margret.

"Look, Desdemona. There's a lot of snow on the top of that mountain," Felix called back to her, pointing.

But there was no answer.

Continuing to walk forward, he repeated what he said before.

Still no answer.

"Desdemona?" Felix asked, turning around to see nothing but an empty trail. His heart stopped for a moment and fear gripped his breath. It seemed like an eternity until he got his breath back and could speak.

And when he could speak, he began yelling.

Felix screamed Desdemona's name, backtracking his steps and even going off the path to search for his sister.

But there was no movement of blonde hair, no flash of a pretty smile, no ring of jubilant laughter.

"Where is she?" Felix asked Kade and Jinx desperately, who silently helped him search.

"We don't know, Felix," Kade answered in a calm, collected voice. "We will find her. We're not going anywhere until we find your sister."

"Jinx, what do you see in the future? There's got to be something," Felix exclaimed. "Even if it just shows us together again. I just need to know she will be okay."

Jinx closed her eyes for what seemed like hours, but in reality was only about five minutes.

Low fog hung just over the horizon. Night had fallen. The crisp air felt colder than before, making Jinx shiver. A tall, triangular rock loomed over Jinx's head as she leaned back on the foot of the formation, breathing heavily.

Jinx watched as a girl struggled against what felt like itchy, scratchy ropes binding her arms, but when she looked closer, she saw no ropes. As she tried to spot the invisible bonds, she saw hair lying flat on a woman's chest. The sun streaked highlights in the beach hair were ones Jinx had only seen on one other person.

Desdemona. Jinx was looking at Desdemona.

Mona's bottom lip quivered with fear and anxiety as she reached around for her bow, which of course had been taken from her hours ago. Out of nowhere, a shadow lurked to her left. Holding back tears, Desdemona tried to make her voice strong and unwavering.

"Who are you?" she asked forcefully.

A deep, hearty laugh came from the shadow, making her wince. "You might not know who I am, but you do know who I am with."

Jinx knew exactly who he meant.

Jane.

Jinx caught a glimpse of a feminine hand brush the man's shoulder in the darkness, followed by a cackle, before something startled her out of the vision.

When Jinx opened her eyes to see Kade and Felix, her face clouded with pain.

"What? What did you see?" Felix begged.

Jinx paused for a moment. "We need to hurry. I saw a man holding Desdemona hostage and I saw…"

Felix waited for her to continue, but she didn't. He only saw glints of tears in her stormy eyes. At that point, he didn't need to know who she saw. It was written, clear as day, on her face.

"Does that mean she's already at the top of the mountain?" Felix questioned, hoping Jinx saw enough to tell them where to find Desdemona.

"No," Jinx answered surely, "She wasn't. I couldn't really tell where she was, but she wasn't there. I think… Jane… came down."

"But why would Jane come down here?" Kade asked.

"Isn't it obvious?" Jinx questioned, turning to him harshly. "Jane wants to kill Desdemona herself."

Jinx whipped around, flipping her hair at Kade and addressed her brother. "That guy you've been hearing. The cockroach. That's who kidnapped her."

"Then Felix can use his powers to read his thoughts and find where they're hiding Desdemona," Kade mentioned. Felix nodded approvingly, while Jinx crossed her arms over her chest, silently giving them the go ahead.

Felix worked to block out the noises of the mountains and focused on the small hum in the back of his mind.

They'll never find her here, the man thought. Felix silently urged him to continue, which he did. But this time, it was not just a simple thought. The man began thinking at Felix.

Ah, Jane did mention her mind reading son. She told me to look out for you. Well, here's a little riddle for you and your sister to think about, Felix.

She does not have much time, for Jane does not believe the killing of a daughter is such a crime.

A place where darkness prevails and light continuously fails.

A setting often overlooked with the Annelida, overtook.

You will not find its shafts on a map for many believe it's one big trap.

If you wish to find your sister, with ropes she is laced I suggest you quit wasting time in my mind and move with haste.

Felix snapped out of his thoughts and stopped dead in his tracks, causing Kade and Jinx to pause as well.

"What did you hear?" Kade asked quickly.

Shakily, Felix recounted the riddle, really worried that Desdemona would be lost forever. Between Jinx's scary vision and Felix's unhinging mind reading, Jinx's area of expertise did not look very bright for Desdemona.

"Annelida? What are Annelida?" Jinx questioned, confused. She'd never liked riddles. She zoned out back in school whenever a teacher would start class with a riddle. Consequently, she had never solved one and didn't really expect to solve one now.

Felix thought for a moment as Kade pondered Jinx's question.

"Annelida…" Felix began. "I think we've heard that word in school somewhere. Don't you think, Jinx?"

"What class are we talking? Because I only listened in the few that I enjoyed," Jinx reminded him. Although Felix didn't know Jinx during school, he could definitely see her as one of the girls that didn't care that much unless it interested her personally.

"Hey, instead of focusing on what we don't know, let's focus on what we can figure out," Kade suggested. "The riddle said it was constantly dark. What place can you guys think of where the light never touches?"

Both Jinx and Felix thought for a moment, in silence. The only sound was the light breeze remaining from the horrible storm that passed through not too long ago.

"What about a cave?" Felix brainstormed. "If they're so far back in the cave, it would be completely dark, right?"

Kade retorted immediately. "No, I don't think that's it. A cave is too obvious for a riddle so confusing. And besides, caves are marked on most maps of mountainous areas."

Felix nodded, agreeing with him and throwing the idea away.

"I don't have anything," Jinx informed everyone. "What about you guys?"

Both boys shook their heads, agreeing with her.

"Well we can't just sit here and do nothing. We need to keep moving, or at least keep… doing something," Felix reminded everyone. He knew it was not a very good idea to continue moving when they didn't know where they were going, but how could anyone expect him to just sit here and do nothing while his sister is an inch away from death?

Jinx's previously blank face grew light with ideas. Suddenly, she smiled and turned to Felix. "You can hear Desdemona, right? You can still hear her thoughts? I know you've always had the best connection with her, so I imagine you would."

Felix closed his eyes, not having to search very far for the sweet, innocent voice of Desdemona's thoughts. "Of course I can hear her," Felix answered. "She's my sister."

"Then why can't we just ask Desdemona where she is?" Jinx pointed out. "She's there. She should know where she is. Or, at least be able to describe her surroundings in more vivid detail than I got from my vision."

Kade nodded coldly at Felix, signaling the go ahead to use his powers once again. Felix slowly pushed the outside world away and focused on the favorite voice inside his head.

Desdemona, Felix began. *Mona, can you hear me?*

The voice inside of his head perked up with excitement and gave a shrill shriek only Desdemona could ever make. *Oh Felix. I'm so glad you can hear me. Listen, you need to come find me soon. They want to kill me.*

Trust me, Mona, we know. We're trying to get there as quickly as possible. The only problem is that we don't know where you are. Do you know where you are? Felix asked her calmly, as if asking a child to share their favorite toy.

No... Desdemona answered sadly. *They must have given me something. I don't remember anything from the moment he took me to the moment I woke up here.*

Well, where is here? Describe where you are. Felix ordered, still treading lightly.

Um... It's dark, really, really dark. And the ceilings are low, so low I can touch them if I'm standing up. And they appear to be made of some sort of dirt or soil. They're definitely squishy. As if they're going to cave in at any moment, Desdemona answered him.

Alright Mona, thank you so much. I'm going to tell Kade and Jinx what you told me, but I'll always be right here. Just yell if you need me, okay?

Okay... Desdemona answered with a depressing tone. *Be safe, Felix. I love you.*

Felix smiled. They really were siblings now. *I love you too, Desdemona.*

"Dirt or soil. That's what she told me the ceiling was made of. What area has a building of dirt and soil?" Felix asked rhetorically, shaking his head in distress. Jinx, actually appearing to care about the turmoil of her sister right now, thought long and hard about a room surrounded with Earth.

Then it hit her.

"Annelida!" Jinx screamed excitedly.

Kade jumped from his own train of thought and bounced onto Jinx's as he waited for her to continue with her realization.

"Felix, think back to your biology classes. This is about domains, kingdoms, phylums, and classes. Remember that?"

Felix thought back in time, to a place where everything in his life was normal. No powers, no sadistic mother, no other species. But also no amazing sisters. It seemed a world away. He'd been a good student in school, but for the life of him, he couldn't connect domains with Annelida.

"You obviously don't," Jinx continued, moving on. "Anyway, Annelida was a phylum of animals. Worms to be exact."

"And worms live in the Earth," Kade finished for her. "Think about it. A place light never touches. A place not on a map. A place where worms live."

A lightbulb went off in Felix's head. "Desdemona is underground."

19

"We need to find her before night," Kade mentioned as they trudged forward. "In my experience, bad things are more apt to happen when the sun goes down."

Dang, he's got that right, Jinx thought to herself, constantly replaying in her head last night's "lapse in judgment," as she is now calling it.

Felix kicked up rocks underneath his sneakers as he trotted along behind Kade. He wasn't exactly sure where they were going, but Kade seemed to know. Felix just continued on, lost in a sea of his own thoughts. He wished to think of something else besides his trapped sister, but worry continuously clouded his mind, filling every crevice of his brain. He knew he could not stop it. Rather than trying to push it out of his mind, Felix simply decided to push someone else into his.

Mona, are you okay? Felix asked Desdemona, hoping, praying she would answer.

Much to his delight, there was a very, very faint *Yes* in Desdemona's sweet tone.

Are you weak? Why are you so quiet? You sound like you're a million miles away.

I'm not sure, Felix. Desdemona answered him. *I'm thinking just like I normally do.*

This is weird.... Felix admitted to her. *Okay, you know how you can scream in your thoughts? I want you to scream as loud as you can.*

Desdemona gave a shrill shriek in her thoughts. Felix knew the screech should have given him an hour long headache, but he could barely hear it. It appeared as a faint whisper, just a little louder than her voice.

Felix felt more nerves creep up into the pit of his stomach. Something wasn't right. But he definitely could not share this with Desdemona. She, of all people, didn't need something else to worry about right now.

Hey Mona, I think Kade wants to talk to me. I need to go. Be safe please. We're on our way to get you.

Felix heard a faint shudder of a heavy hearted goodbye before he pulled himself out of Desdemona's mind.

He noticed Kade still walking confidently in the direction of his choosing. Felix quickened his pace, catching up with Kade quickly.

"Hey… umm… Kade…" Felix began.

After a moment of silence, Kade ordered, "Spit it out, Felix. If it's an Asterian problem, I can help. If it's a personal problem, that's not my job."

"Oh, no, it is an Asterian problem. I was wondering… I was wondering if Asterian's could lose their powers," Felix asked, dearly afraid of the answer.

Kade turned to Felix with a confused expression as he noticed Felix's sweaty hands and furrowed eyebrows. "Unless Jane takes their powers from them, I don't think so. Why do you ask?"

Felix rambled on and began to explain his encounter with a faded Desdemona. How he could hear her just fine before, but how her voice got fainter the farther they walked.

"Felix," Kade patted a hand on Felix's shoulder. "You're not losing your powers. In fact, it's the opposite. Your powers have developed."

Felix's face fell in shock as well as relief, mixed with confusion. "Wait," he paused. "I thought these were my powers. I can see the present. Done. Finished. Complete."

"Oh no, not at all. Far from it, Felix. This is the first of many Embellishments, as we call them, you will experience. As you continue to master your gifts and learn to better manipulate them, they will, in their own way, reward you by expanding. The expansions will always connect back to your core gift. For example, I only used to manipulate sight. Then, as I got my Embellishments, one by one, I gained the power to alter all five senses."

"So you're basically saying this is like puberty for Asterians?" Felix said, flashing back to his dreadful middle school years.

Kade laughed lightly. "Well, I guess that's one way to put it. But I promise, it's better than that."

"Why didn't we learn about these at The House?" Felix questioned.

"Mr. Belton believes it is better to wait to mention Embellishments until a family member actually receives one. He doesn't want new Asterians to feel pressure to get their new powers right away."

"So, what's my Embellishment then?" Felix asked.

Kade stopped in his tracks, turned around and began walking in the other direction. When Felix spun to catch up with him with Jinx on his heels, Kade explained. "You know why I stopped going that way? Because your powers have developed a sense of direction. Desdemona's voice has become quiet because we're farther from her. If we walk this way, it should get louder and tell us we're getting warmer. Listen."

Felix focused in on Desdemona's thoughts without letting her know of his presence. She didn't need to know about their confusion.

But as he listened, her voice still seemed very faint to him, like a continuous buzz of whispers in his head.

And so they kept walking. And walking. And walking. And walking.

Until finally, her sweet thoughts went from a dull murmur to a stage whisper. Felix's feet crunched the ground under him as he continued listening.

"Kade, it's getting louder. I can make out every word she's thinking now," Felix informed Kade excitedly, as if he were a five year old receiving a new toy.

Jinx had been totally silent since they turned around. Or at least everyone but Felix assumed she'd been totally silent. Thoughts appeared to rage inside her head. Felix pushed inside.

Embellishments. I just don't understand why he got his first. If he got his now, mine must be coming any minute, Jinx seethed.

Felix, with half a mind to call her out on it, stopped the words on the tip of his tongue. Was he annoyed by her jealousy while her sister was on the brink of death? Sure. But now wasn't the time to start a fight with Jinx. And besides, that girl can hold a major grudge and she really wasn't the kind of person you wanted as an enemy.

"Felix." Kade snapped Felix out of his own thoughts and back into the moment. "How close are we?"

Felix pushed into Desdemona's mind once again, where her voice was just slightly below normal speaking level.

"I would say we're still a bit away, Kade. It just sounds like she's talking a bit low to me," Felix reported to him. Feeling his mouth grow parched, he reached around to grab water from his bag. When he flipped around, he noticed orange red sunlight shining on the black of his knapsack.

Sunset. They needed to reach Desdemona within a couple of hours.

"We better start moving quicker if we want to save Desdemona before dark, Kade," Felix told him in a determined voice. They needed to start running.

Kade took one glance at the quickly fading sun and nodded before breaking into a slight jog.

"Whoa whoa whoa! I never agreed to any jogging." Jinx called, only slightly quickening her step.

Felix stopped, turned around and let Jinx run smack into his stomach. She fell back, disoriented. "Jinx. Your sister is going to feel a lot more pain being tortured than you will from a little running. Let's go."

Feeling guilty about his indignant tone with her, Felix reached his hand down to help Jinx up. As she brushed herself off, he gave her a quick hug and began to jog. Jinx followed.

At this rate, it wasn't long before Desdemona's voice grew to a shout. And then a yell. And then a scream. To the point where Felix's head began to throb with pain from the volume of her thoughts.

"I'm not so sure I like this Embellishment, Kade." Felix exclaimed in pain.

"Oh, that's natural," Kade reminded him. "Like your other powers, you'll need to learn to control it and control only comes with practice."

After taking a few more steps, Felix didn't know if he could handle the shrieking going on in his mind. "Kade," he began. "I think we're close to…"

Felix stopped mid-sentence as he noticed an enemy they'd seen many times before. With six legs and an abnormally large thorax, the cockroach slithered on the ground in front of them. But just as Felix reached his foot to stomp on it, the brown animal disappeared.

Felix felt a tap on his shoulder and his blood ran cold as ice.

He whipped around only to find himself face to face with the man whose head Felix visited before. With short, black hair and metallic eyes, Felix gazed upon the sad faced man who lost the love of his life. Only here, the man's eyes filled with malicious agony.

Before Felix could react, he felt a silver blade pressed to the base of his throat. The cold metal of the knife made Felix want to quiver with fear, but if he moved an inch, the knife would draw blood.

"Think you're close to Desdemona, do you? I would tell you you're right, but it's not like you'll make it to save her," the man said in a raspy, deep voice.

Both Kade and Jinx began reaching for their weapons, but the man stopped them in their tracks. "Make one more move and your brother's sweet little Embellishment will no longer be of use to him. An Embellishment means nothing to a dead Asterian."

Jinx and Kade shared a look, one lacking all previous awkwardness. Last night now seemed a world away. Much easier than having a knife pressed to her brother's throat and ropes tied to her sister's arms. Jinx couldn't care less about last night.

Jinx silently pleaded with Kade. Her eyes screamed, "What are we going to do?"

Kade nodded slightly, signaling to her he had a plan, just before Felix's small yelp interrupted their eye contact. The man had pressed the knife even harder into Felix's neck. Red blood seeped from the small incision at the base of his throat.

"Hurry," the man said in a sleazy tone. "I'm sure your brother doesn't have a lot of blood to spare."

Kade reacted quickly, deciding to do the thing he knows best - just black him out using his powers. But even when Kade used everything in his ability to take away the man's senses, he didn't budge.

"Ha! He thinks his powers will work on me." The man cackled wildly. "Nice try, Kade, but Jane warned me about you. And to protect me, she shielded me to block out all your tricky moves."

Kade felt himself deflate from the inside out, feeling useless without his powers or his axe. Jinx turned to him, scared, with begging eyes. But Kade didn't know what to do. He racked his brain for solutions. Nothing came.

Instantly, the man holding Felix screamed in pain and dropped his knife to the rocky ground with a clatter. Felix scrambled to get as far away from the enemy as possible, clumsily half crawling, half running towards Jinx and Kade. With the man down, staggering in agony, Jinx threw a single knife, piercing him in the chest. Jinx moved in quickly to examine her kill. Much to her dismay, the wound knocked the man out cold, but his heart still beat.

"What..." Felix stuttered. "What... j-j-just... hap-p-pened?'

Both Jinx and Kade shook their heads. Neither of them understood what initially hurt and stunned the man. As they approached him, a gleam of silver caught the setting sun. The gleam grew brighter and brighter. Inspecting him closer, Jinx noticed the blade of another knife lodged into the man's right leg.

Jinx looked around quickly, trying to identify the person who threw the first knife. The person who really saved Felix's life. The area became motionless and silent.

It's a shame, really. If Jinx had looked up just five seconds earlier, she would have seen the flash of black hair twirl out of sight. Black hair nearly identical to her own.

20

"We can't just leave him here to go tell Jane about all he heard," Kade told them.

"You're saying we need to kill him?" Felix asked, appalled at the thought of taking another man's life.

Jinx turned to him with an angry look on her face. "This man just tried to kill you and he would have succeeded if someone hadn't thrown that knife. You want to let him live?"

"He doesn't deserve to die. You didn't see what I saw. This man has a life. He has feelings. He loved a beautiful woman. He's just lost and heartbroken. He deserves a chance to turn his life around."

Kade turned to Jinx with an equally accusing sneer. "Jinx, violence is our last option here."

"Well what else are we going to do?" Jinx asked, throwing her arms up in the air.

"This," Kade answered. With a quick snap of his fingers, the man gave one last shudder and went still. His chest continued to rise and fall with each beat of his still working heart.

"What did you just do?" Felix asked, craning his neck to get a closer look at the man.

"The knives pierced Jane's force field. I simply blacked out all of his senses, so even when he does wake up, his world will be completely empty. No sights, no sounds, no nothing. Not until I release him, that is."

"When are you planning on releasing him?" Jinx asked.

"As soon as we get far away from here," Kade responded.

Felix glanced at Kade while Jinx practically seethed with anger. She couldn't believe they were going to let this man, who was in cahoots with the enemy, stay alive.

Kade quickly ordered Felix to go ahead and begin looking for the underground entrance. As Felix turned to search, Kade turned to a very displeased Jinx.

"What the heck was that?" Kade asked.

"What do you mean? You mean me trying to protect my siblings from this man in the future? The future is my specialty, you know," Jinx reminded him, crossing her arms defensively over her chest.

"I mean," Kade replied. He tried everything in his power to keep his voice calm. "Your eagerness to kill a man, to take a life. Violence is never a first choice for Asterians. We work for the good. We work to save the lives of other people, not to end them. We are not bloodthirsty."

Kade spun around on his heel to help Felix look for the entrance. Jinx stood, rooted to her spot, totally stunned. Bloodthirsty? Wasn't she only trying to protect her brother and sister? Yes, killing that man seemed to be her only sure option.

Just then, something dawned on her. Was that how Jane rationalized her evil acts? Jinx felt a clawing at her heart. Was she slowly becoming her mother? With each and every day, would Jinx grow more and more bloodthirsty and less and less connected to the lives of others?

It needed to stop this instant. Not a single thing in the world should be allowed to take Jinx to her mother's side. Making a silent vow to act more like a real Asterian, Jinx threw herself into finding the entrance. If there was one thing she could do to make up for almost taking the life of another, it was to save her sister.

Felix and Kade searched and searched. They saw no holes or large rocks in sight. Nothing appeared to be concealing an underground tunnel.

Sighing heavily, Felix glanced towards the almost gone sun. They didn't have much time. They needed to find Desdemona now before it was too late. In his worry, Felix noticed a small leaf on the rocky floor covered in red and different shades of orange, making Felix smile at the myriad of colors covering the usually green leaf.

He needed a little something beautiful in his life right now. Reaching down, Felix took a single step to grab the leaf, but before he could even grab it, his feet appeared to fall out from under him and the ground caved in. Felix began to flail his arms, yelling for help as he tumbled down the tunnel. Abruptly and much sooner than he expected, his butt landed smack on the ground.

"Ow!" Felix exclaimed, not expecting such a brief fall to hurt so much. He dragged himself off the ground and realized why it caused such pain. Felix hadn't just landed on the ground or a normal rock. He fell on two metal tracks, gleaming with shiny silver. The metal tracks continued on and on down a long and dark hallway. A small cart just big enough for a few people straddled the tracks, ready to travel down them. Felix steadied himself and surveyed the area, noticing a pickaxe to the right of the car.

"A mine shaft!" Felix yelled with excitement. "You won't find its shafts on a map. Desdemona is in this mine shaft."

Kade and Jinx both popped their heads over the hole Felix made in the crumbling earth. Realizing Felix survived the short fall, they jumped in, joining Felix in the shaft. Fortunately, neither of them landed bottoms up on the hard metal.

"Felix, can you tell us the right direction?" Kade asked.

Felix dragged himself into Desdemona's mind, where she was practically screaming at him. They were close. Very close. Suddenly, Felix realized the full blessings and burdens of his powers. By being inside Desdemona's mind, he knew he could find her. The price he paid - feeling and living her terror.

We're coming, Mona. We've got you, Felix assured her. The sobs quieted and Desdemona sniffled in agreement.

"That way," Felix said, pointing to the shaft that continued to the right. Kade led the way, first climbing into the mine cart, with Felix and Jinx following suit. The tension between Kade and Jinx could be cut with a knife as they found themselves sitting cramped into the small front part of the cart. The three sat, stunned and motionless for a moment, as if to take in the terrifying events which just transpired.

Felix, realizing the car wasn't going anywhere by itself, hopped out to push a rock out from under the car holding it in place. After he hopped back in the car, the trio began a bumpy ride down the track with no earthly idea where they would end up.

Avoiding eye contact at all costs, neither Jinx nor Kade said a word. Felix, noticing the strange silence, tried to remain calm as the cart picked up speed traveling down the track. Soon, the light in the previous opening faded. Darkness consumed all light.

Felix felt his head pounding as Desdemona's pleas grew to near screams inside his head. So close. Despite the pain, Felix's spirit soared as he thought about being reunited with Desdemona. The last several hours felt like several days.

All three anxiously awaited their arrival to who knew where. A small flicker of light appeared in the distance. As they continued down the track, the flicker grew larger and larger. Finally, its source could be identified - a torch, illuminating a small area surrounded by darkness. At the bottom of the track, the primitive, flickering light revealed Desdemona's beautiful, yet terrified face.

Felix practically jumped out of the moving cart and sprinted at full speed to his sister. She sat on the ground, ropes binding her every limb to the pole holding the torch, with tears rolling down her mud-stained face. Scratches and sores covered much of her once flawless skin, all of which looked minor enough to quickly heal. Except one. A nasty gash trailed from the top of Desdemona's forehead at a diagonal slant through her sad, blue eyes and all the way down to the side of her nose. Blood caked itself around the cut, clotting up. Every time a tear flushed out of her eye, the clear droplet turned red after passing the gash.

But Felix never cared what Desdemona looked like. She was his sister. And she was alive. At this point, nothing else in the entire world mattered.

"Jinx, hand me one of your knives." Felix yelled, not taking his eyes off Desdemona for a moment. Jinx shoved a knife into his hand and Felix slashed quickly, but carefully, at the ropes that bound Desdemona. The ropes fell away, revealing red slashes dug deeply into her skin.

Each rescuer expected a tearful reunion. It didn't happen that way. Instead of jumping for joy, Desdemona remained rooted to her stoop on the metal tracks, motionless.

Felix bent down, sitting next to her and leaned in to kiss her softly on her tear-streaked, dirt-stained, scratch-covered cheek. As he pulled away, he noticed her eyes widen - wider than ever. In fact, if he didn't know she just went through, he would have believed she needed a straitjacket.

Only one word described the look in her once energetic eyes: fear.

"Desdemona?" Felix asked tentatively. "You're safe now. You don't have to worry anymore. We've got you."

When she didn't reply or even so much as look at him, he tried again. "Desdemona, it's going to be okay."

Once again, no words came from her mouth. But this time, Desdemona reached her hand up to her chest, hesitantly gesturing to something none of them noticed.

Her entire body, her entire figure, her entire features mangled with shadows of fear, doubt, and pain. Someone had purposely pinned an untouched piece of tan cloth neatly to her shirt. The unstained, unblemished cloth stood in stark contrast to the blood stains and rope burns covering Desdemona.

Felix reached slowly for the cloth, careful not to scare Desdemona and removed it from her shirt. He held it up to the torch light and cringed when he noticed a small inscription, written in a dark reddish liquid. The author did not use ink.

She got her beauty from me, so I thought I would be the one to take it back. Have fun bearing the weather to come, kids.

It was crudely signed, "Mom." Felix stifled back the urge to blurt out. Mom. She can't be serious. How dare this woman describe herself as a mom.

He passed the note to Kade, letting Kade read it for himself. Neither of them read it aloud, for fear of doing more harm to Desdemona. Turning his attention back to his traumatized sister, Felix sat next to her once again. As he laid his hand on her torn up pants leg, she flinched reflexively and pulled away with a look of pure terror. Felix uttered a quick, silent prayer for her fear of him to subside.

Felix had a thousand questions, but they would have to wait. For now, he wanted to deal with the flinching. Just then, Desdemona inched her leg back towards his.

Desdemona murmured something under her breath, something completely unrecognizable. Felix nodded his head eagerly, hoping she would repeat herself.

When she finally did, her voice shook with instability. Nothing like the Desdemona from just eight short hours ago… "We need to get out of here," Desdemona repeated.

"What?" Felix asked.

Desdemona repeated herself only slightly louder this time. Still, Felix struggled to make out her words.

When he asked her again, her shaky voice turned to an absolutely horrifying shriek. "WE NEED TO GET OUT OF HERE! WE NEED TO GET OUT OF HERE! WE NEED TO GET OUT OF HERE! WE NEED TO GET OUT OF HERE!"

Both Kade and Jinx jumped at her screams, but even after receiving her message, the yelling didn't stop. It became louder. Realizing Desdemona wouldn't or couldn't move on her own, Felix scooped her up in his arms and moved quickly towards the cart. Kade and Jinx followed, each holding their hands over their ears to block the unstoppable screams.

As Kade pumped the cart and it began the roll back to its original destination, Felix's mind raced and his head reeled. His life had taken a turn worse than any horror movie. He could not leave or wake up. And if this was how he felt, something told him Desdemona's worst nightmare had come true.

They found safe shelter for the night in a nearby cave. Kade cleaned the wound on Desdemona's face and announced to Jinx and Felix it would probably heal without too much scarring.

"We need to go back to The House," Jinx told everyone.

"What?" Felix questioned.

Jinx sneered at him. "Oh c'mon. You can't tell me you still think this deathtrap of a mountain is worth it."

Thinking carefully, Felix responded "If I get to save a life, the life of a friend, then yes."

Anger simmered in Jinx's stomach. "You're willing to risk the life of four, perfectly healthy," she glanced first at Desdemona, curled up on the floor shaking and then her arm, which was still wrapped in a sling. "Or soon to be perfectly healthy Asterians for the life of one?"

Felix opened his mouth to retort, but Jinx held up her finger to silence him. "And I'm not done. Isn't it convenient that you, the only sibling who hasn't been hurt up here, are the one who wants to stay? You don't know what it's like to almost have your arm torn off by a cougar or to have your face slashed by your very own mother. Well, let me tell you. It hurts."

"I vote to get off of this mountain as fast as we can. And if Desdemona could vote, I'm sure she would agree with me."

"Wait, Jinx. Think about it. Jane has hurt the both of you. Jane has given you scars, some external and some internal. And she has done the same to so many people before us. She will continue to rein terror on them if we don't end it." Felix sighed. "This isn't just about me, you, Desdemona, or Margret. It's about the whole Asterian race."

Kade stepped forward, finally intervening in their dispute. "Felix is right. We need to end this. Jane is looking forward to a fiery battle with the three of you. Trust me, she plans on getting what she wants. If we tried to leave now, she would eventually find us. This is going to happen one way or another. With Felix's way, we get the chance to do this together, with your combined powers, not to mention the chance to save Margret."

Jinx's jaw fell open in horror as she glared at Kade. "You always side against me, don't you?" She exclaimed, throwing her good arm into the air.

"Jinx," Kade responded calmly "This isn't about you and me right now." He reached across to put a hand on her arm, but she slapped him away.

"So we're staying. That's it. It's been decided," Jinx finalized. Jinx began to sit down next to Desdemona, but then jumped up. "On one condition. We make a game plan."

"A game plan?" Felix asked.

"A game plan. We've been wandering up and around this mountain for days, walking aimlessly into every one of Jane's traps. That has to stop. Now."

As if on cue, the moment Jinx yelled "Now." buckets of rain fell with a clap of thunder. Cold air blew through the wind and the rain, turning it to snow. Luckily for them, the cave blocked out most of the suddenly cold air and kept them fairly warm.

"What just happened?" Felix gasped at the falling snow. It doesn't snow in the midst of a clear, 50 degree night.

"I don't know," Kade answered through gritted teeth. "But I can tell you it's not natural."

All three of them shared a worried look as Jinx brought up the game plan idea one more time. Everyone vowed to brainstorm their own game plan overnight and they would share in the morning.

Sensing an end in the conversation, Felix unwrapped his and Desdemona's sleeping bags and blankets. Tenderly, he pried her hands away from her knees and stopped the shaking long enough to get her changed into clean clothes and the warm bag. Then, he took both of the blankets, his and hers, and placed them over her. Next to Desdemona, Felix curled up in his own sleeping bag.

After a few hours of staring at the ceiling, hoping to fall asleep, Felix heard Desdemona whispering softly to herself.

"Mona?" He whispered back.

She didn't turn to look at him, but spoke just loud enough for him to hear. "I'm scared, Felix."

"We're all scared, Mona," he replied.

"But you're not scared like I am, Felix. I'm terrified. I don't want to fight her." Desdemona admitted to him.

"Do you want to talk about what happened down there?" Felix asked, treading lightly.

"Not right now," Desdemona answered. "Maybe someday, but not right now."

Silence filled the air as Felix's mind raced through all of the horrible possibilities Desdemona could have gone though. Most of them, he hoped, were worse in his imagination. But how she got cut could have been far worse than anything he could dream up.

"Felix…" Desdemona spoke again. "How bad is the cut on my eye?"

Felix thought for a moment, not wanting to lie to her and make it seem better than it was, but also not wanting to make her feel like a pariah. Soon, he figured out a way to avoid both. "It won't matter. If you have a small scar, it will show you've been through something. Something you've grown from."

"You don't think the cut makes me look deformed?" She asked in a voice so small Felix could barely hear it.

"Not one bit," Felix answered confidently. "You're my sister."

Desdemona gave a weak, heartless laugh, but a laugh nonetheless. "So you're saying even if I gained 300 pounds and dyed my hair purple, you would still love me?"

Felix smiled in the darkness. "Of course. I would love you even if you had ten double chins." Felix paused and took a deep breath. "These past few months have been hectic and shocking, but one good thing has come from all the craziness; I've been given the two best sisters a guy could ask for."

21

The group awoke at the crack of dawn to a foot of snow on the mountain floor covering the ground with a blanket of white. The sun beamed down brightly to create a false sense of warmth, but in reality, it did nothing to melt the snow. Snow tickled the edges of the cave and Jinx felt extremely thankful for the shelter they found.

If Jinx hadn't been traveling today, the snow would have been gorgeous. But, since she planned to hike through it, the snow just meant her toes would freeze all day.

Jinx thought long and hard about her plan last night, staying up way past Felix and Desdemona. Through the darkness, she felt her thoughts drift so often towards Kade. She wondered if he was awake, if he was making a plan, if he thought about her, if he thought about the kiss...

But each time Kade infiltrated her thoughts, she forced him away. There was no time for boys in this hectic, magical world. The last thing Jinx needed was a man to drag her down.

Putting the finishing touches on her master plan, Jinx emerged from her sleeping bag and wrapped up in her heavy winter coat. Her hat, scarf, and gloves would soon follow. Quietly, she sat at the front of the cave to admire the slowly falling crystals.

"I've always loved snow, you know?" Kade's voice drifted to Jinx as he too put on his black, woolen coat. Uninvited (and fairly unwanted), Kade sat down next to Jinx. Even a few feet away, Jinx believed this to be way too close for comfort.

"I have great memories of it from when I was a kid," Kade

enthused. "My sister, you know, is also an Asterian. Or was, I guess. And she could manipulate the weather however she liked. She would make it snow and we'd spend hours making forts and having snowball fights."

Jinx felt her heart tug at the image of carefree, joyous Kade, playing in the cold with his older sister. But still, Jinx felt no desire to reply to him. So naturally, he continued.

"But I don't know where she is now. Or even if she's alive, for that matter. She's ten years older than me and disappeared when I was almost seven. Nobody's seen her since the day Mr. Belton came to tell us she fled from The House."

Jinx turned her head towards Kade with a questioning tilt, finally addressing him in some way. "Why are you telling me this? I'm not your friend. I'm your apprentice."

Kade opened and shut his mouth, not seeming to be able to find a response to her question. A few minutes passed as Kade thought, but still, he said nothing. A tense silence grew over the pair until finally Kade asked something to make it more tense.

"Do you…," he stuttered. "Do you ever think about… our kiss?"

Jinx snapped her head to look at him with an expression of disbelief. If anything, she even appeared offended. And just as quickly as her emotions came, they left. Jinx's classic, hardened expression returned. "Kiss? What kiss?"

"Oh, c'mon, J. You can't just pretend it didn't happen," Kade scolded.

Jinx leaned in close, whispering angrily. "Yes, I can. Because it was a mistake, a fluke. It shouldn't have happened and it won't happen again; it would be best if you put it out of your mind." With this, Jinx stood up to wake Felix and Desdemona.

Kade sat, stunned, as he processed what Jinx just told him. Truthful, yes, but it still stung a little. It had taken a lot for Kade to work up the nerve to bring up the magical moment and, obviously, it hadn't gone as expected.

Felix clumsily wobbled into his winter coat before helping a still shaken Desdemona into hers. After last night's talk, Desdemona felt some better about everything she had been through. But even Felix couldn't stop the flashbacks which would soon plague many of her waking and sleeping moments. Only time would do that.

"Alright everyone. I want to hear the plans." Jinx shouted with an excited clap. She sat, criss crossed, like a gleeful child as everyone gathered around in a circle, all prepared to tell their plans. Well, everyone but Desdemona, who they decided would simply vote on her favorite or suggest one of her own on the fly.

"I will start," Jinx began. She took a deep breath and then began to share. "Okay, I think we need to go back. Go down the mountain, fly back, get support from other Asterians at The House and then come to destroy Jane. There's no way we can do this on our own. And sure, we would lose Margret, but Felix said it himself. This is about more than us and it's certainly about more than Margret."

Of course, this plan did not go over well with Felix. He immediately opened his mouth to object, but Jinx held up a finger, silencing him. "Let everyone propose their plans and then we can discuss. Felix, you're next."

"Alright. I think we need to take a different route. We have fallen into all of Jane's traps because we're playing right into her hands. We're being too direct. We need to make at least a half circle around the mountain to try to attack from the other side. And while we're at it, we may miss Jane's other traps and have the element of surprise."

Jinx instinctively wanted to argue, but forced her mouth closed. Nobody likes a critic.

Kade took a deep breath. "Where's the Asterian Jewel?" Kade asked Jinx. She reached around, grabbing her backpack and digging through the side pocket. She pulled out a tan cloth bag, inside of which sat the emerald jewel. But this time, the smooth side of the stone displayed a message of four lines, stacked neatly in gold lettering.

> A daughter among three, disowned
> Her devious powers unstoppable
> To all but her children of three alone

"When did that writing get there?" Felix asked as Jinx passed the Jewel to him. Jinx shook her head. She had no idea. The last time she picked up the Jewel, during the flight, the smooth side contained no message.

Instead, Kade answered. "I'm not sure when the writing got there, but many believe the two sides of the stone, the mountainous and smooth, represent the good and the bad in the world. Maybe the message is trying to say good will soon come."

Jinx squinted skeptically at Kade. "What makes you think the Jewel is so important right now?"

"Because it's about your family, Jinx." Kade exclaimed, incredulously. "Think about it. A daughter among three. Jane had two other siblings. Her devious powers. Whose gifts are more malignant than hers? And then the only ones to stop her will be her children of three? That's you guys."

For a moment, none of them spoke. All three of the Anchor siblings sat, processing the task at hand. In reality, Jinx thought, they knew this all along. But to have it confirmed made her stomach turn inside out. At this point, despite the truth, she wanted to do only one thing: run.

"We have to get out of here, guys. We have to go with my plan and get reinforcements before we attack her," Jinx shook her head anxiously, already getting up to pack her stuff.

"But wait," Desdemona whispered. "Doesn't the stone say 'three alone?' As in just the three of us." Her voice shook as her sentence ended with the thought of facing Jane once more, but Felix took her hand and squeezed it tightly.

"She's right," Kade agreed. "If you do this, it must be you three. And that excludes me. I can try to save Margret while you fight Jane, but I can't be involved in that battle. That is yours and yours alone."

Another spell of silence fell over the family. Jinx shared a look with her brother and sister, one filled with fear, anger, confusion, and apprehension. Jinx didn't believe they could do this on their own.

"Now let's discuss my plan," Kade continued. Jinx slowly let her terror fade away and zeroed in on Kade's plan, focused.

"This jewel will no doubt be crucial to your defeat of Jane. We keep going. But we can't just walk and talk anymore. We have to work together as a team. We can't just use our powers in a crisis. I want all of your powers on high alert 24/7 and I want everything you see reported to the whole group. If we constantly use our powers, Jane will not catch us in any more of her traps. I don't want anyone falling asleep on watches during the night nor do I want any thoughts of failure or death. We can't do this without faith. I need you to be all in. Who's all in?"

Felix raised his hand first. "Count me in," he blurted out. This woman, his mother, hurt both of his sisters and his (hopefully someday) girlfriend. Felix would not allow Jane to come out of this unscathed.

"Thank you, Felix. I am too," Kade announced with a rare, heartfelt smile.

Desdemona cleared her throat next after a few moments of hesitation. "I'm all in." She spoke in a stronger voice than before, with an unwavering sense of courage and self-assurance.

Finally, they all glanced at Jinx, who stared at the cave floor during this entire interaction. She absentmindedly drew on the dirt covering the ground, creating squiggles and zig zags as she hid from the elephant in the room.

"C'mon Jinx," Felix spoke. "Mona has been through hell with Jane. She has every right to want to turn back and hide, but she didn't. Why are you less in than her?"

Jinx felt guilt twist in her gut, making her feel horrible for not being all in. But still, a battle raged on within her, a battle between light and dark. Half of her thought it would simply be easier to turn back and let Jane win. But the other half, the true Asterian half, wanted the opposite.

Only Jinx and Kade knew about Jinx's vision of her turning on Felix and Desdemona to side with Jane. Jinx's mind raced. Was this the real reason for her hesitation? But as Kade said, the future could be changed. It would be up to her to change it. Jinx knew which half must win the foot race inside of her soul.

"I'm all in," Jinx confirmed, without so much as a sigh or further hesitation. She had begun to realize over the past few days the way to suppress the urge to become her mom. Anything

Jane would do, Jinx just did the opposite. That way her dark side could not swallow the light.

"Then it's settled," Kade declared. "Pack your bags, Anchors. We've got a long day of traveling ahead of us."

The snow continued to fall from the sky covering the rocky floor under their feet. The frozen white water reached up well past Desdemona's ankles now, making it difficult for her to take steps forward. She found an easier way by walking in the footsteps of Felix, whose feet were much bigger than her own.

"This snow is really something, isn't it? It's much thicker than the snow at home." Felix enthused, turning his head back to look at Desdemona. But when Desdemona met his eyes, she noticed his face was not normal. All his features were identical, but there was a single, large word written in bold, black ink across his forehead.

"Kind," Desdemona read it aloud, slowly, wondering why Felix wrote something like that on his head.

"What?" Felix asked, confused.

Desdemona squinted to make sure it was really there. Eventually, she reached up to try to smudge the marker. Nothing. "Kind," she repeated. "It's written on your forehead with black marker or something."

"What? There's nothing on my forehead," Felix informed her. He turned to Kade and Jinx, who walked ahead of them. "Hey guys. Is there something on my forehead?"

Jinx and Kade both turned and shook their heads.

"No, wait! There's stuff written on yours, too." Desdemona shouted, pointing to Jinx and Kade. The word "Restricted" appeared across Jinx's forehead, while the word "Forsaken" marked Kade.

"No, there's not, Mona," Jinx informed her, brushing it off to continue walking. Jinx wondered if the time Mona spent underground made her go a little crazy. Maybe she hit her head down there and messed up her vision or something.

"Jinx, wait!" Kade shouted. He came up to Desdemona as Jinx put her hands defiantly on her hips and groaned. Kade reached his hand up to touch Jinx's blank forehead, seeing no writing. But if Desdemona believed their foreheads had words written on them, it wasn't just something Kade could ignore.

Kade took a step back. "What does it say on Jinx's forehead?"

Desdemona took one extra look to make sure the black ink hadn't disappeared. And sure enough, it hadn't. "Restricted," Desdemona answered.

"And what does it say on mine?" Kade asked.

Desdemona shifted her eyes awkwardly. The word on Kade seemed a little too personal to say out loud. Forsaken. A synonym for deserted or abandoned. She opened her mouth, tempted to lie about the word, but then closed it again, deciding against it.

"Desdemona?" Kade questioned. "C'mon, what does it say?"

"I'm really not sure if…" She started.

Kade cut her off in a tone far from his nurturing voice of just a minute ago. Now, it was sharp and forceful. "Tell me."

"Forsaken," Desdemona finally answered. In silence, Desdemona, Jinx, and Felix all shared the same look.

What happened to make his say forsaken? Felix said in his sisters' minds.

I don't know, Jinx answered. *But it isn't good.*

I'm kind of freaked out, Felix, Desdemona thought. *I mean, I was just kidnapped and suddenly there are invisible words written on people's foreheads. I'm going crazy.*

Felix took a deep breath. *Mona, you're not crazy.*

With the awkward air becoming unbearable, Felix decided to share his inference about the words. "Hey, Kade, do you think this could be an Embellishment?"

Kade nodded anxiously, desperately looking for something to change the subject. "Yes! I do," he shouted a little too enthusiastically.

"What's an Embellishment?" Desdemona asked, scrunching up her eyebrows.

Kade gave Desdemona the same explanation he gave Felix when Felix received his first Embellishment. "And because you can see the past, these words on our foreheads must have something to do with our past. Maybe a significant trait."

Once again, the trio shared a tense glance as Desdemona once again looked at the large "forsaken" on Kade's forehead.

With this significant trait in his past, how in the world did he manage to come off so strong and determined?

"Alright, guys, I know Desdemona's new power is pretty cool, but we can't forget about the task at hand. We have three days to reach Margret now. We need to keep moving," Kade reminded them, once again breaking the silence.

All three nodded and began walking once more. Felix and Desdemona chatted excitedly about their newfound powers. Every now and then, Jinx would overhear a snippet of "and my Embellishment" or "it's so cool." And every single time she accidentally heard one of those phrases, her anger would boil over again to fill her veins and run through her entire body. It wasn't fair. Why did they get Embellishments and she didn't? Jinx was just as powerful and talented as them, wasn't she? And she was smarter too. Everything they could do, Jinx could do better, right?

With every step they took closer to that mountain, Jinx felt a tug to join Jane's side, as if Jane called out to her. Jane could get her twenty embellishments. Jane could give her new powers, anything she wanted.

"Calm down," Kade whispered to her, brushing his hand against hers.

Jinx snapped her head around to look at him. "What did you just tell me?"

"I said," Kade repeated. "You need to calm down. I know you. And I know you're angry about not getting an Embellishment like Felix and Desdemona, but you can't be angry. You'll get yours. Every Asterian does, but every Asterian also gets them at different times."

"I want mine now," Jinx ordered.

"Ok, that needs to stop right now. I don't want any pouting for the remainder of this trip," pointing a finger at her. "Jinx, you're fifteen. You need to stop acting like a third grader."

At this point, Kade raised his voice a little more than expected. Felix and Desdemona stopped their giggling just long enough to catch the tone of the conversation.

After their little skirmish, Jinx and Kade didn't speak. Felix and Desdemona simply communicated their excitement about their Embellishments through their minds, so as to not make Jinx jealous. Right now, about the only good thing their group appeared to have going for them was that the snow stopped falling.

In fact, the sun was even nice enough to make an appearance. In a matter of two hours, the snow on the ground drifted from nearly two feet to one foot to only six inches. Desdemona, Felix, Jinx, and Kade removed their winter coats to reveal long sleeve shirts. An hour after that, the snow disappeared completely and long sleeves made way for short sleeves. Before they knew it, the sun blasted down on the group and the temperature rose to 80 degrees.

"What is happening?" Felix panted, removing his sweats to reveal shorts underneath. "How is this even possible?"

Kade took a look at the blinding sun, glanced at the water running down the side of the mountain from the melted snow, then back to the sun. He answered in two simple words. "It's not."

22

Jinx reached down, grazing her hands over the water running down the mountain. The second her skin touched the melted snow, she felt a vision coming on, making her head spin. Immediately, she sat on the wet ground and let the rocky mountainside fade from her view.

Jinx felt her hair drip onto her already soaked clothes, making her shiver even in the warm air. As fast as the rain came, it stopped, just long enough to turn to snow. The temperature dropped drastically as Jinx watched herself, Kade, and her siblings continue their journey up the mountain. The snow continued as Jinx made her way towards the group. She stood right next to herself as silence coated the air, an invisible observer to the scene.

The snow morphed suddenly to hail, making Desdemona scream and cover her head with her arms. Felix folded himself over, shielding her, but putting his own body in grave danger. Jinx watched a single, volleyball sized piece of ice fall, dropping in the exact direction of where Felix kneeled over Desdemona.

"Felix! Watch out!" Jinx screamed as the hail continued to fall. Jinx desperately tried to get their attention, even going as far as to jump at him, pushing him away. But her body passed right though her siblings.

"Felix! You need to move right now." She screeched

even louder. He couldn't hear her. She knew her screaming did no good. Jinx stood, defenseless, as the ice dropped, smashing Felix directly in the back of the head. With a groan of pain, he dropped to the ground, doing even more damage to his head by hitting a hard rock.

As Kade, Desdemona, and Jinx rushed to tend to Felix, the ground began to shake violently. Small trees, firmly rooted to the ground, tumbled down without hesitation. The ground in front of them began to split and Jinx watched as rock went from smooth to jagged, breaking into pieces. The fissure grew, creating a canyon much bigger than the one they spent the night in at the beginning of their journey.

If it weren't such a dire situation, the canyon would have been a beautiful sight. But as lightning and thunder began, Jinx cringed at the wicked laugh nearby.

At first Jinx believed it to be Jane herself. Turning around, she realized she'd been wrong. She didn't recognize the voice at all. A woman's figure emerged, arms thrown in the air, shaking violently. The weather appeared to bend to her every will, as if she were conducting a symphony. As the downpour started again, the woman's long, jagged black hair remained dry. Her mouth turned up in a sneer as she laughed. Her grey blue eyes sparkled with a mischievous and mysterious look which Jinx had only seen on one other person.

Those eyes were eerily similar to Kade's.

Jinx came out from her vision with a gasp. She reached at her hair, expecting it to be soaked, but it was dry as a bone. Glancing around, Jinx hastily searched for Felix. When her eyes landed on his completely intact skull, she let out a sigh of relief.

It took Jinx a minute to control her breathing, but Kade, Desdemona, and Felix watched her like hawks throughout the entire thing.

Eventually, she couldn't take the staring anymore. "Guys," Jinx yelled. "I'll tell you what I saw if you just give me some space for a minute. Please. You two should know how this is," she motioned to her brother and sister. "I need to have space to breathe."

They did as she asked. Jinx cast a hesitant glance in Kade's direction, confirming what she already believed to be true. His eyes, bright blue, yet dulled with flecks of grey, flickered from the sky to the ground and back again. Those eyes were exactly the same ones Jinx saw on the maniacally laughing woman in her vision. The only difference - Kade's eyes were guarded, while the woman displayed all her emotions.

Jinx fought back the urge to ask Kade privately about it right now. But they made a deal to use their powers as a group. Using their powers as a group meant not keeping secrets from one another.

"Alright," Jinx began. "If you guys want to hear it, I'm ready to tell."

It took only a few minutes for Jinx to explain everything up until the woman. When that portion came about, Jinx paused to think how to begin.

"And then I realized..." She paused, contemplating. "This woman controlled all the strange changes in the weather."

"Was it Jane? Because I wouldn't be surprised if she stole some poor girl's power to be able to do that," Felix snapped, huffing.

Jinx shook her head. "Actually, no. This was a woman, but not Jane. She had long black hair and..." She turned to glance at the blue-eyed boy. "And eyes just like Kade's."

Desdemona and Felix both swung their heads to gape at Kade. If Jinx had Felix's power, she knew she would be hearing lots of "what does she mean" and multiple "are they related?"

Jinx finally made the connection.

Kade had mentioned a sister. A sister who could control the weather. A sister who Kade had not seen in over ten years. How could this woman, with hair and eyes a lot like Kade's, not be that sister?

"She's your sister," Jinx stated blatantly. She didn't even need to glance at Kade to know she was right. The way he hadn't spoken for this entire vision told her everything she needed to know.

"I've worried about this," Kade answered. "From the first random snowstorm, I suspected it."

All three Anchor kids remained silent, waiting for their mentor to continue.

"Her name is Hazel," Kade told. He opened his mouth to continue, but Felix cut him off.

"Like the Hazel the cockroach guy thought about?" Felix asked incredulously.

Kade nodded. "Yes. I didn't want to mention anything earlier because I didn't know for sure. It's not a very common name, you know? Hazel. I really hoped it wasn't her."

"But it is," Jinx declared. "Your sister works for Jane. Your sister is trying to kill us."

Desdemona slapped Jinx on the shoulder. "J. Cut the guy a break. He hasn't seen her in a decade and now he's found her fraternizing with the enemy."

Kade jumped up from the place he sat next to Jinx. "Nope. I'm not upset at all. She's made her choice and I made mine." Kade grabbed his bag and slung it over his back. "We need to keep moving. Jinx, when your vision starts to come true, we need to prevent Felix from getting hurt. Hazel won't hurt any of you. Not on my watch."

Jinx felt a pang as she thought of the little boy who used to play in the snow with his older sister. The little boy who laughed at his sister's powers. The little boy who loved his sister more than anything. Jinx knew he felt more than he let on to them. He was upset. There was no doubt about it.

But for their sake, he hid his confusion with a mask of determination because that was what the Anchor kids needed right now.

The weather continued to change rapidly as they continued to climb. It went from blizzard to down pour to heat wave in a matter of thirty minutes. After about an hour of taking clothes off and then putting them back on, the group settled on wearing long sleeves, jeans, and a hat. Their bags became soaked in the very first downpour, meaning soggy bread and old canned goods would be their food source until they confronted Jane. It wasn't ideal by any standards, but for Margret's sake, they needed to keep going.

"Felix," Desdemona whispered in front of him. She slowed her pace to walk alongside him.

Felix turned his head to notice the grief-stricken face of his sister. "Yeah? What's wrong, Mona?" He asked.

"I miss home…" she mumbled, almost ashamed to admit it. She let her dampened hair fall over the wound on her eye to shield her face.

"I know," Felix replied. "I do too. But we will be back at The House within a week, I'm sure."

Desdemona shook her head. "No, that's not what I mean. I mean that I miss *home* home. With Stacy. Where everything was normal and predictable and my biggest worry was the chemistry lab write up."

"You miss chemistry? Are you insane?" Felix joked, trying to lighten the mood a little.

Desdemona laughed halfheartedly. "You know what I mean, Felix. Stacy loved me. I liked believing she was my mom. Then we were just thrown from that life and handed a psychopath mother who likes to cut her kids' faces." At this point, she pushed her hair back behind her ear.

"But we're going to stop her, Mona." Felix reminded her excitedly. "Only we can do this. These powers are such a gift to us. We have been given the opportunity to end over a decade of corruption within the Asterian Society."

"That's a lot of pressure," Desdemona muttered, sighing heavily.

"I know, but I have faith in us. We have strong powers. I still think, in the end, light always overcomes the dark."

Desdemona thought back to all the Disney princess movies she loved so much. In Beauty and the Beast, Gaston tried to kill the Beast. In Snow White, the Evil Queen tried to poison her. In Rapunzel, her own mother locked her in a tower for 16 years.

All of those classics had a bad guy. In all of those classics, the good guys won and the princess ended up with her prince. The only thing Desdemona lacked in her story was a prince, but she knew that would come with time.

"We can do this," Desdemona declared more for herself than for Felix.

Felix beamed at her, giving her a strong pat on the back. "You're exactly right. We can do this."

While Desdemona continued to ponder her Disney similarities and differences, just up ahead, Jinx and Kade appeared to be having the opposite conversation.

"I don't think we can do this," Jinx stated, hands on hips. "I mean, that is your sister up there. If our very own families have turned on us, why would anyone begin to believe we can win?"

"Now that, J, is not the kind of attitude we need up here," Kade reminded her.

"But it's practical," Jinx murmured.

Kade turned to her with a flash of anger in his eyes, but let it soften as he spoke to her. "Do you think I wanted my sister to join Jane's side? Do you think I wanted her to try to kill us?"

Jinx stared at him, speechless, for he obviously wasn't expecting a real answer. When she didn't respond, Kade continued.

"I can't control her actions. The only thing I can do now is forget she is my family. In fact, she's not anymore." Kade sighed shakily. "You three are my family now."

Jinx turned to Kade with an expression of utter shock and disbelief. She wondered if she heard him correctly. Replaying the conversation in her head, she knew she heard him right.

To this, Jinx didn't know how to reply. She's never been good with mushy conversations like this. Stupidly, she responded, "Um… okay…"

"Okay, good," Kade replied. He turned his head in her direction and with a single, curt nod, ended the sympathetic words. Jinx felt herself breathe a sigh of relief. Short and awkward, she could do. In fact, Jinx could handle pretty much anything as long as it didn't involve feelings.

"Jinx," Felix called up to her. "Did you happen to receive a timeline on when I would be getting pegged by that large piece of hail?"

Jinx snorted at his sarcastic comment. They both knew their powers didn't tell when things did or will happen. They just knew, usually, they did and they will.

"Sorry, Bud," Jinx replied. "I wish it worked that way."

"Hey! Who knows? Maybe that will be your first Embellishment." Desdemona added excitedly, but maybe a little too excitedly because Jinx's face immediately fell and she turned back to the front with a scowl.

"Sorry…" Desdemona apologized quietly.

Make a note. Never mention Embellishments to Jinx until she gets one, Felix joked in Desdemona's mind. She shook her head in agreement just as it began to snow again. At this point, changes in the weather began to go unnoticed by the group. They decided panic could wait until the hail came. Until giant ice balls began to fall from the sky, they continued their journey up the hill.

"Hey, can we stop for lunch?" Felix asked. Desdemona mentioned hunger to him earlier, but didn't say anything more about it.

"Yeah, do you guys see shelter anywhere near?" Kade yelled over the blizzard and howling winds. Jinx squinted, glancing in every direction, to no avail. The heavy snow made it hard to see more than twenty feet in front of them. The weather kept changing so much the group hadn't even really noticed snow falling for nearly twenty minutes now.

Jinx first mentioned the continuous snow, which immediately clued her in. Endless snow had been at the beginning of her vision.

"Guys," she called. But the already howling winds grew stronger. "My vision is about to come true," she yelled.

But nobody heard. They continued to look for shelter, not paying attention to the snow until it immediately turned to hail. Jinx found herself screaming, just like she had been as a bystander in her vision. She made every attempt to warn them as the hail began pelt into the fallen snow.

Rushing, she ran over to Kade, struggling to wade through a snow drift.

"This is it! This is my vision," she yelled over the wind. Finally, he heard her and Jinx watched as Kade's eyes grew wide. He whipped around to tell Felix and Desdemona, only to find them both huddled, covering their heads with their backpacks.

When this appeared to work, Jinx and Kade followed suit. With no shelter in sight, what else could they do? Kade hoped if Felix could avoid injury, maybe Hazel wouldn't make her appearance just yet.

As if the elements conspired against them, wind whipped at record speed over Desdemona's head, pulling her backpack out from her hands and leaving her head exposed to the ice. Without even a second thought, Felix draped himself over Desdemona.

Yes, Felix told Kade he wouldn't put himself in harm's way, but under no circumstances would he allow his sister to be hurt again. She had been through enough already. Getting a concussion was the last thing she needed. Felix, on the other hand, could handle a little hit to the head.

In the background, he faintly heard Jinx yelling for him to move, but Felix knew he wouldn't do that. A few seconds later, he heard a thump on his head and everything went black.

Felix came to no more than three minutes later to find Desdemona leaning over him, pressing her hands to his face wildly. Chaos abounded around the outline of her face. Lighting struck in the now darkening sky as Felix heard a very unnerving, high-pitched laugh nearby. When Desdemona noticed his eyes slowly opening, she let out a sigh of relief.

"Oh, thank goodness. Okay, Felix, how old are you?" Desdemona asked, still holding desperately onto his face.

"Um…" he thought for a moment, gathering his bearings. "I'm fifteen, Mona. What's going on?" Felix tried to sit up to see who made the horrible shrieking cackle, but she pressed on his chest.

"Please, stay down. We can risk any more injures to your head," she told him. Desdemona winced as she realized the snow under Felix's head was coated in bright red.

"Where are we?" She asked another question, trying to judge if he suffered a concussion or not.

"We're climbing a mountain. Now why are you asking me all these questions? My head is fine." Felix wondered aloud, trying to sit up again. He placed his hand on the back of his head, rubbing his injury, trying to conceal his mild panic when it came away covered in blood. After a moment of thought, he reached down to his shirt and tore off the bottom half. He wrapped it quickly around his head, making sure it was tight to clot the blood. When he placed his hand there again and it came away clean, Felix got up, ignoring Desdemona's protests.

"You need to stay sitting," she yelled, grabbing onto his arm to pull him back. But he didn't budge.

"Mona," Felix whipped around to look her in the eyes. Slowly, she released her grip on his arm. "My head feels fine right now. I've slowed the bleeding for the time being. Look, Mona, Jinx and Kade are in trouble and there's no way I'm sitting this one out. I told you, I'm not letting Jane hurt any of you again."

"But this isn't Jane. It's Hazel, Kade's sister." Desdemona called in a final, desperate attempt to get him to stay.

Of course it didn't work. "But Jane sent her here, which means if Jinx gets hurt right now, then Jane hurt her."

"If you're going, I'm coming too," Desdemona told him. Felix smirked at her as he got out his sword and Desdemona picked up her bow and arrow.

"Let's do this," Felix inspired. Desdemona smiled at him and then they both ran over to join Jinx and Kade, who stood a good distance from Hazel. Once they got closer, Felix realized they weren't fighting yet. They were talking.

"Should have known my little brother would be on the losing side," Hazel snorted, staring directly at Kade. Desdemona looked up at Hazel's forehead to find "Lost" written in black letters.

Kade stood tall, pulling his axe from his belt. "Should have known my older sister would join the enemy."

Hazel laughed maliciously once more. "The enemy? Jane is the opposite of the enemy. She is the future of the Asterian race. These three children? They're just a big waste of your time."

Desdemona reached for an arrow and loaded it into her bow.

The ground began to shake vigorously, making Desdemona lose her balance and drop the arrow she planned to fire at Hazel. Jinx and Felix soon fell as well, leaving Kade and Hazel as the last ones standing.

"Oh, Sister, you never stayed around long enough to find out the extent of my powers," Kade said confidently. "You may control the weather, but my power to control the senses is much stronger." At first, Hazel laughed out loud, but her eyes slowly lost their humor. The ground stopped shaking. It became obvious Hazel lost her battle focus.

Her eyes, the ones perfectly mimicking Kade's, turned from mocking to shocked. Kade planted her mind in another place, far from Truchas Peak.

But unlike the other times Jinx saw Kade take someone's senses, Hazel did not scream. She appeared to almost be in awe of the scene in front of her. She shivered with her teeth chattering as the weather in the scene changed against her will.

Jinx didn't know what Kade had shown Hazel. She suspected it differed from his usual scenes.

"We used to be happy, Hazel," Kade called to her. "But then you went and joined Jane." Hazel gasped quickly as the current scene apparently came back to her. Her eyes glazed over, staring into the distance.

"Don't follow us, Hazel," Kade ordered. "I can take you to terrifying places and I swear, if you lay a hand on any one of these kids, I won't be afraid to give you my worst."

Hazel nodded furiously, again with glazed over eyes. Kade picked up his discarded bag, keeping his axe out and began to walk around Hazel. There she stood, too stunned to even acknowledge the three Anchor kids passing by her. And sure enough, as Kade ordered, she didn't lay a finger on any of them.

23

The weather grew steadily colder as the Asterians continued to climb Truchas Peak. Instead of changing every ten minutes, a wintery chill settled in on the Anchor kids. They all put on their coats once again, knowing this time they would be staying on until the end of their journey up the mountain. The atmosphere began to change, making it slightly harder to breathe, but Felix had no intention of stopping. They didn't have much higher to go.

"Maybe just a day or so more of climbing," Kade informed them as he gazed up towards the top of the mountain. These were the first words shared among the group since their encounter with Hazel. In fact, it became so eerily quiet that all three kids hesitated to respond to Kade's analysis.

Desdemona spoke first and she, along with her siblings, turned her head towards their goal: Truchas Peak. "Yeah, I would imagine you're right, Kade," nodding her head.

"So..." Desdemona added after a moment. "What did you show Hazel?"

"The usual," Kade responded, maybe a little too quickly. "I took all of her senses and make snakes bite at her ankles and birds flap around her head. It was nothing too serious, but it definitely scared her enough. She's always been a wimp."

To anyone who didn't know much about Kade, this answer would seem nonchalant and simple. Predictable even. But to Jinx, this answer was much too obvious. His voice seemed unusually emotionless and stiff, making him appear colder than normal.

Desdemona and Felix simply believed Kade saw his sister for the first time in over a decade. But Jinx, who now knew Kade better than most, realized the truth must be more complicated.

Jinx felt the urge to press Kade on it, to call him out for his strange answer. But she thought better of it. If she asked now, Kade would grow defensive and skirt around her question entirely. She would find a correct place and time for this conversation, but here, with Desdemona and Felix listening, was definitely not it.

They continued in a tense, uneasy silence.

It wasn't until a couple of hours later when Jinx broke that silence.

"Hey, we need to stop. I think I'm getting a vision," Jinx told everyone. Kade, knowing every vision at this point could help, didn't protest. Meanwhile, everyone decided to make dinner and get some rest before they travelled further. Jinx, on the other hand, didn't appear to be getting rest anytime soon. Her stomach tossed and turned until, finally, her powers took over.

> In the pitch black room, Jinx couldn't see her hand in front of her face. Jinx turned her head from side to side, searching for any sign of movement within her vision. Nothing happened.
>
> This vision differed from all others Jinx experienced before. This time she had not been thrown into an action scene with Asterians running, screaming, jumping, and using their powers. Jinx had grown used to those. She did not fear those visions. Darkness unnerved her.
>
> "Hello?" Jinx eventually yelled, hoping someone would answer. Still, she heard no voices.
>
> Nothing moved until a bright, yellow light shone on a pedestal in the middle of the room. The pedestal rose to Jinx's waist and appeared to be made completely of white marble. On top of this marble, a light illuminated a stone Jinx now knew very well.
>
> The Asterian Jewel.

Jinx watched as an alternate version of herself emerged from the darkness of the room. Slowly, with steady hands, Jinx observed as she reached to cup the stone in her hands. The stone began to emit a faint, white glow.

Desdemona came from the dark, her blonde hair pulled back in a high, tight ponytail. Without hesitation, Desdemona put a single hand on the jewel and the glow grew brighter.

Felix joined his siblings and the stone. He confidently touched it and watched, in awe, as the jewel erupted with light. The entire room glowed with the white, blinding light of the stone. Just as Jinx's eyes began to adjust, she tried to take in her surroundings. Before she could focus, the scene in front of her began to fade. Just before the scene went black, she heard the familiar, malignant laugh of Jane Anchor.

Jinx opened her eyes slowly, taking in the cold mountainous air. Laughing and giggling about who knows what, Desdemona and Felix stood just a few feet away. Kade sat right beside Jinx as he patiently waited for her to exit the vision.

"Hey, J," Kade whispered tentatively, making sure she wasn't planning on snapping at him.

Lucky for Kade, Jinx wasn't in the mood to anger him. "Hey," she replied just as quietly.

"What did you see?" Kade asked. He raised his hand, waving over Felix and Desdemona, so they could all gather to hear Jinx's vision. After they settled in, Jinx recounted the events of the past few minutes in full detail, emphasizing Jane's ominous cackle at the end. When she finished, both siblings seemed uneasy, with visibly nervous, shifty eyes.

"So, what do you think it means?" Kade quizzed. Lately, he encouraged the Anchor kids to sharpen interpretations of their visions. Kade thought better interpretations could be better relied upon to affect future events.

"I think…" Jinx commented, running her vision once over again in her mind. "I think the jewel has something to do with whether we will defeat Jane."

"How," Felix corrected.

"What?" Desdemona asked Felix.

"How we defeat Jane. Not whether we defeat her," he clarified with a fire in his eyes Jinx had not seen before. Felix had become noticeably stronger and tougher since they rescued Desdemona. Ever since, when anyone mentioned Jane, Felix looked like he wanted nothing more than to put an end to her reign of terror.

In fact, that was exactly what he intended to do.

"I think," Jinx continued. "We need to use this Jewel when we finally meet Jane."

"But your vision didn't even show Jane," Desdemona pointed out.

"That's true, but I did hear her laugh. And I have a feeling we weren't actually in a black room. I have a feeling the dream blacked out the surroundings. If I had been able to see, I'm almost 100% sure I would have seen Jane," she declared. Everyone stopped to ponder this for a moment, but of course, none of them had been there first hand like Jinx. Neither Kade, Desdemona, nor Felix could get a good handle on what really happened in this vision. For now, they would just have to take her word for it.

"Hey," Desdemona looked up towards to setting sun. "It's getting pretty dark. Can we have dinner and get some sleep?"

Felix opened his mouth to argue, wanting to say they needed to reach Margret as soon as possible, but Kade silenced him with his finger. "Yes, Mona. I think we all need some rest anyway. It's been a long, hard day."

Desdemona sighed with relief at his agreement and looked around for shelter of some sort. Snow flurries falling from the sky blurred her sight.

"Where are we going to sleep?" Felix asked, scanning around in all directions. Jinx and Kade did the same, but nothing popped out at them.

"I guess we just need to keep walking," Kade shook his head in disappointment.

Felix watched as Desdemona's face fell and tears began to well in her big blue eyes. She didn't protest, choosing to silently hold back her cries as she walked. Instead of calling her out, Felix pushed into his sister's mind.

Hey, what's wrong? We're going to find some place to sleep really soon, Mona, Felix reassured her.

Much to his dismay, the voice in his head sounded a lot like the voice Felix heard from her while she was underground. Defeated. Disappointed. Distraught. *I need to go to sleep...*

We're going to find some cave or something really soon, I promise, Felix reminded her, but he feared words and thoughts couldn't comfort her at this point.

Felix, this time last night my own mother cut my face. I've been left with a physical scar which might heal, but an emotional one which never will. I'm in the middle of nowhere with two siblings I met six months ago and a seventeen year old boy with an axe on his belt. I'm scared out of my mind and I need to sleep. I need to sleep to escape.

Felix felt a knot in the pit of his stomach. He might not have been able to end Jane right now, but he could find Mona a place to sleep.

The search for shelter continued into the darkness of night. The moon rose high into the sky and stars managed to shine through clouds filled with frozen rain. With each passing moment, Desdemona felt herself wishing harder and harder they could find a place to call it a night. Her fingers and toes felt numb with cold as they ventured onward, continuing towards the top of the mountain.

"Hey!" Jinx called from the front of the line. "Look! I think I see a cave over there." She pointed a little to their left, where a large hole had been weathered out of an oversized boulder.

"Perfect," Kade called, breaking into a jog towards the rock. He held his hand out to the others, motioning for them to wait while he went in to scout the cave. When nothing attacked him, Kade sighed in relief and began to set down his stuff. The three kids followed suit and devoured their rations of food before setting up for bed. The insulated boulder kept most of the snow flurries outside their hideaway and the ones trickling in melted instantaneously. Desdemona snuggled into her sleeping bag and

Felix, hovering over her ever since they reached the shelter, set up very close to her.

Kade and Jinx, of course, sat awake, side by side as they watched the falling snow.

"What did you show Hazel?" Jinx asked finally.

Kade stared straight ahead not even glancing at her. "I told you what I showed her. I told all three of you."

"No, Kade," Jinx stopped him. "I know when you're lying. What did you really show her?"

Kade finally snapped his head over to glance at Jinx, who stared him down intensely. "Why do you care?" He replied. "It's not like I'm your boyfriend. I'm nothing more than your mentor and you made that very clear the other day."

Jinx shook her head at his answer. "Kade, just because you can't go around kissing me all day doesn't mean you can't talk to me."

"I know. I don't want to go around kissing you all day," Kade clarified. "Now, as I told you previously, I simply made bugs crawl around her ankles and birds fly around her head."

"You said snakes last time," Jinx pointed out. "You said snakes crawled around her ankles, not bugs."

At this, Kade turned his head angrily, knowing Jinx busted him. When he didn't offer anything further, Jinx continued.

"And if you don't want to tell me, that's fine," Jinx nodded with finality. Quickly, she got up off the ground and began to go over to her sleeping bag.

"I showed her the snow," Kade whispered under his breath, just loud enough for Jinx to hear. She stopped rustling her bag and came back to sit down next to him once again. He continued. "I showed her us in the snow as kids. The time I told you about how we would make snow angels and have snowball fights. And then when it got too cold to bear, we would go inside and have hot chocolate and watch a movie. That is what I showed her. I wanted to show her how far she fell. And maybe a part of me just wanted her to remember."

Jinx's jaw dropped slightly before she pulled it shut. She expected something harsh from Kade, maybe something different from snakes. She never anticipated this sentimental approach.

In truth, with their difficult circumstances where harsh actions were required, Jinx couldn't decide if it made her love him or hate him.

While Jinx and Kade sat in silence, both thinking about his childhood, just a couple miles up the mountain, two women had a somewhat related but very different conversation.

"I was crystal clear. You were to capture the three kids, separate them from their mentor, then bring them to me. Why are those three kids asleep in some cave right now, warm and safe?" Jane shrieked, throwing her arms up in the air, glaring in disapproval.

Giving Jane the answer she wanted, Hazel shook her head. "Yes, I know I failed you. I know I messed up. I just couldn't continue to hunt them like animals."

Jane shot Hazel a glare as they continued to walk towards their headquarters at the top of the mountain. So angry at Hazel for not capturing her kids, Jane took the liberty of meeting her subject at the halfway point from the headquarters and where Hazel met the kids. "And what stopped you from hunting them?" Jane asked, not looking at Hazel.

Hazel debated a lie, wanting to say Kade blinded and froze her, unwillingly, to the spot to prevent her from chasing after them. Hazel knew that wouldn't work. One of the powers Jane stole from some helpless Asterian was a lie detector. Ever since, Jane had an uncanny knack for pointing out even the whitest lie, then persecuting the liar.

Hazel had no real choice. She had to be honest.

"Kade took my senses and gave me a vision," Hazel began. When Jane didn't respond, she continued. "And it wasn't what I expected him to show me. He didn't torture me with snakes or spiders or murderers. He reminded me of something I've kept buried for a very long time."

"The vision started on a hot, summer day. I was fifteen and I just received my powers. Kade was five, barely learning how to read and write. Kade never liked summer. He never liked to sweat or wear shorts or feel the sun on his face. In fact, my little brother always preferred winter. With my new powers, wanting to make him happy, I decided to make it snow. I dropped the temperature from ninety to twenty in our backyard alone. The rain held in the puffy, summer clouds froze instantly. Oh, Jane. You should have seen his face when he saw the snow."

Hazel didn't even wait for Jane to say something. She continued recollecting her story in a wistful voice with her hands folded together in front of her.

"We both got our snow clothes on as fast as possible and ran out into the winter wonderland which I created with my own hands. And you know the first thing he did? That little stinker threw a cold, frozen snowball at me. A full blown snow ball fight broke out. We spent the next two hours making forts and piling up ammo. We threw and laughed and ran until we crushed all the snowballs and the forts. Then, we sat down on the winter ground in the dead of summer and made snow angels. I remember our mother taking a picture of the two of us near our angels. My angel made his look tiny, but the smile on his face that day made mine look like a frown."

"Eventually, the snow became too cold for us and we went inside. Our mom stripped us of our snow pants and the two of us put on pajamas and drank hot chocolate near the fire in our living room. Later that day, our parents went to get the photo of the snow angels developed at a local film shop. She gave one to me and I put it in my room. You know, that picture still sat on my bedside table the day I decided to leave home. Sometimes, I wonder if it's still there."

Hazel felt herself get so lost in her thoughts she didn't even realize Jane stopped walking. Hazel's stopped dead in her tracks as Jane whipped around with fire in her eyes.

"You know what that story was?" Jane asked. When Hazel opened her mouth to respond, Jane cut her off. "That story was the reason you failed on your mission today. That story was one giant weakness. And you know how I feel about weakness. I've seen this flaw in families before and I know only one thing will end it: kill Kade. When Kade comes with my three kids, he is your responsibility. I want him dead by the time I take their powers or I will personally see to your demise."

Jane paused, smirking devilishly before providing the final sentence of her ultimatum. "Put an end to him or I will put an end to you."

24

When the sun finally peaked out from under the horizon, Jinx awoke to find her head against Kade's shoulder, his arm pulling her closer. Surprised, Jinx tried to move quickly, but gently, away from him to not wake him up. Much to her dismay, Kade slept lightly. The second Jinx moved his arm away, Kade's eyes shot open.

"Oh!" Kade yelled in surprise, moving his arm away instantly. "Oh, gosh. I'm sorry. Really sorry." He nervously scanned his eyes across the cave floor, trying to look anywhere but at Jinx.

"It's um, it's okay," Jinx replied awkwardly. Kade let the silence hang for another moment before abruptly standing up in hopes of ending the tension in the air. It didn't work. Jinx stood up at the exact same time and accidentally bumped her head against his.

"Ow! Sorry," Kade exclaimed, rubbing his head. Jinx did the same and skirted her eyes away from his very handsome, disheveled bedhead, mentally cursing herself for even noticing a thing like that in the first place.

"You know what?" Jinx said, embarrassed. "I'm just going to go check the... weather... and stuff outside."

Kade knew very well Jinx could "check the weather" by simply looking out the mouth of the cave, but at this point, he was glad the exchange came to a close. Most of his confrontations with Jinx ended in awkward silences or tense glances. Kade wondered if things would always be this way...

"Hey! Kade!" Felix shouted from behind him, breaking Kade's inner monologue. "How far are we from Jane?"

"That's actually what I was about to bring up during breakfast. Wake your sister and we'll discuss it." While Felix instantly turned around to shake Desdemona, Kade took a step, hesitantly, outside, where he noticed Jinx dutifully inspecting the sky.

"I'd say it looks like a sunny day," Jinx noted after ample observation. "It will be nice. We haven't had a sunny day in a while."

"Well, it's still cold and you'd be advised to put on a coat before you get frostbite, J," Kade ordered her. "And while you're at it, come inside and have breakfast. We have things to discuss." Kade turned on his heel to go back inside. At this point, he figured a snippy reply from Jinx would only bring back the awkwardness.

When Jinx came in and Desdemona groggily dragged herself out of her sleeping bag, Kade answered Felix's previous question. "If my estimation is right, we should be within a day's walk from Jane's headquarters at the top of the mountain. We might be able to get there by sundown if we start now."

Felix practically shot up and out the door with joy. "Well, then what are we waiting for? We're going to save Margret today."

"Just in the brink of time. If we were just a few days later, she would've been chopped liver," Jinx sadistically joked, laughing. Felix shot her an angry glance, obviously disapproving of her choice of words, before setting up their only remaining breakfast: oatmeal.

"Remember now," Kade started, pausing to take a bite. "When we get there, I'm not coming with you. I plan on breaking off a few miles before we reach her base."

"We need the jewel," Jinx ordered in between mouthfuls of goopy oats.

"What?" Kade asked.

"The jewel," Jinx repeated. "We need the Asterian Jewel. I can feel it."

"The jewel may help, Jinx, but if you think a stone can beat Jane, you're underestimating her. There is a reason the three of you have been brought to this point at this time. Don't forget that." Kade replied.

Once Jinx made sure the Jewel was still in her bag, the group finished up breakfast and headed out. All the coats, hats, gloves, scarves, and extra socks would be brought out once they continued their climb into the frosty heights. The group settled into their normal hiking routine. Jinx and Kade led the pack while Desdemona and Felix brought up the rear.

"Hey," Felix turned to Desdemona. "Can I ask you a question?"

Desdemona turned to him with a confused look. "Umm… sure, I guess."

"What was it like?" Felix asked. "What was it like down there with Jane?"

Desdemona didn't respond, choosing instead to stare at the ground at her moving feet. She opened her mouth to speak, but promptly closed it again after thinking once more. She pondered over her brother's question for a full minute before finally answering.

"It felt like someone brought a vacuum into the mine shaft and used it to suck all the joy out of the air," Desdemona started. She looked at Felix with sad, reflective eyes before continuing. Felix began to questions further, but at the sound of Felix's voice, she felt the vision coming.

Desdemona once again found herself in the darkness of the abandoned mine shaft. She grabbed at her chest, wishing to have any vision but this one, wishing to relive anything besides this. But once a vision started, it couldn't be stopped. Jane emerged from the shadows, knives gleaming in her belt. A smile curled on her lips as she watched her helpless daughter struggle against the ropes.

"Don't struggle, sweet one. There's no point in wasting any energy," Jane advised in a deceivingly delicate tone. Jane took three slow, small steps towards Desdemona before kneeling down to eye level. Desdemona, in a desperate effort to get as far from her as possible, pressed

against the metal wire digging into her back. Reaching one hand to touch her face, Jane smiled. "How are your brother and sister?"

When Desdemona refused to answer, Jane reached for one of the knives on her belt. Desdemona felt fear grip her, but refused to open her mouth. Again, Jane spoke. "Where are they? If you tell me, I will leave you alone. Who knows? Maybe I'll even let you go."

Both Desdemona and Jane knew this would never happen. Desdemona would be here until Jane had her way. "I don't know where they are, Jane," Desdemona answered through gritted teeth.

"Jane? Why so formal? Please, call me Mom," Jane responded. Desdemona shook her head wildly in refusal. Jane again reached for her knife, but this time, actually unsheathed it, allowing the silver to glow in the torchlight above. Horrified at the sight of the knife once again, Desdemona shrieked. As Jane brought the knife closer and closer to her face, Desdemona felt herself being quickly pulled out of the vision.

Desdemona came out of her vision shaking, but still on her feet. She felt a single tear run down her cheek, passing the wound inflicted by the same knife she saw just moments ago. Felix, looking on at her tears, shook his head.

"No, please, don't answer that. I'm very sorry I asked at all," Felix apologized.

Desdemona volunteered anyway. Eventually, she would need to talk about this. If she didn't, she might never stop reliving that moment. "It felt completely devoid of hope. With Jane, you think you can't be saved."

"I wish we found you sooner. But with our powers, working together, we came out of it. We had hope and it came true." Felix answered proudly, offering a comforting hand on Desdemona's shoulder.

"And that was the weird thing, really. All that hope came back to me the minute she was gone and I saw the outside air above ground. It was as if someone breathed life back into me," Desdemona replied, with a deep, solemn sigh.

Felix nodded, able to sympathize, but not empathize with his sister. Desdemona turned and gave him a half-hearted smile. In fact, it wasn't much of a smile at all, more like a simple turn of the lips with no real emotion behind it besides sadness.

Feeling the connection with Desdemona's pain, desperately trying to elicit a real smile, Felix cheered, "Well, in less than twenty-four hours, Jane will be no more."

Desdemona giggled at her brother's excitement and smiled broadly at him. Felix, satisfied with his work, let the air around them go quiet. Kade and Jinx, avidly avoiding another awkward confrontation, allowed the silence to continue as they walked.

The sun rose quickly, going from a tiny speck above the horizon to a giant ball right above their heads. Before they knew it, high noon arrived, yet the air grew even colder since early morning.

Just as Felix looked to his left, seeing a small, brown bush on the ground, he felt a voice inside of his head.

Oh, Felix. A woman's voice beckoned quietly. Although he only heard her voice one other time, he recognized the unmistakable tone.

Jane, he replied calmly, trying not to freak out about the fact that he was hearing his mother's thoughts.

My son! You heard me. Jane exclaimed.

Yes, I heard you. That's my power. And I'm not your son, Felix reminded her sharply.

Well, of course you're my son. I gave birth to you. I was there, I saw it and I'm sure my beautiful blonde daughter saw it too in one of her visions of the past, Jane cooed.

Felix had half a mind not to answer, to silence the voice in his head, but he decided against it. Maybe he could get some good information out of her. *What do you want, Jane?* Felix asked bluntly.

Oh! I only wanted to speak to my only son. She told him sweetly. Now, had Jane not been a habitual liar and murderer, this sentence might have been endearing.

I know that's a load of bull, Jane. Now what do you want? Felix repeated.

Jane gasped in her thoughts. *Felix! I won't have my son using that kind of tone with his mother.*

Felix walked forward and waited for Jane to drop the act. For a while, it was silent, until Felix heard her take a sharp breath and continue.

I just wanted to remind you guys to hurry because I have moved the deadline of Margret's death up to tonight. Jane laughed manically.

Felix's mind raced at a hundred miles per hour, but he knew he couldn't let Jane see his panic. Keeping a steady, calm voice, Felix offered his mother one word. *What?*

You heard me, Felix. If the three of you don't speed it up, then poor, sweet, beautiful Margret will be chopped liver, Jane yelled, although the voice was still quiet in his mind.

Felix hesitated for a moment, realizing the "chopped liver" joke was the same one Jinx made earlier. Only this time, it wasn't a joke. This time, Margret really could be made into chopped liver if they didn't make it in time.

Jane continued to banter on about Margret in her thoughts. Felix, knowing he couldn't handle her right now, closed her off and turned to his sisters and Kade.

"Guys, we need to hurry up," he ordered them.

Jinx gave a weak laugh, "You don't think we know that, idiot? We're going as fast as we can."

"No," Felix countered. "This can't be our fastest because if we can't speed it up, Margret will die."

"Chill out, Felix," Desdemona put her hand on Felix's shoulder in an attempt to comfort him. "Margret still has a two day lead."

"No, she doesn't," Felix shouted, near hysterics. "I just heard Jane's thoughts. She said she's moving the deadline up to tonight at nightfall."

"What?" Desdemona shrieked. "She can't do that. We were supposed to have seven days."

Kade shook his head. "Jane can do whatever she wants. It's said she has the powers of over 1,000 Asterians in her hands. I promise you, she can move up a deadline."

"Well, we're not going to reach her in time by walking," Jinx reminded them. "Let's run a couple miles and then walk one to catch our breath."

Nobody argued with this plan and within a minute all four broke into a steady run.

I've never been more thankful for all the conditioning we did at The House, Desdemona laughed in Felix's mind.

Honestly, Felix replied. *I never thought I would actually need it in a life or death situation.*

Well here we are, Desdemona said bluntly before her thoughts changed from sentences to deep, heavy breaths as she ran.

Suddenly, the miserable, cold weather felt cool, crisp, and perfect. As Felix's body temperature rose, he slowly shed his many layers of clothing. As he ran, the sun slowly dipped on its downfall to sunset.

25

Jane watched the sun begin to go down below the horizon as the four helpless Asterians busted their butts to reach the headquarters. As they moved within viewing distance, Jane thoroughly enjoyed observing them struggle up the last few miles. Her plan worked perfectly. The running would exhaust the kids to the point where they would be unable to fight.

"Margret," Jane shouted loudly to the pretty girl standing just a few steps behind her.

"Yes, ma'am?" Margret asked sweetly, ready to execute their plan.

"I want to congratulate you for fooling these naive kids from the very beginning at The House. Not even Mr. Belton saw it coming," praised Jane.

"Now, tell everyone to get into position. The time has finally come," Jane cackled. Margret laughed along with her and turned to warn the others. Just before she left, Jane stopped her once more.

"Oh and remind Hazel she's assigned to Kade. I expect he will be breaking off from the group just before they get here. Tell Hazel I want him dead as soon as possible."

Margret nodded quickly and turned to walk out of the room, entering a large arena. The walls of the arena rose over three stories high, allowing bleachers to rise to the top of the structure. "Why all the bleachers?" Many of Jane's followers asked. Well, Margret explained, the word of her children's powers spread quickly. Jane wanted the spectacle of her assumption of their powers to be a public matter.

In fact, Jane always desired a crowd. Whenever she would come to the arena to practice with her weapon of choice, knives, nearly all her people came to "admire" her skills.

On occasion, a lucky Asterian would be invited into the arena with her for a duel. Every time Jane would bring her subject to near death only to stop before delivering the final blow. The medics, Asterians with healing powers, rushed in to aid their injured ally.

Jane never met her match. Or so it seemed. In reality, Jane's people followed an unspoken rule. Don't give Jane a run for her money. Jane never liked to be challenged. An actual dual would have been an Asterian death sentence for any true opponent.

Margret liked to believe Jane did this to her subjects to remind them of her invincibility. But how could they forget? She could take powers with a single, purposeful touch. Only a fool would cross her.

"Attention," Margret shouted to all those assembled in the arena, some of whom dueled in separate areas of the circle. Immediately, everyone stopped. Margret had become Jane's latest right hand man, the second in line, the sidekick. Piss Margret off and you wouldn't live to see the next sunrise.

"The time has come. Jane's children will be here in less than half an hour. All not directly involved in the plan, please take your seats in the bleachers. All those handpicked by Jane, follow me."

Only five Asterians standing in the center of the arena pressed up the stairs towards Margret. Three large men had varying degrees of invincible brute strength. The fourth, a tall, lean woman, sported extreme gifts with every weapon, no matter its weight, size, or shape. The fifth, however, was perhaps the most integral to Jane's plans. A short, pale girl no older than eighteen, Annaliese had the power to stop time.

To Jane, Annaliese's powers had a downfall. Only Annaliese could move while she paused time. Of course, Jane couldn't surrender that sort of power during her showdown with the Anchor kids. However, Jane kept Annaliese as a backup plan if the other four failed.

Margret herself served as the sixth of Jane's chosen ones. After all, the Anchor kids left The House for Margret. After begging Jane to allow her to further prove her strength, Jane gave Margret the task of capturing Felix himself. Which should be a breeze, Margret figured. She knew Felix was head over heels for her and Margret's powers always worked when boys loved her. Felix will be following at her heels with a simple smile, right to his demise. Margret knew it.

After they gathered their weapons of choice (more than one for the tall woman), Margret led them to Jane's perch just above the top floor of the arena.

"The team is ready," Margret announced. Jane turned around slowly, assessing each of her handpicked members thoroughly.

"Perfect," Jane noted. "It shouldn't be long now. We need to make our way down to the entrance."

All six of them nodded furiously, not daring to disagree with Jane. Before they began to descend the stairs to ground level, Margret gazed at the hill which hid the headquarters of Jane Anchor - Margret's new home. Just as they began their final descent, Hazel brushed past Margret's shoulder going up the staircase.

"Hazel," Margret stopped her dead in her tracks. "Jane wants you waiting outside to get Kade when he breaks off from the group. She thinks he will break off a little before reaching the headquarters."

"Why is Kade planning on breaking off from the group?" Hazel asked.

"I don't know," Margret answered. "But Jane seems very sure of it. And you don't want to be the one to mess up her master plan, right?"

"Of course not," Hazel answered with fake enthusiasm. Two days ago, this declaration would have been the most truthful thing Hazel ever said. But now as she began to slowly escape Jane's tight hold, hope began creeping in. Now, she wasn't too sure.

Despite her doubts, she knew she couldn't let Jane in on her feelings. With the first sign of disloyalty, her powers would be gone in the blink of an eye.

Kade broke off from the group about a fourth of a mile before they reached the foot of their destination. All four gasped for air, but they couldn't stop now. Stopping now could cost them their lives as well as Margret's.

"Alright guys, this is where I peel off," Kade announced. "I think I caught a glimpse of the headquarters - not far from here in that direction." Kade pointed down the path towards the hill which hid the arena and headquarters.

Felix and Desdemona gave Kade hearty hugs, squeezing him tightly and thanking him for everything.

"You're not allowed to die on us," Desdemona ordered as they hugged.

"And you guys won't get yourselves killed, right?" Kade asked Felix, who answered for the group with a weak laugh and a slight nod. But the truth - they were all scared. They couldn't make any promises about coming out alive, much less with their powers. For all they knew, the Anchor kids would face death within the hour.

Jinx, watching tight hugs and sentimental words being shared, stood back and waited for her brother and sister to say their last goodbyes.

When they were done, Desdemona turned to Jinx. "Aren't you going to tell Kade goodbye?"

"Oh, yeah," Jinx answered. "You guys go on and walk ahead a little. I'll catch up with you in a minute."

"No," Felix shouted. "We're not leaving you here. We're so close to the headquarters."

"Felix, let her. We will meet up with her soon," Desdemona said through gritted teeth. Just as Felix began to argue again, Desdemona began to think very loudly.

Felix, she needs to do this alone, okay? Let's just go over the crest of this hill and crouch behind the rock. We're not going anywhere.

Felix sighed back to her. *I guess you're right. She needs this.*

Desdemona smiled. "We'll walk slowly so you can catch up. Be quick though. We want to beat sunset." Desdemona and Felix turned and continued along the trail.

Jinx waved a slight goodbye to her siblings and then turned back to Kade, who stood just a few feet away. Not knowing what to say, Jinx let the silence hang.

"C'mon J, this is it. We can't let this be awkward," Kade told her.

"Yeah, I guess you're right," she responded. "I just… I just have so much I want to say to you."

"Honestly, me too, but I really don't think there are words to describe all those things in this short time," Kade admitted. "Luckily, I know another way to show it."

Kade took one large step towards Jinx and placed his hands on her cheeks. Quickly, but firmly, he gave her their second kiss. But this time, it wasn't tense and awkward and sad. This time, Kade felt confident in his feelings. And he sure as heck wasn't planning on letting this girl leave without one more amazing moment.

When he finally pulled away, Kade leaned his forehead against Jinx's. "Come back to me, J, okay?"

Jinx nodded, not realizing tears welling in her eyes until one fell to her cheek. Kade pulled away and reached a hand to wipe the tear from Jinx's face. He flashed that small smirk, much like the one on that first day in the training room.

In reply, Jinx scoffed, just like she did when they met. But this time she smiled softly before turning around to catch up with her brother and sister.

Jinx didn't turn to look back at Kade as she walked to catch up with Desdemona and Felix. Just like they promised, they walked slowly. Jinx caught up quickly. The sun, barely over the horizon, shone the remaining glimmer of red and gold daylight on the mountain. Without Kade, the Anchor kids were alone now. Nobody felt more nervous than Felix.

Urging his sisters to hurry up, Felix's heart fluttered in his chest at the thought of seeing Margret, at the thought of saving Margret. The adrenaline pumping through his veins overpowered the tense fear sitting in the pit of his stomach, screaming at him to turn around right now. In nearly five minutes they would be face to face with evil herself.

"Hey guys, I love you," Desdemona panted from behind Felix, meeting the eyes of Jinx behind her. "And I know it's been crazy. In some ways we just met, but I want to say you guys mean a lot to me."

Felix stopped and hugged his sister quickly in response. Jinx, strangely quiet since leaving Kade, offered a small, warm smile, one more genuine than Desdemona had ever seen. Just as Desdemona planned on giving Jinx a hug too, she heard a familiar cackle agonizingly close. Desdemona sucked in a sharp breath and prepared herself for what she was sure to see above this hill – their mother.

And sure enough, Jane already had the upper hand. She saw them before they noticed her. The team Jane assembled, weapons at the ready, stood three on each side of their leader, with Margret directly to her right. Just as they poised for the attack, Jane held up her hand in hesitation.

Jane smiled maliciously. "Hang on, let's have some fun."

26

When Felix, Desdemona, and Jinx finally met Jane's eye, Felix immediately turned to Margret.

"Let her go," Felix shouted at Jane, ignoring fear and channeling adrenaline. He'd spent the last week preparing for this moment. He had no intention of screwing it up.

"Why should I?" Jane asked, raising a single, black eyebrow.

Felix held up his sword, trying his best to stop it from shaking within his grasp. "Well, we're here, aren't we? You said we had seven days to bring ourselves to you and you would let Margret go."

Jane turned to address Margret specifically. "Margret, would you like to go with Felix?" Jane winked quickly, so discreetly all three of her children missed it.

Margret knew exactly what Jane wanted from her. She took about fifteen steps towards Felix and put her hand on his shoulder. "Felix, put down your weapon."

"What?" Felix asked, confused. "Why would I do that? Jane is trying to hurt you, Margret."

"Felix, put down your weapon, please," Margret said with emphasis on her last word. Felix nodded, bending to her every word as he felt the influence of her powers.

Jinx's eyes grew wide, realizing what had been going on this entire time. Taking a small step towards Desdemona, she whispered just loud enough for her sister to hear. "Mona, Margret has been playing us. She wasn't kidnapped. She went with Jane willingly."

"Yeah, I gathered that. But I don't think Felix did," Desdemona noted. Despite how much she wanted to scream and yell and punch Margret in the face, Desdemona knew that would accomplish nothing. She needed to do this calmly, to convince her brother not to listen to Margret without getting angry.

Desdemona reached towards Felix, glancing over at Jane who watched the entire interaction with judgmental, squinting eyes, much like the ones Desdemona saw on Jinx many times before.

"Felix, I think you need to come with me, okay?" Desdemona asked tentatively. In all actuality, Desdemona didn't know where they planned on going. She only knew Felix needed to step away from Margret right this second.

Felix turned towards Desdemona and smiled at her, taking a step towards his sister.

"Felix," Margret didn't need to say anything more. Felix stopped dead in his tracks and turned towards Margret with affection-clouded eyes.

Desdemona felt rage building in her stomach. "Felix, I'm your sister. Come with me," Desdemona ordered through gritted teeth.

Just as Felix took another step towards Desdemona, Jinx noticed Jane give a slight nod towards one of warriors standing to her left. The man, who looked like a lineman for a professional football team, instantaneously raised his fists and rushed over to where Desdemona continued to coax Felix away from Margret.

"Mona, watch out," Jinx shouted. Immediately, Desdemona whipped around and pulled an arrow out of her quiver on her back. Loading it quickly, she fired and hit the burly man directly in the neck.

Internally celebrating her good shot, Desdemona felt the urge to pat herself on the back. That is, until she realized the man barely halted, pulling the arrow out of his neck and continuing his rush towards her.

"Help me!" Desdemona shouted at Jinx and Felix. As Desdemona continued to fire her arrows, Jinx slashed knives through the air, hitting the man in the legs repeatedly. Each time, the man pulled them out in nearly a dead run and tossed them on the ground as blood flowed from his legs.

"Hardey!" Jane shouted. "Stop!" Without hesitation, the man stopped his charge and went back to Jane. "Go to the Asterian healers now. Thank you for your service."

Hardey nodded solemnly and jogged past the rest of his team as he headed into the entrance of the headquarters. Desdemona stared in shock at the man's strength and pain tolerance. With that many wounds, he shouldn't be breathing, much less walking and talking.

For the first time on their journey, Desdemona felt not just subdued, but truly outmatched. She reached up and touched the healing wound on her face, briefly shivering as she remembered the mine shaft.

"I see the cut is healing slowly Mona - that's going to leave a scar as a reminder of our time together," Jane observed, sarcastically.

"That's not my name, as far as your concerned, Jane. My name is Desdemona," Desdemona retorted, trying to steady her voice.

"And I noticed Jinx has been handed down my old nickname. Your brother and sister call you "J", don't they?" Jane asked, addressing her other daughter now.

Jinx nodded sharply. "But I'm nothing like you."

Jane laughed loudly, "And yet I see you've taken up my weapon - knives. You don't think that's just a coincidence, do you?" Not waiting for an answer to her rhetorical question, Jane turned towards the two remaining men as well as the tall woman. "Get them," she ordered.

And that's when all hell broke loose.

Weapons came from the woman's hands at terrifying speeds, whizzing right past Felix's head, snapping him back to reality. With a small, simple glance at Margret, Felix shook his head in disappointment and began to fight with a burly man coming at him. He slashed his sword with great precision, displaying every skill he learned at The House. By his side, Jinx and Desdemona fended off their attackers, fighting with more passion and vigor than ever before.

But when it came down to it, the Anchor kids' worst fears came true. Jane's warriors overwhelmed them. One by one, after only a few minutes of battle, each lost consciousness - knocked out cold.

Kade paced around, circling a small tree which, despite the high altitude, grew fruitfully next to him. His mind wandered to Desdemona, Felix, and Jinx. He hoped and prayed for their safety, second-guessing himself. He wished Jane had never found them. He hoped they could somehow free Margret without a battle.

But he knew better than that.

Kade knew they were face to face with Jane right now. Kade hoped their strength and talent would overcome their inexperience. The three chosen ones from the greatest Asterian family would find a way to overcome, right?

As he continued to pace, Kade felt a strange, soft wind blow across his cheek. On a windless, cloudless day, this felt strange and out of place. Nothing about this wind seemed natural. Only one person could make the wind blow like that.

When Kade stopped pacing to turn around, sure enough, his sister stood about ten feet away, small sword in hand.

"Hazel. Good to see you again," Kade greeted her flatly. He had no interest in whatever his sister said at this point.

"Kade, I…" Hazel began. But then she closed her mouth to think for a bit, tapping her fingers as if listing off things she needed to say to him. "Kade, I've been ordered here to kill you."

Kade raised his eyebrows. "Go ahead then. What are you waiting for?" Kade answered.

"And I'm going to do it. I'm going to do it because my alliance is with Jane," Hazel bantered nervously.

"Is it?" Kade asked. "Why do you have an alliance with Jane?"

"Because she's going to rise up against all Asterians and I want to be on the winning side when she does it," Hazel answered stiffly, as if she rehearsed the statement in her mind and repeated it hundreds of times.

Kade took a step closer to her. "Do you really think she's going to win? Forget for a moment about what happens today. In the end, we have an entire Asterian race on our side."

Hazel stared at the ground, flustered, until finally meeting Kade's eyes again. "Why did you show me that?"

"The scene from when we were younger? Kade replied. "Because no matter how much things have changed, I know in the back of our minds neither of us can forget that day. We have thousands of those memories and that's who we really are. Remember when our biggest concern was which one of us would get to watch our favorite episode of SpongeBob next? Hazel, I guess I just wanted you to know you still have a choice. You can choose to leave Jane and be a big sister again.

"I'm happy with Jane." Hazel countered, raising her sword higher than before as rain began to fall over Kade's head.

"Hazel," Kade said, looking up. "Stop it now."

And as he ordered, the rain let up to just a slight drizzle over the pair.

"Show me something else…" Hazel trailed off, hoping Kade would give her another scene. And when she asked, he delivered.

This time, Kade took Hazel back to their childhood home, decked out in green garland on the steps, red candles on the dining room table, with the smell of cranberries wafting from the kitchen. A moving Santa singing "We Wish You a Merry Christmas" played softly in the corner of the living room. In the den, a Christmas tree towered to the ceiling, showered with homemade ornaments and sloppy strands of popcorn. Multicolored bulbs twinkled, lighting up the many presents under the tree, all addressed to "Hazel" or "Kade."

In the study, illuminated with a smaller red Christmas tree, sat the hopeful beneficiaries of the many gifts in the den. Kade, no more than five, leaned eagerly over his older sister's shoulder as she searched the internet for the Santa Tracker. Although Hazel surely didn't believe in Santa anymore, she wouldn't dare ruin it for her younger brother. Excitedly, Kade waited for the Santa Tracker to show the latest location. "Look Hazel, Santa is just two states away from our house." He jumped up and down eagerly, throwing both arms around Hazel's neck, squeezing her. After he let go, he promptly told his sister, in a sweet voice, "We need to go to bed this instant or Santa will skip our house."

Laughing, she agreed. Together always, they walked up the garland lined staircase towards their bedrooms.

Hazel smiled lightly at Kade once she got her senses back, then frowned as she remembered what Jane sent her to do: kill him. But for the first time since her last scene from Kade, Hazel felt alive. Joy, love and excitement began to nudge aside a deep, dark cloud of fear and insecurity.

"Hazel, why are you siding with Jane?" Kade asked softly.

"I told you already. Because Jane is going to win. I want to be on the winning side," she reminded him, hands shaking.

"Hazel," Kade repeated. "Why are you siding with Jane?"

Hazel looked up at the brother, remembering all the snowstorms she made and all the love they shared. How many snowstorms and how much love had she missed?

Feeling confused, yet enlightened, Hazel finally answered truthfully. "I don't... I don't know."

When Jinx finally began to open her eyes, the light shining from above surprised her. Shielding her eyes from the light, Jinx reached over to shake Felix and Desdemona, who were just waking up as well.

"Where are we?" Desdemona asked.

It was then Jinx remembered the day's events thus far. "Uhhh... guys..." Jinx started. "I don't think we're really in a safe place right now..."

Felix's face melted with realization as he heard Jane's voice once again. "J, you would be incorrect about that. This is the safest place you'll ever be, as long as you choose to cooperate."

Finally, Jinx's eyes adjusted to the light and her ears filled with shouts of excitement and cheer. Looking around, she was astounded to find herself in a large arena. Bleachers, filled with Asterians, yelled encouragements to Jane. Jinx winced when she heard one man yell, "just kill them already!" As she scanned her eyes around the many Asterians in the arena, her gaze fell on Margret, standing on a bleacher while everyone else sat. For a split second, Jinx's eyes met Margret's and Margret smiled innocently. Jinx resisted the burning urge to forget about Jane and to go after Margret.

Jinx staggered to her feet, followed by Desdemona and Felix. Speaking up, Jinx turned to Jane.

"If you wanted to kill us, why didn't you do it while we were out cold?" Jinx raised her eyebrows.

Jane raised her eyebrows, mimicking her daughter exactly. In fact, everything about her mimicked Jinx right now. Her black hair, cut short and jagged like Jinx's, was tucked behind her left ear. Her eyes squinted, taking in the scene around her like her daughter so often did. The smirk on her lips was one Jinx found herself giving on more than one occasion. "Because I wanted to give you guys a chance. Remember when Felix was trapped with a blade to his neck, only to be saved because the man was suddenly hit in the leg with a knife? That was yours truly. You're my children. Do you really think I'm so cruel as to mercilessly take the powers of my own kids without giving them a choice?"

Yeah, we actually do, Desdemona refuted in her thoughts. Felix nodded, silently agreeing with her.

"I want to let you choose. Come with me and help me defeat the Asterians who won't join us. Asterians are much more powerful than Mr. Belton, The House and the Asterian Society think we are. We are good for much more than benevolent deeds. We can rule the world." Jane shouted, throwing her arms up. At this, the crowd erupted in applause, cheering and yelling into oblivion.

"Join me, children," Jane offered, extending her hand. "Or forfeit your powers forever."

Felix and Desdemona knew their answers immediately. They wouldn't side with Jane, dead or alive, powers or no powers.

Jinx, on the other hand, wasn't so sure. She felt a familiar tug in her stomach; a tug that urged her to go to Jane. And for a moment, she entertained the tug, wondering what she would do with all the power Jane could give. Thousands of Asterians under her control, bending to her every will as she predicted their futures and foresaw how Jane's plans would work to their benefit. Margret would be tossed aside like a dishrag, leaving

Jinx to be her mother's right hand man. Upon Jane's death, Jinx would not just rule Asterians - she might rule the entire universe.

These images of power and wealth played across Jinx's mind like a vision, sucking her into a world where everyone answered to her and only her.

But then she felt a tingle on her lips and Kade ran across her thoughts. Kade - a boy who made her promise to come back alive and well.

Turning over to darkness was the opposite of returning alive and well. Jinx would become broken, alone, and consumed to the point where her old self would be unrecognizable. She would become a ruthless, power-hungry leader, no better than Hitler himself.

Jinx didn't need to think anymore. She looked up and met Jane's eyes, speaking for the entire group. "No. If you want our powers, you're going to have to go through us."

Jane sneered and, quick as lighting, drew a knife from her belt and threw it. It whizzed right by Desdemona's head, where her scar rested across her eye. But Jinx was surprised to find Desdemona didn't even flinch. She didn't move away, she didn't scream or yell. Calmly, she drew her bow and loaded an arrow.

"I'm not afraid of you, Jane. So what if there's a scar on my face? From this day forward, it will only be a reminder of the day Jane Anchor's own kids put an end to her terror," and with this, Desdemona fired her arrow, a direct shot at Jane's chest.

But Jane snapped her fingers effortlessly and the arrow bounced off course and flew the other direction. Desdemona lowered her bow, trying not to look phased as Jane's Asterians cheered at her formidable power.

Girls, I think this is going to be a harder battle than we thought. We need a new game plan, Felix said in his sister's minds. Both girls agreed with him and thought quickly on their feet.

When Jinx remembered a weight in her knapsack a plan formed. *Felix.* She shouted in her thoughts. *The Asterian Jewel. I had a vision about it and I think the vision is happening right now. This stone is the only way we will ever defeat her.*

"Exactly," Kade nodded his head at his nervous, shaking sister. "You don't know why you're doing it. So, why is it still happening then? Do something you know you want to do."

Hazel lifted her sword once more and the wind began to blow at astonishing rates, whipping around Kade's hair. "I have to kill you, Kade."

Kade took a couple of steps closer to Hazel, reaching out his hand to grasp the handle of the sword, putting his hand on top of hers. He tried to ignore Hazel's flinch as they touched for the first time in over ten years. "No, you don't."

Kade suppressed feelings of fear as he realized if Hazel wanted to kill him, she could do it in a heartbeat as he stood so close to her. But he knew his sister. And he knew she wouldn't.

"Yes I do," She shouted. All at once, she ripped the sword away from his grasp, allowing it to clip the skin of his arm. Red blood oozed from the small, but deep wound as Kade glanced down at his arm. Hazel also stared, gasping, seemingly horrified at what she did. In her frozen disarray, Kade acted swiftly, knocking Hazel's arm with a forceful punch. The sword clattered to the ground, deserted.

While Hazel stood in shock, Kade moved calmly to pick up the forgotten sword. His mind flashed to the one other person he knew used a sword: Felix. And for a split second, he forgot about Hazel and worried about the triplets.

But he knew worrying wouldn't help them. There was only one way Kade could help them and he planned on doing just that.

"Hazel, think about it," Kade started. "How much happier have you felt since I showed you the first scene?"

Hazel didn't hesitate. Staring at the ground, she answered, "Much happier."

"And I imagine all those other Asterians under Jane's mind tricks will be the same way."

"Mind tricks?" Hazel asked, looking at Kade. "What mind tricks?"

Kade took a deep breath, prepared to share his undisclosed theory. "I've been thinking maybe Jane's followers don't fight for her because it's what they believe. Maybe she makes them think that's what they believe. She steals their memories and happiness of the past so they will blindly follow her without question."

"What are you trying to say?" Hazel asked, shaking.

"I'm saying Jane has stolen your hope and the visions of our childhood have restored it," Kade clarified.

At this point, Hazel reached her epiphany. "You're right," she shouted. "We have to free them, all of them."

Hazel stopped shaking and began to think hard, devising a plan to save all of Jane's followers. Kade was one step ahead.

Sharing his scheme with his sister, Kade felt a weight lifted off of his chest, like a long-lasting problem resolved. For the first time in ten years, he didn't have to worry about where his sister was or if she was alive or if she was on the right track. Because for the first time in ten years, he knew.

Felix moved, carefully and discreetly, just a few steps at a time, closer towards Jinx's backpack. The jewel was in her left side pocket and he knew they could not defeat Jane without it. But he also knew if he got caught, Jane would take the jewel and the battle could be over before it even began.

While Felix tried to tiptoe towards her backpack, Desdemona and Jinx carried a tense, terrifying conversation with Jane to delay her attack.

"I wonder how Hazel is doing," Jane cackled. "I ordered her to kill Kade, you know. And there is no way she would let him get away again."

Jinx felt her heart beat rapidly in her chest at the idea of Kade being murdered. She tried to smother her gasps at the thought of losing him, knowing she could not bear to go back to The House without him. All at once, calm replaced her panic.

Jane lunged forward towards them. Desdemona side stepped out of the way just as Felix grabbed the Asterian Jewel from Jinx's backpack and clenched it in his fist. But time appeared to be moving in slow motion in this moment. Jinx could see everything so clearly and distinctly, enough to realize Jane noticed Felix pulling the stone from her backpack.

And then, time sped up, with Jane popping back into the spot where she stood before she lunged. The cackle Jinx heard before she lunged continued and Jinx felt her panic return.

It was then Jinx realized the lunge never happened. Or at least it hadn't happened yet. In fact, nearly no time passed since Jinx felt her panic leave and return.

It was like blinking. Whatever Jinx had just seen was as fast as the blink of an eye. And she felt nearly sure Jane planned on lunging once Felix grabbed the jewel.

Right on schedule, Jinx felt Felix's hand touch her backpack and, sure enough, Jane lunged at the triplets. Desdemona side-stepped from her attack as Felix pulled the jewel from the pocket. Running to the opposite side of the arena, Jinx felt the calm come over her again as she sprinted. Again, in the blink of an eye, it happened.

Felix, Desdemona, and herself, with their hands on the Asterian Jewel, stood in a perfect triangle as Jane threw knives. All the knives bounced off them without damage, just as Desdemona's arrow did earlier.

Immediately, Jinx felt her gasping breath come back as she continued to run. A smile crawled on her face as she realized she had what she really wanted: her first Embellishment.

Jinx could now see the immediate future without any real effect on her movement or thoughts in the present.

27

Jinx did everything in her power to block out the deafening screams of the crowd as Jane hurled knife after knife in their direction. With difficulty, the trio managed to jump and dodge each one. That was, until one landed directly into the skin of Felix's forearm.

Stopping for a moment, Felix glanced at the knife and pulled it out without a moment's hesitation, wincing only slightly. To his delight, the knife hit him slightly sideways, with a wound not as deep as he expected. Angrily, he gripped the knife and flung it back at Jane with surprising accuracy. Felix turned quickly to run to his sisters. The knife blade grazed Jane's ankle, drawing blood.

Desdemona stared back at Jane, seeing the blood, when her Embellishment kicked in. One word in large black letters spread across Jane's forehead: PRECARIOUS. Desdemona thought for a moment, finding this word fairly odd since Jane, on the outside, appeared the exact opposite of uncertain or unstable.

Standing near Desdemona, Jinx held the jewel up in the palm of her hand, reaching for the sky. Desdemona looked at Jinx with a weird expression. "What are you doing?" She yelled over the noisy Asterians.

"Put your hand on it. Trust me," Jinx yelled back.

"What's that going to do?" Desdemona demanded.

Felix, from a few yards away, quickly pushed himself into Desdemona's mind, urging, *do what Jinx says, now!*

Jinx, pleading with her eyes, shouted. "I'm your sister. Trust me." Without a second more of hesitation, Desdemona complied and placed her soft palm over the emerald stone. Felix, finally reaching them, followed suit and touched the jewel immediately.

Felix, Desdemona, and Jinx heard a loud sizzle as the stone began its magic, glowing from an emerald green, to faded lavender, to angry red, then ocean blue. Jane, seeing them stand in one spot now, laughed with giddy maliciousness and came closer, throwing more knives with extreme precision and speed.

One moment, the knives shot at the trio. The next moment, they clattered to the ground, as if they hit a wall.

In fact, they did.

What's happening? Felix asked in his sisters' heads.

Not quite sure, but I think it had something to do us being able to come together at just the right time with the jewel. I think it might have put up a shield, Jinx thought back, excitedly.

Jane interrupted their moment of excitement with another, unfazed bout of laughter. "You might be protected from my physical attacks, but no tiny jewel can match my unstoppable powers."

Desdemona felt fear in the pit of her stomach as her mother lifted her hands and summoned one of her many powers. Desdemona cringed and closed her eyes, readying herself for the attack, but nothing happened.

There was not a sound.

Not a noise.

Not a murmur.

Until the world swept out from under the Anchors' feet. Together, for the first time, they saw one another's visions.

Desdemona found herself back in the operating room, much like the one in her first vision. But this time she realized the doctor was their uncle, Marcus, and the old woman with grey hair was none other than their grandmother, Hilga. The black hair that fell on Desdemona's shoulders was definitely not hers. Rather, that hair belonged to their aunt Stacy. Glancing over to the entryway of the operating room, Desdemona noticed Felix and Jinx standing, dumbfounded, as they watched their own birth. Marcus completely subdued Jane and for the first time in their lives, they watched her lay silent, as if asleep. Desdemona rushed around the operating room, helping Marcus deliver her and her siblings.

She tried to ignore the odd feeling as she realized her life changed completely in the last few months. On her birthday, when she first saw this image, confusion washed over her mind and body, numbing her to the oddities of her new world. And now here she was. Here they were. Fifteen years old and watching their own births live, in action.

Before they knew it, the operating room swirled out of focus and the triplets left Desdemona's vision, only to enter Felix's.

Felix recalled the look of the inside of his father's- or uncle's - mind the minute they entered it again. Felix watched as he and his sisters walked along the windy roads and mountains of Marcus's life, all tearing up a little as they watched Marcus grieve over the loss of his wife and work endlessly to hide his depression from his only son, Felix. Felix saw his uncle's life from a different perspective. Felix noticed the hidden tears and the distraught gulps when anyone mentioned her name.

Felix, too, watched as his life came full circle before his eyes. When he first had this vision, he screamed at the terror of being inside of his uncle's mind. He hardly paid attention to the ongoing grief in the vision. But now, it was all he could focus on. Making a mental note to call Marcus the minute he got home, Felix and his sisters swept out of the vision.

It didn't take much for the Felix and Desdemona to realize the jewel gave each of them their very first vision back. But they soon realized one vision was missing from the mix.

"Jinx?" Felix yelled. "Where is your vision?"

Jinx took a deep breath and looked around her. "Felix, the jewel isn't showing us my first vision because right here, right now, WE ARE LIVING IT."

Jane screamed at the top of her lungs, interrupting their conversation. "WHERE ARE MY POWERS?"

Jinx, Desdemona, and Felix all shared incredulous glances. Everyone told them so much about Jane's unbeatable array of stolen powers and now, when the Anchors finally found themselves face to face with her, something rendered those powers useless.

Jane continued to yell, screaming out powers she wished to summon. She clenched her hands into fists and then opened them again. She hit her palms and wiped them on her clothes. She did everything she could to restore her abilities. Nothing worked.

As Jane screamed in agony, the earth began to shake. Bleachers began to rattle against the ground, making the Asterians in the stands begin to scream along with Jane, who hardly noticed the crumbling stone around her.

The shaking began to grow and grow and grow until a large chunk of the roof came tumbling down onto the center of the arena. Asterians stood up and began to evacuate the arena, running outside to avoid falling debris.

But the Anchors stayed put. All four of them.

Jane continued to yell and scream in despair and confusion at the loss of her powers, her screams barely audible over the tumbling arena. As the earthquake continued, a giant chunk of the ceiling broke free from its connecting pieces and began to fall directly on Jinx, Desdemona, and Felix. Desdemona began to yell, but Jinx stayed perfectly calm and kept the siblings together. She saw this moment in her mind only minutes ago.

A large chunk broke from the ceiling, moving in slow motion as Jinx observed her new Embellishment. It fell, causing her sister to scream at the top of her lungs, but when it finally reached ground level, the large piece of plaster simply bounced right off the shield created by the Asterian Jewel. The Anchor kids breathed out, unharmed.

And sure enough, the events played out just as Jinx expected. The large ceiling piece fell on their force field, trapping them in a bubble of security as the quake began to tear the entire arena to shreds.

Jinx stood, watching with her hand firmly on the jewel as a gaping hole appeared in the side of the arena with a crash. The passageway revealed two people, one of whom, just a few minutes before, Jinx thought she might never see again.

On the other side of the hole stood Kade and his sister Hazel, with her hands raised slightly. A broad smile spread across Hazel's face as she saw the triplets, unharmed, in the midst of the chaos Hazel caused. Jinx locked eyes with Kade, smirked slyly at him, and shook her head. He did the same, melting her heart with his grin, while the arena continued to tumble down around them. Crashing noises blocked out Jane's yells of despair, so much that nobody noticed when they came to a halt in the midst of the blasts.

Eventually, when the last piece of the arena came tumbling down, Hazel let her hands fall down to her thighs, smiling with excitement.

"That was awesome! I haven't felt so alive in years." She enthused, jumping up and down. Kade hugged her tightly, thanking her.

Jinx was the first to let her hand fall from the stone, followed by Felix and then Desdemona. Desdemona tossed the jewel back to Jinx, who caught it swiftly.

"So…" Felix began. "Where is Jane?"

"I think that's her over there," Desdemona shouted from a few feet over. She pointed to where tresses of black hair and a pale, white hand stuck out from under a very large piece of rubble.

"Kade," Jinx called him over to where they were examining Jane. "Is she dead?"

Kade leaned down, placing his fingers on her outstretched wrist. After a few seconds, he sighed and stood up to announce, "Jane Anchor is no longer a menace to the Asterian World."

Her children beamed with excitement and the realization they succeeded in their mission. Hugs were shared between brothers and sisters (and crushes, in Jinx and Kade's case) before the plaguing question was finally brought up.

"But…" Desdemona started. "How did that work? Why couldn't Jane use her powers?"

"I'm not sure," Kade answered. "But I think the Asterian Jewel might have a knack for picking out the good from the bad. I think it protects those who follow Asterian purposes and renders useless those who torture."

"And does it just work for the three of us? The jewel has words about me and my brother and sister," Jinx noted, holding her hand out to show the jewel again to Kade. But when she looked, the golden prophecy had disappeared without a trace. The words once so prominent left a blank, emerald stone. Beautiful, but blank.

"Well... That's what it did say," Jinx shrugged, placing the jewel back in her backpack. Her curious mind wondered why the words disappeared, but she figured she would save that mystery for another day. Right now, they needed to get back to The House.

Felix sighed lightly, glancing around the rubble, halfheartedly wishing to see Margret's red hair, but reminded himself she wasn't who he thought she was.

Desdemona came over and placed her hand on his shoulder. "Are you okay? I mean, with Margret and stuff."

Felix kicked a piece of rubble with his foot. "Not really, but I will be. I swear, I really thought she was worth it. I thought something was going to come of us- Margret and me. And I went this whole way, excited to see her and save her and be her knight in shining armor, but she played us. This whole trip seems like it was for nothing."

Desdemona let her jaw drop. "Felix, this trip was *not* for nothing. We defeated the most evil woman in all of Asterian history. Look at the Asterians around here who are no longer under her spell. There's no telling how many lives you saved today."

Felix thought for moment, glancing at Jane's outstretched hand and feeling slightly better. "I guess you're right. We did what we were created to do."

"You're right," Desdemona agreed. "We really did."

Kade came over to Jinx and conspicuously wrapped his hand around Jinx's shoulder, winking discreetly at her. Jinx jeered at him and nudged back. Desdemona noticed this and looked at

Felix with wide eyes. Felix stifled a gasp and a giggle at their sudden feelings, choosing not to embarrass them.

Because above all, this was a time for hope and joy. This was a time to celebrate their victory and one of the greatest ascensions in Asterian history.

"Alright guys, let's get home," Kade announced. "I think I saw a confused Asterian over there who has long distance teleportation powers. I remember him from The House. We can go back together. You're coming, right, Hazel?"

Hazel nodded. "I wouldn't miss it for the world, little brother."

And so the four, now five, members of our team turned around and climbed out of the rubble, walking into the moonlit night.

But if they stayed for just one more minute, they would have noticed a slight twitch in the outstretched hand of Jane Anchor.

For the light may have eradicated the darkness, but as soon as light turns a blind eye, the shadows of darkness always rise again.

Acknowledgments

This book, although my name is on the front cover, was ultimately a team effort and could not have been completed without a myriad of people standing in my corner.

For reading this novel over and over again without complaint and providing invaluable critiques and ideas, I thank my father, Robert Hudson, who encouraged me to make this world inside my head a reality.

For always taking care of me and easing me away from the computer when writer's block had a strong hold, I acknowledge my marvelous mother, Melissa Hudson.

A huge shout out to my brother, Robbie Hudson, for being the basis of nearly every interaction between the Anchor siblings and giving me so many great memories.

I would like to acknowledge my extended family, Cynthia Branstetter, Cheryl, Elizabeth, and Odell Martin, and Pasty and D.D. Hudson, who have read the manuscripts of my novels in rough- no, really rough- drafts and for encouraging me to put on the finishing touches.

For always listening to me rant about finding the perfect title during biology class or enthuse about a new plot twist during AP European History, I thank my amazing friends: Lauren Nieman, Gabbie Caple, Hanna Baehner, Kyle Rose, Madison Webster, Sydney Jones and so many more.

I also wish to recognize my AP English Language and Composition teacher, Mrs. Jennifer Henry at Dixie Heights High School, for improving my writing immensely over the course of my sophomore year and tearing apart just about everything I wrote in her class to make it the best it could be.

For taking a chance on this novel as well as my past book, I recognize Cathy Teets, my unbelievable publisher and owner of Headline Books. It takes a bold publisher to publish the manuscripts of a teenage author.

Special thanks to Joseph Beth Booksellers, who consistently advocated for my previous book and play. It's hard to believe they agreed, in advance of its publication, to throw this novel a fantastic launch party.

Lastly, I would like to thank God for giving me such a love for writing that acts as an outlet for my over-active imagination. We accomplish nothing without him.